D0256120

my SOUL to *Save*

RACHEL VINCENT

All the characters in this book have no existence outside the imagination of the author, and have no relation whatsoever to anyone bearing the same name or names. They are not even distantly inspired by any individual known or unknown to the author, and all the incidents are pure invention.

Published in Great Britain 2011
MIRA Books, Eton House, 18-24 Paradise Road,
Richmond, Surrey, TW9 1SR

© Rachel Vincent 2010

ISBN 978 0 7783 0435 7

47-0311

Printed and bound by CPI Group (UK)
Ltd, Croydon, CR0 4YY

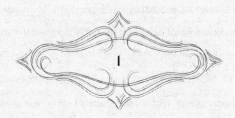

1

ADDISON PAGE had the world at her feet. She had the face, the body, the voice, the moves, and the money. Let's not forget the money. But advantages like that come with a price. I should have known it was all too good to be true....

"What?" I yelled, my throat already raw from shouting over the roar of the crowd and the music blasting from dozens of huge speakers. Around us, thousands of bodies bobbed in time to the beat, hands in the air, lips forming the words, shouting the lyrics along with the beautiful, glittery girl strutting across the stage, seen close-up on a pair of giant digital screens.

Nash and I had great seats, thanks to his brother, Tod, but no one was sitting. Excitement bounced off every solid surface, fed by the crowd and growing with each passing second until the auditorium seemed to swell with the communal high. Energy buzzed through me, setting my nerve endings on fire with enough kick to keep me pinging off the walls through high school and well into college.

I didn't want to know how Tod had scored seats a mere fifteen rows from the stage, but even my darkest suspicion hadn't kept me at home. I couldn't pass up a chance to see Eden live in concert, even though it meant giving up a Saturday night alone with Nash, during my dad's extra shift at work.

And this was only Eden's opening act….

Nash pulled me closer, one hand on my hip, and shouted into my ear. "I said, Tod used to date her!"

I rode the wave of adrenaline through my veins as I inhaled his scent. Six weeks together, and I still smiled every time he looked at me, and flushed every time he *really* looked at me. My lips brushed his ear as I spoke. "Tod used to date who?" There were several thousand possible suspects dancing all around us.

"Her!" Nash shouted back, nodding over the sea of concertgoers toward the main attraction, his spiky, deliberately messy brown hair momentarily highlighted by a roaming spotlight.

Addison Page, Eden's opening act, strutted across the stage in slim black boots; low-cut, ripped jeans; a tight white halter; and a sparkly silver belt, wailing a bitter yet up-tempo lament about the one who got away. The glittery blue streak in her straight, white-blond hair sparkled beneath the lights and fanned out behind her when she whirled to face the audience from center stage, her voice rising easily into the clear, res-onant notes she was famous for.

I stared, suddenly still while everyone around me swayed along with the crescendo. I couldn't help it.

"Tod dated Addison Page?"

Nash couldn't have heard me. *I* barely heard me. But he nodded and leaned into me again, and I wrapped my arm around him for balance as the cowboy on my other side swung one eager, pumping fist dangerously close to my shoulder. "Three years ago. She's local, you know."

Like us, the hometown crowd had turned out as much for Texas's own rising star as for the headliner. "She's from Hurst, right?" Less than twenty minutes from my own Arlington address.

"Yeah. Addy and I were freshmen together, before

we moved back to Arlington. She and Tod dated for most of that year. He was a sophomore."

"So what happened?" I asked as the music faded and the lighting changed for the second song.

I pressed closer to Nash as he spoke into my ear, though he didn't really have to at that point; the new song was a melodic, angsty tune of regret. "Addy got cast in a pilot for the HOT network. The show took off and she moved to L.A." He shrugged. "Long distance is hard enough when you're fifteen, and impossible when your girlfriend's famous."

"So why didn't he come tonight?" I wouldn't have been able to resist watching a celebrity ex strut on stage, and hopefully fall on his face, assuming I was the dumpee.

"He's here somewhere." Nash glanced around at the crowd as it settled a bit for the softer song. "But it's not like he needs a ticket." As a grim reaper, Tod could choose whether or not he wanted to be seen or heard, and by whom. Which meant he could be standing on stage right next to Addison Page, and we'd never know it.

And knowing Tod, that's exactly where he was.

After Addison's set, there was a brief, loud intermission while the stage was set for the headliner. I expected

Tod to show up during the break, but there was still no sign of him when the stadium suddenly went black.

For a moment, there was only dark silence, emphasized by surprised whispers, and glowing wristbands and cell-phone screens. Then a dark blue glow came from the stage and the crowd erupted into frenzied cheers. Another light flared to life, illuminating a new platform in the middle of the stage. Two bursts of red flames exploded near the wings. When they faded, but for the imprint behind my eyelids, *she* appeared center stage, as if she'd been there all along.

Eden.

She wore a white tailored jacket open over a pink leather bra and a short pink-fringed skirt that exaggerated every twitch of her famous hips. Her long, dark hair swung with each toss of her head, and the fevered screaming of the crowed buzzed in my head as Eden dropped into a crouch, microphone in hand.

She rose slowly, hips swaying with the rhythm of her own song. Her voice was low and throaty, a moan set to music, and no one was immune to the siren song of sex she sold.

Eden was hypnotic. Spellbinding. Her voice flowed like honey, sweet and sticky. To hear it was to crave it, whether you wanted to or not.

The sound wound through me like blood in my

veins, and I knew that hours from then, when I lay awake in my bed, Eden would still sing in my mind, and that when I closed my eyes, I would still see her.

It was even stronger for Nash; I could see that at a glance. He couldn't tear his gaze from her, and we were so close to the stage that his view was virtually uninterrupted. His eyes swirled with emotion—with need—but not for me.

A violent, irrational surge of jealousy spiked in me as fresh sweat dampened his forehead. He clenched his hands at his sides, the long, tight muscles in his arms bulging beneath his sleeves. As if he were concentrating. Oblivious to everything else.

I had to pry his fingers open to lace them with mine. He turned to grin at me and squeezed my hand, beautiful hazel eyes settling into a slower churn as his gaze met mine. The yearning was still there—for me this time—but was both deeper and more coherent. What he wanted from me went beyond mindless lust, though that was there, too, thank goodness.

I'd broken the spell. For the moment. I didn't know whether to thank Tod for the tickets or ream him.

Onstage, soft lights illuminated dancers strutting out to join Eden as the huge screen tracked her every movement. The dancers closed in on her, writhing in sync, hands gliding lightly over her arms, shoulders, and bare stomach. Then they paired off so she could strut down the catwalk stretching several rows into the crowd.

Suddenly I was glad we didn't have front-row seats. I'd have had to scrape a puddle of Nash goo into a jar just to get him home.

Warm breath puffed against my neck an instant before the sound hit my ear. "Hey, Kaylee!"

I jumped, so badly startled I nearly fell into my chair. Tod stood on my right, and when the cowboy's swinging arm went *through* him, I knew the reaper was there for my viewing pleasure only.

"Don't do that!" I snapped beneath my breath. He probably couldn't hear me, but I wasn't going to raise my voice and risk the guy next to me thinking I was talking to myself. Or worse, to *him*.

"Grab Nash and come on!" From the front pocket of his baggy, faded jeans, Tod pulled two plastic-coated, official-looking cards attached to lanyards. His mischievous grin could do nothing to darken the cherubic features he'd inherited from his mother, and I had to remind myself that no matter how innocent he looked, Tod was trouble. Always.

"What's that?" I asked, and the cowboy frowned at me in question. I ignored him—so much for not looking crazy—and elbowed Nash. "Tod," I mouthed when he raised both brows at me.

Nash rolled his eyes and glanced past me, but I could tell from his roving stare that he couldn't see his brother. And that, as always, he was pissed that Tod had appeared to me, but not to him.

"Backstage passes." Tod reached through the cowboy to grab my hand, and if I hadn't jerked back from the reaper's grasp, I'd have gotten a very intimate feel of one of Eden's rudest fans.

I stood on my toes to reach Nash's ear. "He has backstage passes."

Nash's scowl made an irritated mask of his entire face, while on stage, Eden shed her jacket, now clad only in a bikini top and short skirt. "Where did he get them?"

"Do you really want to know?" Reapers weren't paid in money—at least, not the human kind—so he certainly hadn't bought the passes. Or the tickets.

"No," Nash grumbled. But he followed me, anyway.

Keeping up with Tod was a lost cause. He didn't have to edge past row after row of ecstatic fans, or stop and apologize when he stepped on one girl's foot or spilled her date's drink. He just walked right through seats and concertgoers alike, as if they didn't exist in his world.

They probably didn't.

Like all reapers, Tod's natural state of existence—if it could even be called natural—was somewhere between our world, where humans and the occasional *bean sidhe* reside in relative peace, and the Netherworld, where most things dark and dangerous dwell. He could exist completely in either one, if he chose, but he rarely did, because when he was corporeal, he typically forgot to avoid obstacles like chairs, tables, and doors. And people.

Of course, he could easily become visible to both me and Nash, but it was evidently much more fun to mess with his brother. I'd never met a set of siblings with less in common than Nash and Tod. They weren't even the same species; at least, not anymore.

The Hudson brothers were both born *bean sidhes*— that was the correct spelling, though most people knew us as banshees—from normal *bean sidhe* parents. As was I. But Tod had died two years earlier, when he was seventeen, and that's when things got weird, even for *bean sidhes*. Tod was recruited by the grim reapers.

As a reaper, Tod would live on in his own unaging body. In exchange, he worked a twelve-hour shift every day, collecting souls from humans whose time had come to die. He didn't have to eat or sleep, so he got pretty bored for those other twelve hours of each day. And since Nash and I were among the few who knew about him, he typically took that boredom out on us.

Which was how we'd gotten kicked out of a mall, a skating rink, and a bowling alley, all in the past month. And as I bumped my way through the crowd after Tod, I had a feeling the concert would be next on the list.

One glance at the irritation glowing in Nash's cheeks told me he still couldn't see his brother, so I pulled him along as I tracked the headful of blond curls now several rows ahead of us, heading toward a side door beneath a red exit sign.

Eden's first song ended in a huge flash of purple light, reflected on the thousands of faces around me, then the lights went out.

I stopped, unwilling to move in the dark for fear that I'd trip over someone and land in an unidentified puddle. Or a lap.

Seconds later, the stage exploded with swirling, pulsing light, and Eden now swayed to the new beat in a different but equally skimpy costume. I glanced at her, then back at Tod, but caught only a fleeting glimpse of his curls disappearing through the closed side door.

Nash and I rushed after him, stepping on a series of toes and vaulting over a half-empty bottle of Coke someone had smuggled in. We were out of breath when we reached the door, so I glanced one last time at the stage, then shoved the door, grateful when it actually opened. Doors Tod walks through usually turn out to be locked.

Tod stood in the hall beyond, grinning, both backstage passes looped over one arm. "What'd you do, crawl all the way here?"

The door closed behind us, and I was surprised to realize I could barely hear the music, though it had been loud enough to drown out my thoughts in the auditorium. But I could still feel the thump of the bass, pulsing up through my feet from the floor.

Nash let go of my hand and glared at his brother. "Some of us are bound by the laws of physics."

"Not my problem." Tod waved the passes, then tossed one to each of us. "Snoozin', loozin', and all that crap."

I slipped the nylon lanyard over my neck and pulled my long brown hair over it. Now that I wore the pass, it would be seen by anyone who saw me; everything Tod holds is only as visible as he is at the time.

The reaper went fully corporeal then, his sneakers squeaking on the floor as he led us down a series of wide white hallways and through several doors, until we hit one that was locked. Tod shot us a mischievous grin, then walked through the door and pushed it open from the other side.

"Thanks." I brushed past him into the new hall, and the sudden upsurge of music warned that we were getting close to the stage. In spite of the questionable source of our backstage passes, my pulse jumped with excitement when we rounded the next corner and the building opened into a long, wide hall with a cavernous ceiling. Equipment was stacked against the walls—soundboards, speakers, instruments, and lights. People milled everywhere, carrying clothes, food, and clipboards. They spoke into two-way radios and headset microphones, and most wore badges similar to ours, though theirs read "Crew" in bold black letters.

Security guards in black tees and matching hats loitered, thick arms crossed over their chests. Background dancers raced across the open space in all stages of the next costume change, while a woman with a clipboard pointed and rushed them along.

No one noticed me and Nash, and I could tell Tod had gone non-corporeal again by the silence of his steps. We headed slowly toward the stage, where light pulsed and music thumped, much too loud for any of the backstage racket to be heard out front. I touched nothing, irrationally afraid that sneaking a cookie from the snack table would finally expose us as backstage-pass thieves.

In the wings of the stage, a small crowd had gathered to watch the show. Everyone wore badges similar to ours, and several people held equipment or props, most notably a small monkey, wearing a collar and a funny, brightly colored hat.

I laughed out loud, wondering what on earth America's reigning pop queen would do on stage with a monkey.

From our vantage point, we saw Eden in profile, now grinding in skintight white leather pants and a matching half top. The new song was gritty, with a crunchy guitar riff, and her dancing had changed to suit it; she popped each pose hard, and her hair swung out behind her. Guys in jeans and tight, dark shirts danced around and behind her, each taking her hand in turn, and lifting her on occasion.

Eden gave it her all, even several songs into the performance. The magazines and news stories hyped her hard work and dedication to her career, and the hours and hours a day she trained, rehearsed, and planned. And it showed. No one put on a show like Eden. She was the entertainment industry's golden girl, rolling in money and fame. Rumor had it she'd signed on for the lead in her first film, to begin shooting after the conclusion of her sold-out tour.

Everything Eden touched turned to gold.

We watched her, enthralled by each pose she struck, mesmerized by each note. We were under such a spell that at first no one noticed when something went wrong. During the guitar solo, Eden's arms fell to her side and she stopped dancing.

I thought it was another dramatic transition to the next song, so when her head fell forward, I assumed she was counting silently, ready to look up with those hypnotic, piercing black eyes and captivate her fans all over again.

But then the other dancers noticed, and several stopped moving. Then several more. And when the guitar solo ended, Eden still stood there, silent, a virtual vacuum sucking life from the background music.

Her chest heaved. Her shoulders shook. The microphone fell from her hand and crashed to the stage.

Feedback squealed across the auditorium, and the drummer stopped drumming. The guitarists—both lead and bass—turned toward Eden and stopped playing when they saw her.

Eden collapsed, legs bent, long, dark hair spilling around her on the floor.

Someone screamed from behind me in the sudden

hush, and I jumped, startled. A woman raced past me and onto the stage, followed by several large men. My hair blew back in the draft created by the sudden rush, but I barely noticed. My gaze was glued to Eden who lay unmoving on the floor.

People bent over her, and I recognized the woman as her mother, the most famous stage parent/manager in the country. Eden's mom was crying, trying to shake her daughter awake as a member of security tried to pull her away. "She's not breathing!" the mother shouted, and we all heard her clearly, because the crowd of thousands had gone silent with shock. "Somebody help her, she's not breathing!"

And suddenly neither was I.

My hand clenched Nash's, and my heart raced in dreadful anticipation of the keening that would rip its way from my throat as the pop star's soul left her body. A *bean sidhe*'s wail can shatter not just glass, but eardrums. The frequency resonates painfully in the human brain, so that the sound seems to rattle from both outside and within.

"Breathe, Kaylee," Nash whispered into my ear, wrapping both arms around me as his voice cocooned my heart, his Influence soothing, comforting. A male *bean sidhe*'s voice is like an audio-sedative, without the side effects of the chemical version. Nash could make the screaming stop, or at least lower its volume and intensity. "Just breathe through it." So I did. I watched the stage over his shoulder and breathed, waiting for Eden to die.

Waiting for the scream to build deep inside me.

But the scream didn't come.

Onstage, someone's foot hit Eden's microphone, and it rolled across the floor and into the pit. No one noticed, because Eden still wasn't breathing. But I wasn't wailing, either.

Slowly, I loosened my grip on Nash and felt relief settle through me as logic prevailed over my dread. Eden wasn't wearing a death shroud—a translucent black haze surrounding the soon-to-be-dead, visible only to female *bean sidhes*. "She's fine." I smiled in spite of the horrified expressions surrounding me. "She's gonna be fine." Because if she were going to die, I'd already be screaming.

I'm a female *bean sidhe*. That's what we do.

"No, she isn't," Tod said softly, and we turned to find him still staring at the stage. The reaper pointed, and I followed his finger until my gaze found Eden again, surrounded by her mother, bodyguards, and odd members of the crew, one of whom was now giving her mouth-to-mouth. And as I watched, a foggy, ethereal substance began to rise slowly from the star's body like a snake from its charmer's basket.

Rather than floating toward the ceiling, as a soul should, Eden's seemed *heavy,* like it might sink to the ground around her instead. It was thick, yet colorless. And undulating through it were ribbons of darkness, swirling as if stirred by an unfelt breeze.

My breath caught in my throat, but I let it go almost immediately, because though I had no idea what that substance was, I knew without a doubt what it *wasn't*.

Eden had no soul.

2

"WHAT IS THAT?" I whispered frantically, tugging Nash's hand. "It's not a soul. And if she's dead, how come I'm not screaming?"

"What is what?" Nash hissed, and I realized he couldn't see Eden's not-soul. Male *bean sidhes* can only see elements of the Netherworld—including freed souls—when a female *bean sidhe* wails. Apparently the same held true for whatever ethereal sludge was oozing from Eden's body.

Nash glanced around to make sure no one was listening to us, but there was really no need. Eden was the center of attention.

Tod rolled his eyes and pulled one hand from the

pocket of his baggy jeans. "Look over there." He pointed not toward the stage, but across it, where more people watched the spectacle from the opposite wing. "Do you see her?"

"I see lots of hers." People scrambled on the other side of the stage, most speaking into cell phones. A couple of vultures even snapped pictures of the fallen singer, and indignation burned deep in my chest.

But Tod continued to point, so I squinted into the dark wing. Whatever he wanted me to see probably wasn't native to the human world so it wouldn't be immediately obvious.

And that's when I found her.

The woman's tall, slim form created a darker spot in the already-thick shadows, a mere suggestion of a shape. Her eyes were the only part of her I could focus on, glowing like green embers in the gloom. "Who is she?" I glanced at Nash and he nodded, telling me he could see her too. Which likely meant she was *letting* us see her…

"That's Libby, from Special Projects." An odd, eager light shone in blue eyes Tod usually kept shadowed by brows drawn low. "When this week's list came down, she came with it, for this one job."

He was talking about the reapers' list, which contained the names and the exact place and time of death of everyone scheduled to die in the local area within a one-week span.

"You knew this was going to happen?" Even knowing he was a reaper, I couldn't believe how different Tod's reaction to death was from mine. Unlike most people, it wasn't my own death I feared—it was everyone else's. The sight of the deceased's soul would mark my own descent into madness. At least, that's what most people thought of my screaming fits. Humans had no idea that my "hysterical shrieking" actually suspended a person's soul as it leaves its body.

Sometimes I wished I still lived in human ignorance, but those days were over for me, for better or for worse.

"I couldn't turn down the chance to watch Libby work. She's a legend." Tod shrugged. "And seeing Addy was a bonus."

"Well, thanks so much for dragging us along!" Nash snapped.

"What is she?" I asked as another cluster of people rushed past us—two more bodyguards and a short, slight man whose face looked pinched with professional concern and curiosity. Probably a doctor. "And what's so special about this assignment?"

"Libby's a very special reaper." Tod's short, blond goatee glinted in the blue-tinted overhead lights as he spoke. "She was called in because that—" he pointed to the substance the female reaper now was steadily *inhaling* from Eden's body, over a twenty-foot span and dozens of heads "—isn't a soul. It's Demon's Breath."

Suddenly I was very glad no one else could hear Tod. I wished they couldn't hear me, either. "Demon, as in hellion?" I whispered, as low as I could speak and still be heard.

Tod nodded with his usual slow, grim smile. The very word *hellion* sent a jolt of terror through me, but Tod's eyes sparkled with excitement, as if he could actually get high on danger. I guess that's what you get when you mix boredom with the afterlife.

"She sold her soul…." Nash whispered, revulsion echoing within the sudden understanding in his voice.

I'd never met a hellion—they couldn't leave the Netherworld, fortunately—but I was intimately familiar with their appetite for human souls. Six weeks earlier, my aunt had tried to trade five poached teenage souls in exchange for her own eternal youth and beauty, but her plan went bad in the end, and she wound up paying in part with her own soul. But not before four girls died for her vanity.

Tod shrugged. "That's what it looks like to me."

Horror filled me. "Why would anyone do that?"

Nash looked like he shared my revulsion, but Tod

only shrugged again, clearly unbothered by the most horrifying concept I'd ever encountered. "They usually ask for fame, fortune, and beauty."

All of which Eden had in spades.

"Okay, so she sold her soul to a hellion." That statement sound wrong in *sooo* many ways…. "Do I even want to know how Demon's Breath got into Eden's body in its place?"

"Probably not," Nash whispered, as heavy black curtains began to slide across the front of the stage, cutting off the shocked, horrified chatter from the auditorium.

But as usual, Tod was happy to give me a morbid peek into the Netherworld—complete with irreverent hand gestures. "When the hellion literally sucked out her soul, he replaced it with his own breath. That kept her alive until her time to die. Which is why Libby's here. Demon's Breath is a controlled substance in the Netherworld, and it has to be disposed of very carefully. Libby's trained to do that."

"A controlled substance?" I felt my brows dip in confusion. "Like plutonium?"

Tod chuckled, running his fingers across a panel of dead electronic equipment propped against the wall. "More like heroin."

I sighed and leaned into Nash, letting the warmth

of his body comfort me. "The Netherworld is soooo weird."

"You have no idea." Tod's curls bounced when he turned to face Libby again, where the lady reaper had now inhaled most of the sluggish Demon's Breath. It swirled slowly into her mouth in a long, thick strand, like a ghostly trail of rotting spaghetti. "Come on, I want to talk to her." He took off toward the stage without waiting for our reply, and I lunged after him, hoping he was solid enough to touch.

He was—at least for me. Though I was sure Nash's hand would have gone right through the reaper.

"Wait." I hauled him back in spite of the weird look I got from some random stagehand in a black tee. "We can't just trot across the stage without being seen." Though, there were certainly times I wished I could go invisible. Like, during P.E. The girls' basketball coach was out to get me, I was sure of it.

"And I don't think I want to meet this super-reaper." Nash stuffed his hands in his front pockets. "The garden variety's weird enough."

Plus, most reapers hold no fondness for *bean sidhes*. The combined natural abilities of a male and female *bean sidhe*—the potential to return a soul to its body— are in direct opposition with a reaper's entire purpose in life. Or, the afterlife.

Tod was the rare exception to this mutual species aversion, by virtue of being both *bean sidhe* and reaper.

"Fine, but don't expect me to pass on any pearls of wisdom she coughs up...." Tod's gaze settled on me, and his full, perfect lips turned up into a wicked smile. He knew he had me; I was trying to learn everything I could about the Netherworld, to make up for living the first sixteen years of my life in total ignorance, thanks to my family's misguided attempt to keep me safe. And as creeped-out as I was by Eden's sudden, soulless death, I wouldn't pass up the opportunity to learn something neither Tod nor Nash could teach me.

"Nash, please?" I pulled his hand from his pocket and wound my fingers through his. I would go without him, but I'd rather have his company, and I was pretty sure I'd get it. He wouldn't leave me alone with Tod, because he didn't entirely trust his undead brother.

Neither did I.

I saw Nash's decision in the frown lines around his mouth before he nodded, so I stood on my toes to kiss him. Excitement tingled along the length of my spine and settled to burn lower when our lips touched, and when I pulled away, his hazel eyes churned with swirls of green and brown, a sure sign that a *bean sidhe* was feeling something strong. Not that humans could see it.

Nash nodded again to answer my unspoken question. "Yours are swirling, too."

I dared a grin in spite of the solemn circumstances, and Tod rolled his eyes at our display. Then he stomped off silently to meet this "special" reaper.

The fluttering in my stomach settled into a heavy anchor of dread as we followed Tod behind the stage, dodging shell-shocked technicians and stagehands on our way to the opposite wing. I needed all the information I could find about the Netherworld to keep myself from accidentally stumbling into something dangerous, but I didn't exactly look forward to meeting more reapers. Especially the creepy, intimidating woman swallowing the ominous life-source that had kept Eden up and singing for who knew how long.

"So what makes this reaper such a legend?" I whispered, walking between Nash and Tod, whose shoes still made no sound on the floor.

For a moment, Tod gaped at me like I'd just asked what made grass green. Then he seemed to remember my ignorance. "She's ancient. The oldest reaper still reaping. Maybe the oldest reaper ever. No one knows what name she was born with, but back in ancient Rome she took on the name of the goddess of death. Libitina."

I arched both brows at Tod. "So, you address the oldest, scariest grim reaper in history by a nickname?"

Tod shrugged, but I thought I saw him blush. Though, that could have been the red satin backdrop panels showing through his nearly translucent cheek. "I've never actually addressed her as anything. We haven't officially met."

"Great," I breathed, rolling my eyes. We were accompanying Tod-the-reaper-fanboy to meet his hero. It couldn't get any lamer without a *Star Trek* convention and an English-to-Klingon dictionary.

When we rounded the corner, my gaze found Libby just as she sucked the last bit of Demon's Breath from the air. The end of the strand whipped up to smack her cheek before sliding between her pursed lips, and the ancient reaper swiped the back of one black-leather-clad arm across her mouth, as if to wipe a smudge of sauce from her face.

I didn't want to know what kind of sauce Demon's Breath swam in.

"There she is," Tod said, and the eerie, awed quality of his voice drew my gaze to his face. He looked… shy.

My own intimidation faded in the face of the first obvious nerves I'd seen from the rookie reaper, and I couldn't resist a grin. "Okay, let's go." I took Tod's hand and had tugged him two steps in Libby's direction before his fingers suddenly faded out of existence around my own.

I stopped and glanced down, irritated to see that he had dialed both his appearance and his physical presence down to barely-there, to escape my grasp. "What's wrong?"

"Nothing a little dignity wouldn't fix," Tod snapped. "So could we please *not* mob the three-thousand-plus-year-old reaper like tweens at a boy-band concert?" He ran transparent hands over his equally transparent tee and marched toward Libby with his shoulders square, evidently satisfied that his composure was intact.

He grew a little more solid with each step, and I glanced around, afraid someone would notice him suddenly appearing in our midst. But when his shoes continued to make no sound, I realized he hadn't stepped into human sight. Not that it mattered. All eyes were glued to the stage, where the doctor still worked tirelessly—and fruitlessly—on Eden.

We followed Tod, and I knew by the sudden confidence in Nash's step that he could now see his brother. And that he was probably secretly hoping Tod would do or say something stupid in front of the foremost expert in his field.

We caught up with him as he stopped, and since they

were the same height, Libby's bright green eyes stared straight into Tod's blue with enough intensity to make even me squirm. "Hi," Tod started, and I had to give him credit for not stuttering.

My own tongue was completely paralyzed.

Libitina was very old, very experienced, and clearly very powerful—all obvious in her bearing alone. She was also so impossibly beautiful that I was suddenly embarrassed by the makeup I'd probably sweated off during the concert and the long brown hair I could see frizzing on the edge of my vision, in spite of my efforts with a flatiron.

Libby wore a long, black leather trench coat, cinched at her tiny waist to show off slim hips. I would have said the coat was cliché for someone intimately involved with Death, except that as old as she was, she'd probably been wearing black leather much longer than it had been in vogue for hookers and superheroes alike.

Her hair was pulled back from her face in a severe ponytail that trailed tight, black curls halfway down her back. Her skin was dark and flawless, and so smooth I wanted to touch her cheek, just to assure myself she wasn't as perfect as she looked. She couldn't be.

Could she?

"Yes?" Libby said, her piercing gaze still trained on Tod. She hadn't acknowledged either me or Nash, and

I was suddenly sure that, like most reapers, she hated *bean sidhes*. Maybe we shouldn't have tagged along after all.

Yet she hadn't become invisible to us....

"My name is Tod, and I work for the local branch office." He paused, and I was amused to realize Tod's cheeks were blazing—and this time that had nothing to do with the stage backdrop. "Can I ask you a couple of questions?"

Libby scowled, and a chill shot up my spine. "You are dissatisfied with my services?" She bit off the ends of her words in anger, distorting an accent I couldn't place, and we all three stepped back in unison, unwilling to stand in the face of her fury.

"No!" Tod held up both hands, and I was too busy choking on my own fear to be amused by his. "This has nothing to do with the local office. I'm off duty tonight. I'm just curious. About the process…"

Libby's thin, black brows arched, and I thought I saw amusement flicker behind her eyes. "Ask," she said finally, and suddenly I liked her—even if she didn't like *bean sidhes*—because she could easily have made Tod feel about an inch tall.

Tod stuffed his hands into his pockets and inhaled slowly. "What does it feel like? Demon's Breath. You hold it…inside. Right?"

Libby nodded briefly, then turned and walked away, headed toward a hallway identical to the one we'd followed to the stage.

We hesitated, glancing at one another in question. Then Tod shrugged and hurried after her. We actually had to jog to keep up as her boots moved silently but quickly over the floor.

"You breathe it in, deep into your lungs." Her rich accent spoke of dead languages, of cultures long ago lost to the ravages of time and fickle memory. Her voice was low and gruff. Aged. Powerful. It sent shivers through me, as if I were hearing something I shouldn't be able to. Something no one else had heard in centuries. "It fills you. It burns like frostbite, as if the Breath will consume your insides. Feed on them. But that is good. If the burning stops, you have held it too long. Demon's Breath will kill your soul."

The shivers grew until I noticed my hands trembling. I took Nash's in my left, and shoved the right into my pocket.

A couple of technicians passed us carrying equipment, and Tod waited until they were gone to pose his next question. "How long do you have?" He paced beside the female reaper now. Nash and I were content to trail behind, just close enough to hear.

"An hour." Her lips moved in profile against the

white wall as she turned to half face him. "Any longer, and you risk much."

"What do you do with it?" I asked—I couldn't help it—and Libby froze in midstep. She pivoted slowly to look at me, and I saw *time* in her eyes. Years of life and death, and existence without end. The shivers in my hands became tremors echoing the length of my body.

I should not have drawn her attention.

"Who is this?" Libby faced Tod again.

"A friend. My brother's girlfriend." He nodded toward Nash, who stood tall beneath her hair-curling, nerve-crunching scrutiny. Then Libby whirled on one booted heel and marched on.

Cool relief sifted through me, and only then did I realize Tod hadn't given her either of our names. Nash had practically beaten that precaution into him; it was never wise to give your name to Death's emissaries. Though, if a reaper wanted to know your name, it was easy enough to find, especially in today's world. Which is why it was also unwise to catch a reaper's attention.

Sirens warbled outside the stadium then, and another gaggle of official-looking people rushed down the hall toward the stage, but Libby didn't seem to notice them. "There are places for proper disposal of Demon's Breath. In the Nether," she added, as if there were any question about that.

"If a reaper wanted to get into that—collecting Demon's Breath instead of souls—how might he get started?" Tod asked as we followed Libby around a sharp white corner, her feet silent on the slick linoleum.

"By surviving the next thousand years." Her accent grew sharper, her words thick with warning. "If you still live then, find me. I will show you. But do not try it alone. Fools suffer miserable deaths, boy."

"I won't," Tod assured her. "But it was awesome to watch."

Libby stopped, eyeing him with a strange expression caught on her features, as if she didn't quite know what she intended to say until the words came out. "You may watch again. I will return in five days."

"For more Demon's Breath?" I asked, and again her creepy green gaze slid my way, seeming to burn through my eyes and into my brain.

"Of course. The other fool will release hers on Thursday."

"What other fool?" Tod demanded through clenched teeth, and I glanced at him, surprised by his sharp tone. His brows were furrowed, his beautiful lips thinned by dread.

"Addison Page. The singer," Libby said, like it should have been obvious.

Tod actually stumbled backward, and Nash put a

hand on his shoulder, but it went right through him. For a moment, I was afraid he'd fall through the featureless white wall. "Addy sold her soul?" Tod rubbed one hand across his own nearly transparent forehead. "Are you sure?"

Libby raised her brows, as if to ask if he were serious. "When?"

"That is not my concern." The reaper slid her slim, dark hands into the pockets of her coat, watching Tod with disdain now, as if her hunch that he wasn't yet ready to collect Demon's Breath had just been confirmed. "Mine is to gather what I come for and dispose of it properly. Time marches on, boy, and so must I."

"Wait!" Tod grabbed her arm, and I wasn't sure who was more surprised—Libby or Nash. But Tod rushed on as if he hadn't noticed. "Addy's going to die?"

Libby nodded, then disappeared without so much as a wink to warn us. She was just suddenly gone, yet her voice remained for a moment longer, an echo of her very existence.

"She will release the Demon's Breath by taking her own life. And I shall be there to claim it."

3

"ADDY SOLD HER SOUL." Tod's voice sounded odd. Distant. I think he was in shock. Or maybe that was just an echo from the empty hallway.

If a voice isn't audible in the human range of hearing, can it echo?

"Um, yeah. Sounds like it," I said. The very thought sent chills through me, and I rubbed my arms through my sleeves, trying to get rid of the goose bumps.

"She's gonna kill herself." Tod's eyes were wide with panic and horror. I'd never seen him scared, and I didn't like how fear pressed his lips into a tense, thin line and wrinkled his forehead. "We have to stop her. Warn her, or something." Tod took off down the hall, and Nash and I ran after him. If we didn't keep up, he'd disappear through a wall or something, and we'd never find him. At least, not in time to finish arguing with him.

"Warn her of what? That she's going to kill herself?" Nash's shoes squeaked as we rounded a corner. "Don't you think she already knows that?"

"Maybe not." Tod stopped when the hallway ended in a T, glancing both ways in indecision. "Maybe whatever's supposed to drive her to suicide hasn't happened yet." He looked to the left again, then took off toward the right.

"Wait!" I lunged forward and grabbed his arm, relieved when my hand didn't pass right through him. "Do you even know where you're going?"

"No clue." He shrugged, looking more like his brother in that moment than ever before. "I know where her dressing room is, but I don't know how to get there from here, and I can't just pop in without losing you two."

I didn't want to know how he knew where her dressing room was, but considering how often he'd gone invisible to spy on me, the answer seemed obvious.

"Yeah, physics is a real bitch." Nash rolled his beautiful hazel eyes and leaned with one shoulder against the wall like he had nowhere better to be.

"You don't have to wait for us." As cool as it would

have been to meet Addison Page, telling a rising star that she was going to end both her career and her life in less than a week was so not on my to-do list. "I think I'm going to sit this one out." I propped my hands on my hips and glanced at Nash to see if he was with me, but he and Tod wore identical, half amused, half reluctant expressions. "What?"

"I'm dead, Kaylee." Tod stopped in front of the first door we'd come to, his hand on the knob. "Addy came to my funeral. I can't show up in her dressing room two years after I was buried and tell her not to kill herself. That would just be rude."

I laughed at his idea of post-death etiquette, pretty sure that "rude" was a bit of an understatement. But I sobered quickly when his point sank in. "Wait, you want us to tell her?"

"If she sees me, she'll freak out and spend the last days of her life in the psych ward."

I bristled, irritated by the reminder of my own brief stay in the land of sedatives and straitjackets. "It's called the mental health unit, thank you. And we are *not* going to go tell your famous ex-girlfriend to lighten up or she'll be joining you six feet under. *That* would be rude."

"She wouldn't believe us, anyway," Nash said, crossing his arms over his chest in a show of solidarity. "She'd probably call Security and have us arrested."

"So *make* her believe you." Tod gestured in exasperation. Like it'd be that easy. "I'll be there to help. She just won't be able to see me."

I glanced at Nash and was relieved to see my reluctance still reflected in his features. As much as I wanted to help—to hopefully save Addison Page's life—I did *not* want to be taken from her dressing room in handcuffs.

And my dad would be soooo pissed if he had to bail me out of jail.

But before I could even contemplate how bad that would be, something else sank in….

"Tod, wait a minute." He let go of the knob when I stepped between him and the door, but his oddly angelic frown said he wasn't happy about it. "How do we know this will even work? I mean, say she believes us and decides not to kill herself. Won't she just die of some other cause next week, at the same time she would have killed herself? If her name's really on the list, she's going to die one way or another, right? You can't stop Libby from coming for her, and frankly, I think you'd be an idiot to even try."

Nash and Tod had explained to me how the whole death business works right after I found out I was a *bean sidhe,* during the single most stressful week of my life. Evidently people come with expiration dates stamped on them at birth—much like food in the grocery store. It was the reapers' job to enforce that expiration date, then collect the dead person's soul and take it to be recycled.

As far as I knew, the only way to extend a person's life was to exchange his or her death date for someone else's, to keep life and death in balance. So if we saved Addison Page's life—which, as *bean sidhes,* Nash and I could technically do—someone else would have to die in her place, and that someone could be anyone. Me or Nash, or some random, nearby stranger.

As much as I wanted to help both Tod and Addison, I was not willing to pay that price, nor would I ask someone else to.

Tod blinked at me, and while his scowl remained in place, his sad eyes revealed the truth. "I know." He sighed, and his broad shoulders fell with the movement. "But I haven't actually seen the list yet, so I'm not going to worry about that right now. What I *am* going to do is try to talk her out of suicide. But I need help. Please, guys." His gaze trailed from me to Nash, then back.

Nash frowned and leaned against the wall beside the door again, striking the I-cannot-be-moved posture I recognized from several of our own past arguments.

"Tod, you're the one who says it's dangerous for *bean sidhes* to mess in reaper business."

"And that knowing when they're going to die only makes a human's last days miserable," I added, perversely pleased by the chance to throw his own words back at him.

Tod shrugged. "I know, but this is different."

"Why?" Nash demanded, his gaze going hard as he glared at Tod. "Because this time it's an ex? One you've obviously never gotten over…"

Anger flashed across the reaper's face, mirroring his brother's, but beneath it lay a foundation of pain and vulnerability even he could not hide. "This is different because she sold her soul, Nash. You know what that means."

Nash's eyes closed for a moment, and he inhaled deeply. When he met Tod's gaze again, his held more sympathy than anger. "That was her choice."

"She didn't know what she was getting into! She couldn't have!" the reaper shouted, and I was floored by the depth of his anger and frustration. I'd never seen him put so much raw emotion on display.

"What was she getting into?" I glanced from brother to brother and crossed my own arms, waiting for an answer. I hate always being the clueless one.

Finally Nash sighed and turned his attention to me.

"She sold her soul to a hellion, but he won't have full use of it until she dies. When she does, her soul is his for eternity. Forever. He can do whatever he wants with it, but since hellions feed on pain and chaos, he'll probably torture Addison's soul—and thus what remains of Addison—until the end of time. Or the end of the Netherworld. Whichever comes first."

My stomach churned around the dinner we'd grabbed before the concert, threatening to send the burger back up. "Is that what happened to the souls Aunt Val traded to Belphegore?" Nash nodded grimly, and horror drew my hands into cold, damp fists. "But that's not fair. Those girls did nothing wrong, and now their souls are going to be tortured for all of eternity?"

"That's why soul-poaching is illegal." Tod's voice was soft with sympathy and heavy with grief.

"Is selling your soul illegal, too?" A spark of hope zinged through me. Maybe Addison could get her soul back on a technicality!

But the reaper shook his head. "Souls can't be stolen from the living. They can only be given away or sold by the owner, or poached after death, once they're released from the body. There's a huge market for human souls in the Netherworld, and what Addy did was perfectly legal. But she had no idea what she was getting into. She couldn't have."

I didn't know what to say. I couldn't decide whether I was more horrified for those four innocent souls or for my aunt, who'd given up her own soul to save her daughter's. Or for Addison Page, who would soon suffer the same fate.

"We have to tell her." I looked into Nash's eyes and found the greens and browns once again swirling, this time with fear and reluctance, based on the expression framing the windows of his soul. "I couldn't live with myself if we didn't at least try."

"Kaylee, this is not our responsibility," he said, his protest fortified with a solid dose of ordinary common sense. "The hellion already has her soul. What are we supposed to do?"

I shrugged. "I don't know. Maybe we could help her break her demon contract, or something. Is that possible?"

Nash nodded reluctantly. "There are procedures built in, but Kaylee, it's way too dangerous…." But he knew he couldn't change my mind. Not this time. I could see it on his face.

"I can't walk away and leave her soul to be tortured if there's anything I can do to help. Can you?"

He didn't answer, and his heavy silence frightened me more than the thought of the hellion waiting for full possession of Addison's soul. Then he took my hand,

and I exhaled deeply in relief. "Lead the way, reaper," he said. "And you better hurry. With Eden dead, Addy probably won't stick around for the finale." The previous shows had each closed with a duet from Addison's forthcoming album.

With Nash's warning in mind, we wound our way through the backstage area, Tod popping into locked rooms and side hallways occasionally to make sure we were on the right track. He also popped into Addison's dressing room twice, to make sure she was still there.

The closer we got, the more people we saw in the halls, and they were all talking about Eden's onstage collapse. She'd been rushed to the hospital moments after we left the stage, and though the EMTs had been giving her CPR and mouth-to-mouth when they left, no one seemed to think she would live.

Which we already knew for sure.

Thanks to the badges around our necks, no one tried to throw us out, or even ask where we were headed, so when we finally made it to Addison's dressing room, I couldn't help thinking the whole thing had been too easy.

I was right. There was a security guard posted outside her door. He had a newspaper rolled up in one fist and biceps the size of cannons.

"Now what?" I whispered, bending for a drink from the water fountain twenty feet from the closed door.

"Let me make sure she's still alone," Tod said, and I flinched over how loud he was speaking until I realized no one else could hear him. "Then I'll get rid of the guard."

Before we could ask how he planned to do that, the reaper disappeared.

Nash and I strolled arm in arm down the hall, trying not to look suspicious, and I grew more grateful by the second that he'd come with us—because I would have done it even without him. The security guard wore sunglasses, though it was night and we were inside, so I couldn't tell whether or not he was watching us, but I would have bet money that he was.

Out of nowhere, a hand touched my elbow, and Tod suddenly appeared at my side. I nearly jumped out of my skin, and the guard's head swiveled slowly in my direction.

"Don't do that!" I whispered angrily.

"Sorry," Tod said. But he didn't look very sorry. "Her mom's in there with her now, but she's about to leave to call the car."

He'd barely spoken the last word when the dressing room door opened, and an older, darker version of Addison Page emerged. She nodded to the guard, then clacked off down the hall past us, without a word or a glance in our direction.

"Okay…" This time Tod whispered, as if setting the tone for the Acme tiptoe routine we were about to pull. "You guys duck into the bathroom around the corner. I'll draw the guard away while you sneak into Addy's room, then I'll pop in with you. Get her attention fast, and don't let her scream."

But something told me that would be easier said than done.

"I'm gonna kill you if this goes bad," Nash hissed as we followed the reaper around the corner toward the public restroom.

"It's a little late for that," Tod snapped. Then he was gone again.

I opened the door to the ladies' room to make sure it was empty, then waved Nash inside and left the door slightly ajar. While he looked around in awe at the cleanliness and the fresh flowers, I peeked through the crack, waiting for some all-clear sign from Tod.

We'd only been in the bathroom a few seconds when rapid footsteps clomped toward us from the direction of Addison's dressing room. Tod appeared around the corner, fully corporeal now, a wild grin on his face, the security guard's newspaper tucked under one arm. The guard raced after him, but the poor man was obviously built for strength rather than speed, because Tod put more distance between them with every step.

"Get back here, you little punk!" the guard shouted, huge arms pumping uselessly at his sides.

Tod glanced at me as he passed the bathroom, and I could swear I saw him wink. Then he rounded the next corner, and the guard trailed after him.

As soon as they were gone, Nash and I jogged back to the dressing room, hearts pounding with exhilaration, afraid the guard would return at any moment. We stood in front of the door, hand in hand, and my pulse raced with nerves. Nash met my eyes, then nodded toward the doorknob.

"You do it," I whispered. "She doesn't know me, but she may remember you."

Nash rolled his eyes but reached toward the door. His hand hesitated over the knob for a second, then I saw determination—or was that resignation?—flash across his face. He twisted the knob and opened the door in one smooth motion, so brash I almost envied his nerve.

He stepped inside and pulled me in with him, then closed the door.

I braced myself, expecting to hear Addison scream for Security. Instead, I heard nothing and saw no sign of Addison Page.

But her room was *awesome*. A rack of flashy costumes stood against one wall, beside a full-length stand-alone mirror. Which was next to a vanity lit by several large, frosted bulbs. In one corner stood a small round table covered in an array of meats, cheeses, fruit, and bite-size desserts. And in the center of the room, a couch and two chairs were gathered around a flat-screen television hooked up to a PlayStation 3.

But no Addison Page.

Nash glanced at me with his brows raised in question, and I shrugged. Then jumped when the sound of running water drew my focus to an open door I hadn't noticed before. The dressing room had a private restroom. And Addison Page was in it.

"Is the car ready?" The singer stepped out of the restroom and crossed the floor toward her vanity, head tilted away from us as she pulled an earring from her left ear. Then she looked up and froze. For just a second, I thought she might actually scream. But then Nash spoke, and her features relaxed, just enough to hold true fear at bay.

"Hi, Addison," he said, and his Influence flowed over the room like a warm, comforting breeze, smoothing her ruffled feathers and taking the edge off my own nerves. Male *bean sidhes* rocked the whole audio-anesthesia thing, whereas the females of our species sported only an eardrum-bursting scream.

Not fair, right? But convenient at times.

A brief flicker of annoyance flashed across Addison's famous, pixieish features, replaced an instant later by a gracious, bright white smile. "Um, this isn't really a good time. I'm on my way to the hospital to check on Eden," she said, brushing back the blue streak in her pale hair while she grabbed a pen from the vanity. "But I guess I have time for a quick autograph."

She thought we were fans. And she didn't know Eden was dead. I wasn't sure which misunderstanding to correct first, so I started with the lesser of two evils.

"Oh, we're not fans." I shrugged, stuffing my hands into my pockets. But then she frowned, and I realized how that had sounded. "I mean, we *are* fans. We love your music. But that's not why we're here."

Her frown deepened. Even with Nash's Influence, by my best guess, we had less than a minute before she would yell for the guard, who had surely returned to his post by now. "Then what do you want?" Addison narrowed beautiful, impossibly pale blue eyes, though her smile stayed friendly. Or at least cautious.

I glanced at Nash, hoping for some help, but he only shrugged and gestured for me to start talking. After all, I'd gotten him into this.

"We have to tell you something." I hesitated, glancing at the couch. "Could we maybe sit down?"

"Why?" She was openly suspicious now, and her hand snuck into her pocket, where a bulge betrayed her cell phone. "Who are you?"

"My name is Kaylee Cavanaugh, and this is Nash Hudson. I think you two used to know each other."

The lines in her brow deepened, and she propped one hand on her hip. "No, I... Wait. Hudson?" Understanding flickered behind her eyes.

Nash nodded.

"Tod's brother." Addison pulled her hand from her pocket and laid it across her chest, like she was crossing her heart. "I'm sorry I didn't recognize you. I haven't seen you since the funeral. How are you?"

"I'm fine." Nash gave her a small, sad smile. "But you're not."

Alarm flashed across her face and her hand slid into her pocket again, her thin, gold chain-link bracelet pushed up her arm with the motion. "What is this?"

Before I could answer, Tod appeared at my side, still winded from his race with the security guard. "What'd I miss?"

"Nothing," Nash said, having obviously heard, if not seen, him. "We haven't told her yet."

"Told who what?" Addison pulled the phone from

her pocket and flipped it open, truly frightened now. "What's going on?"

"Say something," Tod urged, elbowing me. I glared at him, and Addison followed my gaze to…nothing. She couldn't see him, and she obviously couldn't hear him. "Start talking or she's going to call someone."

"I know!" I whispered, elbowing him back. There was no use pretending he wasn't there on her account. She already thought we were nuts. "Addison, please sit down. We have to tell you something, and it's going to sound very…strange."

"It already does. I think you should go." She edged toward the door, stretching one arm ahead of her, as if to point the way. "You're creeping me out."

"*Do* something!" Tod yelled this time, eyes wide and desperate.

Nash sighed heavily, and I knew what he was going to do a moment before the words left his mouth. But not soon enough to prevent them. "Okay, here's the deal. You're going to kill yourself in five days, and we're here to talk you out of it."

Addison blinked, and for a moment her fear gave way to confusion, then anger as her empty hand clenched the back of the sofa. "Get out. Now."

"What, you couldn't put a little Influence behind that one?" I snapped, glaring at Nash.

"Not if you want her to understand." His gaze shifted past me to Tod. "I told you she wouldn't listen."

"Who are you talking to?" Addison demanded, her voice rising in both pitch and volume.

"You're gonna have to show her," I told Tod, hyper-conscious of the singer's near panic. "She won't listen to us, but she can't ignore *you*."

Tod glanced at Nash for a second opinion, but his brother only nodded, leaning with one hip against the arm of an overstuffed chair. "I don't see any other way."

Tod sighed, and I knew from the surprise on Addison's face that she'd heard him. A second later she jumped backward and her free hand went to her throat in shock. "No…"

She could see him.

4

"Addy, please don't freak out." Tod held his hands palms out, as if to calm her.

"There's another option?" Addison backed slowly toward her vanity, planting one wedge-heeled foot carefully behind the other with each step. "You're dead. I saw you in your coffin."

She had? I turned to Tod with one hand propped on my hip, surprised. "Wait, you were actually *in* the coffin?"

"Not for long," he mumbled. Then, "Not the point, Kay."

Oh, yeah. Soulless pop star contemplating suicide. *Focus, Kaylee.*

"Who are you?" Addison demanded. The backs of her thighs hit the vanity and she gripped the edge of it to steady herself. "How did you do that?"

It took me a second to realize she meant his sudden appearance out of nowhere. And maybe the whole coming-back-to-life thing.

"Addison, it's Tod. You know it's him," I said, desperately hoping that was true. That she was even listening to me, though her shocked, wide-eyed gaze was glued to her undead ex-boyfriend.

Her breathing slowed and her pale blue eyes narrowed. She was studying him, probably trying to decide whether to freak out and shout for help, or to calm down and listen. I honestly don't know which I would have chosen in her position. But then she shook her head once, as if she were trying to toss off sleep, and denial shone bright in her eyes again.

"No. You're not him. You can't be. This is some kind of joke, or stunt. I'm being *Punk'd,* right? Ashton, if you're out there, this is *not funny!*" Her face flushed with anger, and tears formed in her eyes.

"You're gonna have to prove it," I whispered, glancing sideways at Tod.

He sighed, and I was impressed with how calm he stayed. "You know me, Addy. We went out for eight months in high school, back in Hurst, before you got the pilot. You were a freshman and I was a sophomore. Remember?"

Instead of answering, Addy crossed her arms over her chest and rolled her eyes. "Lots of people know that. I mentioned Tod in an interview once, and paparazzi followed me to his funeral. Nice try, but you're done. Get out before I yell for Security."

She talked about Tod to reporters? Wow. *They must have been really close....*

"Addy, you remember our first date? You didn't talk to the press about that, did you?"

She shook her head slowly, listening, though her arms remained crossed.

"We went to the West End for ice cream at Marble Slab, and we got a caricature done together by a guy with an easel set up on the sidewalk. I still have it. Then you got carsick on the way home and threw up on the side of the road. Do you remember? You didn't tell anyone else about that, did you?"

She shook her head again, her eyes wide. "Tod?" Addison's famous voice went squeaky, and broke on that one syllable. He nodded, and she hugged herself. "How...? That's impossible. I saw you, and you were dead. You were *dead!*"

"Yeah, well, it turns out that's not always as permanent as it sounds." Nash spoke calmly, softly, and the tension in my own body seemed to ease at his first words. "He was dead. But he's not anymore. Kind of."

Addison's shoulders relaxed as her gaze traveled from Tod to his still-living brother. "How? That doesn't make sense." Yet she wasn't as upset by that as she should have been. With any luck, Nash could strike a balance between too-terrified-to-listen and too-relaxed-to-understand.

"It doesn't make sense up here—" Nash tapped his temple "—but I think you know the truth inside. You've seen strange things, haven't you, Addy?" His voice lilted up with the question and he stepped forward, capturing her gaze. "You sold your soul, and you must have seen some pretty weird stuff in the process...."

Addison's shock broke through her mild daze for a moment, and she opened her mouth, but before she could ask how he knew about her soul, Nash continued. "But all of that was real, and so is this. So is Tod."

Her gaze slid to the reaper again, and now that Nash had calmed her fear and quieted that stubborn human denial, I could tell she really *saw* him. "How did you... get here?"

The reaper shrugged, and mild mischief turned up the corners of his lips. "I distracted the guard at the door, then doubled back."

Addison frowned, then a small smile began at her mouth and spread to include those famous, eerily pale eyes. "I see death hasn't killed your sense of humor."

Though, the great dirt nap hadn't exactly revived it, either....

She laughed over her own lame joke. "Wow. That's not a sentence I ever expected to say."

"So, are you okay with all this?" I asked, crossing my arms over my chest. "Done freaking out?"

She shrugged and propped both hands at her waist. "I can't promise there won't be a relapse, but Tod's clearly here and alive. I can't really argue with the facts."

I liked her already.

"So, can we sit?" Tod gestured toward the plush seating arrangement.

"Yeah." Addy rounded one of the stiff-looking, green-upholstered armchairs and sank into it, waving a hand at the matching green-striped couch. "But my mom will be back in a few minutes, and she's not going to take this anywhere near as well as I am."

"No doubt," Tod mumbled. He sat in the chair opposite Addy's, while I took the couch. At Tod's signal, Nash locked the door to give us warning when her mother returned, then he joined me on the couch. "You remember my brother, right?"

"Of course. Nash. It's been a while." She crossed her

legs and smiled, as if we hadn't come to discuss her immortal soul and impending suicide. Addison was much more poised than I would have been in her position, and I have to admit I was a little jealous of her composure. But then, maybe that was one of the advantages of being an actress.

That, and massive fame and fortune.

Her gaze slid my way, and she made actual eye contact. "And you're Kaylee, right?"

I nodded and gave her a genuine smile. People hardly ever remembered my name after only one introduction. I was pretty forgettable. At least, when I wasn't screaming.

Tod cleared his throat to get everyone's attention, and I turned to see him watching Addison intently from the chair opposite hers. One impeccably solid foot tapped the thick carpet. "Addy, you can't kill yourself," he said, and it took the rest of us a second to absorb his abrupt launch into a conversation no one else seemed prepared for.

Addison recovered first. "Hadn't planned to." She shrugged and smiled, then launched into a question of her own. "So, how are you alive now, when you were dead two years ago? Did your mom freak out, or what?" Unbridled curiosity illuminated her flawless features better than any stage lights could have.

"It's complicated." Tod tugged briefly on the blond fuzz at the end of his chin. "I'll tell you all about it later, but right now I just need to know you're not going to kill yourself." The gravity in his voice surprised me, and I'd never seen Tod look so frightened. So genuinely concerned for someone else. "Please," he said, and that last word wrung a bruising pang of sympathy from my heart, though I wasn't sure which of them I felt worse for: the soulless pop star with five days to live, or the reaper who would lose her again.

Addison's brows furrowed. "I said I won't. I love my life." She spread her arms to take in the entire room, as if to ask who *wouldn't* love her life.

Tod exhaled slowly, his features weighted by doubt and worry. He didn't believe her. How could he, considering Libby's inside information?

"Maybe she's not planning it yet." I shifted to lean against Nash's chest. His arm wound around me, his fingers spread across my ribs, and my pulse raced in response. "Maybe whatever drives her to it hasn't happened yet."

Tod nodded, and his gaze went distant. "Yeah." He turned back to Addison. "Is there anything wrong, Addy? You're probably under a lot of stress. Is your mother pushing you into this? Are you *on* something? There were rumors a couple of months ago…."

"No." Addison cut him off, her smile wilting like a cut flower. "Nothing's wrong, Tod. Nothing serious, anyway. There's pressure, but that's true no matter who you are or what you do."

Isn't that *the truth*....

"And am I *on* something...?" Her brows formed a hard line, and she clenched the arms of her chair, bracelet pressed into the upholstery. "I can't believe you'd even ask me that, with my mom still strung out on those damn pain pills."

Tod sighed and leaned forward with his elbows on his knees. I'd never seen him look so tense. So worried. "Is it bad again?"

Addy twisted her bracelet. "Nothing I can't handle."

"You sure?" Tod asked, obviously thinking the same thing I was. A strung-out parent could be a lot of stress. Especially for someone like Addison Page, for whom privacy was only a vague concept.

"As sure as I am that you're sitting there." Addy forced an awkward laugh at her own joke, and the reaper rolled his eyes. "Nothing's wrong, Tod. Other than Eden collapsing onstage. We're going to see her in a couple of minutes." She paused and glanced at the hands now twisted together in her lap. "You guys want to come? I don't think they'll let you in to see her, but I could use the company."

"Addison…" I began, but then hesitated. I'd never been the bearer of such bad news before, but someone had to tell her. "Eden died onstage."

Addison shook her head in echo of her earlier denial. "How do you know…?" She stopped as something occurred to her, and glanced at both of the guys. "Does this have anything to do with me…killing myself?"

I deferred to Tod, unsure about that one.

"We don't know," he said finally. "But, Addy, I need you to promise me…."

Suddenly the doorknob turned behind us, and was followed by a wooden *thunk* when someone walked into the door, obviously expecting it to open. "Addy?" a woman's nasal voice called. "What are you doing? Open the door."

Addison stood so quickly *my* head spun, rubbing her palms nervously on the sides of her jeans. "Just a minute, Mom," she called. "I'm…in the bathroom."

I stood and pulled Nash off of the couch, my pulse racing now. No human mother—even one strung out on painkillers—would understand what we'd come to tell Addy. But Tod could go invisible, and Nash and I could pretend to be fans.

If Addison hadn't already panicked and lied…

She glanced at the door in dread, but before she could say anything else, Tod grabbed her hand. "Addy, promise me that no matter what happens, you won't kill yourself. *Promise* me."

"I…" Addison's gaze flicked from his face, lined in desperation, to the door, which her mother was now pounding on.

"Addison Renee Page, let me in right now! My nose is bleeding!"

"Are you okay in there?" her bodyguard called, and the knob twisted again.

Nash tugged me toward the wall, either to give the ex-couple more space or to put us out of the line of fire when the door gave way.

"*Promise* me!" Tod hissed, loud enough that I knew he'd gone inaudible to everyone outside the room. "You do *not* want to die without your soul. Trust me on this."

Addy's breaths came rapidly. Her jugular vein stood out in her neck, jiggling wildly in fear and confusion. Her voice was an uneven whisper. "How do you guys know about that?"

"The same way we know Eden's dead." Tod pulled her close, speaking almost directly into her ear, his voice low and gravelly with fear. "Addison, if you die while that hellion has your soul, he'll give you form in the Netherworld and will own you forever. *Forever,* Addy. He'll feed on your pain. He'll slice you open and let you bleed. He'll wear your intestines around his neck and peel your skin off inch by inch while you scream."

Tears formed in Addison's eyes, and her hands began to shake as she tried to push Tod away. But he wasn't done. "He'll twist your sanity with your own memories. He'll exploit your every fear, and every twinge of guilt you've ever felt. Then he'll heal you—inside and out—and start all over again."

Tod held her at arm's length so he could see her, and I jumped in, hissing softly as I tried to pull him away from her while Nash tried to hold me back. "Tod, stop it! You're scaring her!" And me.

But he meant to. He was scaring her to keep her alive. Though surely he knew such an effort was pointless. He'd taught me that you can't cheat death. Not without paying the price…

"Addison!" Ms. Page shouted from outside the door, and a fresh jolt of alarm shot up my spine and raced down my limbs. "Open up or I'll have Roger break down the door." But this time we barely heard her.

"You're serious?" Addison's terrified gaze was glued to Tod, her hands shaking worse than ever.

He nodded. "You have to get out of it, Addy. Get your soul back. There's an out-clause in your contract, right? That's hellion law. There has to be an out-clause."

Oh… He wasn't just trying to save her life, which was probably impossible, anyway. He was trying to save her soul.

Addison nodded, tears rolling down her face. "Eden did it, too," she sobbed softly. "Is she… Does he…*have* her now?"

Tod nodded and let her go, then wrapped his arms around her when she collapsed against him. "They didn't tell us that. About the torture." She sniffled against his shoulder. "They just said humans don't need their souls, and that if we sold ours, we could have everything. *Everything.*" She shook silently, then stepped back to look at him, eyes flashing with terror and indignation. Delirium, maybe. "He said we don't need souls!"

"You don't need them to keep you alive," Nash said softly. "Demon's Breath will do that just as well. But while a hellion has your soul, you can't move on. You'll be stuck there, a plaything for whoever owns you."

"You have to get it back, Addison," I ventured, hugging myself in horror. I hadn't known much about hellions, either. "You have to get your soul back, with this…out-clause." Whatever that was.

Addison eyed Tod fiercely, clutching at his arms. "Help me!" she begged softly. "I don't know what I'm doing. You have to help me. Please!" She glanced over his shoulder at me and Nash. "All of you, please!"

I had no idea what to say, but Tod nodded. "Of course we will."

Nash went stiff at my side, but before he could protest, more shouting came from the hallway.

"Okay, break it down!" the stage mother called, and Addison glanced around frantically, probably looking for somewhere to hide us.

"Wait, I'm coming!" she shouted. "Here," she whispered, pulling me toward the door by my arm. Nash followed, and she pressed us against the wall behind the door, so we'd be hidden when it opened. She tried to pull Tod into line with us, but he only smiled and shook his head.

"I can hide myself." He forced a smile, and Addy nodded, wiping tears from her face with her bare hands.

"Oh, yeah." She hesitated, then glanced at the door again. "Just a minute, Mom!" Then she turned to Tod and whispered, "I'm staying at the Adolphus, as Lisa Hawthorne. Call me tomorrow night and I'll sneak you guys up. Please?"

Tod nodded, but his smile was grimmer than I'd ever seen it. "I'll call you at eight."

"Thank you," she mouthed.

Tod winked at me and Nash, then blinked out of sight. Addy pressed one finger to her mouth in the world-wide signal for "shhhh," then unlocked the door and pulled it open.

"Mom! Are you okay? What happened?" Shoes brushed the carpet as she ushered her mother to the bathroom, but all I could see was the back of the door, an inch from my nose. Nash's hand curled around mine, and our pulses raced together.

"I didn't expect your door to be locked," her mother snapped as water ran, and I couldn't resist a grin. "Addy, you look like a tomato. Have you been crying?"

"I'm just worried about Eden. Hurry and get cleaned up so we can go." More footsteps brushed toward us, and Addy called out, "Roger, can you go get some wet rags or something?"

"Sure, Ms. Page," a deep voice said from outside the room. Heavy footsteps headed away, and Addy swung the door open, signaling the all clear.

I spared her one last, sympathetic smile, then Nash tugged me into the hall, still blessedly deserted.

We speed-walked through the maze of hallways, through the empty auditorium, and out to the half-empty parking lot, where Tod leaned against the closed passenger door of their mother's car.

Nash's hand went stiff in mine the moment he saw the reaper, and Tod had his hands up to ward off his brother's anger long before we got within hearing distance.

"What was I supposed to do?" he asked, before either of us could get a word out.

"Not my problem!" Nash tried to shove Tod out of the way so he could unlock my door, but the reaper went non-corporeal at the last second, and Nash went right through him. His shoulder slammed into the car just above the window, and when he turned, anger blazed in his swirling eyes. "You could have done anything! *Except* tell her we'd get her soul back for her."

He pulled open the passenger side door and shoved it closed when I was settled in my seat and was still yelling when he opened his own door. "How are we supposed to do that? Wander around the Netherworld asking random hellions if they took possession of a human pop star's soul, and if so, would they please consider giving it back out of the kindness of their decayed hearts?"

Nash slid into his seat and slammed the door, leaving Tod alone in the dark parking lot with a handful of humans now watching us warily. He turned the key in the ignition, shifted into Drive, then took off across the asphalt, headed toward the exit with his parking receipt already in one fist.

As soon as we turned out of the lot, something caught my eye from the side-view mirror and I twisted in my seat to see Tod staring back at me, his usual scowl unusually fierce. "Don't do that!" I said, for at least the thousandth time since we'd met. "Normal people don't get in the car while it's still moving!"

Nash glared at him in the rearview mirror. "But as long as you're here, you need to understand something, and I'm only going to say this once—we are not tracking down Addison Page's soul. It's not our responsibility, and we wouldn't even know where to start. But most important, it's—*too. Damn. Dangerous.*"

"Fine," Tod said through teeth clenched with either fear or anger. Or both.

"What?" Nash stopped for a red light and glanced in the mirror again, his brows low in confusion. He'd obviously expected an argument, as had I.

Tod shifted on the cloth seat, his corporeal clothes rustling with the movement. "I said fine. This is my problem, not yours. I'll do it myself."

"This isn't your problem, either," Nash insisted, and I turned in my seat again so I could see them both at once. "She sold her soul of her own free will for fame and fortune. The contract is legally binding, and it has a legally binding out-clause. Let her get it back herself." He stomped on the gas when the light changed, and the tires squealed beneath us as I grabbed the armrest.

"She didn't know what she was doing, Nash, and she still doesn't." Tod leaned forward, glaring into the rearview mirror. "She has no idea what rights she has in the Netherworld, and she can't even get there on her own. The out-clause is no good if you can't enforce it. You know that."

"Wait…" I loosened my seat belt and found a more comfortable sideways position as dread twisted my stomach into knots a scout couldn't untie. "She really can't do this on her own?"

Tod shook his head. "She doesn't stand a chance."

I sighed and sank back into my seat.

Nash glanced away from the road long enough to read my expression, shadows shifting over his face as we drove under a series of streetlights. "No, Kaylee. We can't. We could get killed."

"I know." I closed my eyes and let my head fall against the headrest. "I *know.*"

"No!" he repeated, his knuckles white on the steering wheel, jaw clenched in either fear or anger. Probably both.

"Nash, we have to. I have to, anyway." I stared at his profile, desperate for the words to make him understand. "I couldn't save the souls Aunt Val sold. Heidi, and Alyson, and Meredith, and Julie are going to be tortured forever, because I couldn't save them." My throat felt thick, and my voice cracked as tears burned my eyes.

"Kaylee, that's not your fau—"

"I know, but, Nash, I *can* help Addison. I can stop the same thing from happening to her." I wasn't sure how, but Tod wouldn't have offered our help if there was nothing we could do. Right? "I have to do this."

Nash clutched the wheel even tighter, and he looked like he wanted to twist it into a pretzel. Then he exhaled, and his hands relaxed. He'd made his decision, and I held my breath, waiting for it. "Fine. If you're in, I'm in." His focus shifted to the rearview mirror, where he glared at Tod. "But I'm in this for Kaylee, not for you, and not for your idiot pop princess." The look he shot me then was part disappointment, part anger, part loyalty, and all Nash. His gaze scalded me from the inside out, and I squirmed in my seat as that heat settled low within me.

But when he turned back to the road, the flames sputtered beneath a wash of cold fear. Nash would get involved for me, but the truth was that I had no idea what I was doing.

What had I just gotten us into?

5

"OKAY, KAYLEE, FOCUS…." Harmony Hudson, Nash's
mother, leaned forward on the faded olive couch, licking
her lips in concentration as she watched me. She wore
jeans and another snug tee, her blond curls pulled into
the usual ponytail, a few ringlets hanging loose around
her face. Harmony was the hottest mom I'd ever personally met. She looked thirty years old, at the most,
but I'd seen her blow out her birthday candles a month
earlier.

All eighty-two of them.

"Close your eyes and think about the last time it happened," she continued, and I sucked in a lungful of the

fudge-brownie-scented air. "The last time you knew someone was going to die."

And that's where I lost my motivation. I didn't want to think about the last time. It still gave me nightmares.

Pale brows dipped low over Harmony's bright blue eyes—exact copies of Tod's—and her dimple deepened when she frowned. "What's wrong?"

I stared at the scarred hardwood floor. "Last time was…with Sophie and Aunt Val."

"Oh…" Harmony's eyes took on a familiar glint of wisdom, which, at first glance, seemed at odds with her youthful appearance. She was there when the rogue reaper killed my cousin and tried to take her soul. She saw my aunt give her life instead of Sophie's—a last-minute act of courage and selflessness that had gone a long way toward redeeming her in my eyes.

Until I'd learned that the other souls she'd sold to Belphegore would be tortured for eternity along with my aunt's. Now I was leaning decidedly toward the Aunt-Val-deserved-what-she-got school of thought.

Harmony watched emotions flit across my face, but as usual, she reserved her own judgment. That was why I liked her. Well, that, and the fact that she always had fresh-baked goodies ready to be devoured after our how-to-be-a-*bean-sidhe* lessons. "Okay, then, pick a different time. Just think back to any death premonition. One that was less traumatic."

But the truth was that they were all traumatic. I'd only known I was a *bean sidhe* for six weeks, and so far every premonition I'd ever suffered through had thoroughly freaked me out. And every wail was largely uncontrollable.

Thus the lessons.

"Okay…" I closed my eyes and leaned against the soft, faded couch cushions, thinking back to the most memorable premonition—other than that last one.

Emma.

My best friend's death had been unbearably awful, made even worse because I'd known it was coming. I'd seen Em wearing the death shroud for at least two minutes before she collapsed on the gym floor, surrounded by hundreds of other students and parents, gathered to mourn a dead classmate.

But I chose Emma's death to focus on because hers had a happy ending.

Okay, a bittersweet ending, but that was better than the screaming, panicking, clawing-my-way-out-of-the-Netherfog ending most of them had. I'd suspended Emma's soul above her body with my wail to keep it from the reaper who'd killed her, while Nash had directed it back into her body. Emma had lived.

But someone else had died instead. That was the price, and the decision we'd made. I'd felt guilty about it ever since, but I'd do it all over again if I had to, because I couldn't let Emma die before her time, no matter who took her place.

So two months later I sat on Nash's couch beside his mother, picturing my best friend's death.

Emma, in the gym, several steps ahead. Voices buzzing around us. Nash's arm around my waist. His fingers curled over my hip. Then the death shroud.

It smeared her blond hair with thin, runny black, like a child's watercolors. Streaks smudged her clothes and her arms, and the scream built inside me. It clawed at my throat, scraping my skin raw even as I clenched my jaws shut, denying it exit.

As in memory, so in life.

The scream rose again, and my throat felt full. Hot. Bruised from the inside out.

My eyes flew open in panic, and Harmony stared calmly back at me. She smiled, a tiny upturn of full lips both of her sons had inherited. "You've got it!" she whispered, eyes shining with pride. "Okay, now here comes the hard part."

It gets harder?

I couldn't ask my question because once a *bean sidhe's* wail takes over, her throat can be used for nothing else until that scream has either burst loose or been swallowed. I couldn't swallow it—not without Nash's voice to calm me, to coax my birthright into submission—and I wasn't willing to let it loose. Never again, if I could help it.

This lesson was on harnessing my wail. Making it work for me, rather than the other way around. So I nodded, telling Harmony I was ready for the hard part.

"Good. I want you to keep a tight rein on it. Then let it out a little at a time—like a very slow leak—without actually opening your mouth. Only keep the volume down. You want to just barely hear it."

Because the whole point was for me to be able to see and hear the Netherworld through my wail, without humans noticing anything weird. Like me screaming loud enough to shatter their minds. But that was easier said than done, especially considering how much time I'd spent trying to hold back my wail. Evidently suppressing it completely and letting just a little leak through were two very different skill sets.

But I tried.

Keeping my lips sealed, I opened my throat a tiny bit, forcing my jaws to relax. That's where the whole thing went downhill. Instead of that little leak of sound

Harmony had mentioned, the entire wail ruptured from my throat, shoving my mouth open wide.

My screech filled the room. The entire house. My whole body hummed with the keening, a violent chord of discordant sounds no human could have produced. My head throbbed, my brain seeming to bounce around within my skull.

I closed my eyes. I couldn't take it.

Cold, smooth fingers brushed my arm, and I opened my eyes again to find Harmony speaking to me. The room around her had become a blur of colors and textures, thanks to my inability to focus on it. Her pretty face was twisted into a constant wince of pain from the shards of steel my scream was no doubt driving into her brain. Male *bean sidhes* hear a female's wail as an eerie, beautiful soul song. They crave the sound, and are pulled toward it. Almost seduced by it.

Female *bean sidhes* hear it as it is. As humans hear it. As a titanic racket loud enough to deafen, and sharp enough to shatter not just glass, but your ever-loving sanity.

Harmony glanced at her living-room window, the glass trembling in its frame. Because we shared a gender and species—though I was fuzzy on exactly how the whole thing worked—I could hear her words through my own screaming, but they sounded like they came from within my own head.

Calm down. Take a breath. Close your mouth….

I snapped my jaws shut, muffling the sound, but not eradicating it. It buzzed in my mouth now, rattling my teeth, and still seeped out like a moan on steroids. But I could hear her normally now.

"Breathe deeply, Kaylee," Harmony soothed, rubbing my arms until goose bumps stood up beneath my sleeves. "Close your eyes and draw it back in. All but that last little bit."

I let my eyelids fall, though that small effort took a lot of courage, because closing my eyes meant blocking her out and embracing my own private darkness. Being alone with the ruthless keening. With the memory of Emma's death, before I'd known it would be temporary.

But I did it.

"Okay, now pull it back. Deep inside you. Picture swallowing your wail—forcing it down past your throat into your heart. You can set it free in there. Let it bounce around. Ricochet. The human heart is a fragile thing, all thin vessels and delicate pumps. But the *bean sidhe* heart is armored. It has to be, for us to survive."

I pictured my heart with iron plating. I forced my arms to relax, my hands to fall into my lap. I listened

to my wail as it seeped from my throat, forcing myself
to hear each inharmonic note individually. And slowly,
painfully, I drew them back into myself. Forced them
down into my center.

I felt the wail in my throat, in reverse. It was tangible,
and the sensation was eerie. Downright creepy. It was
like swallowing smoke, if smoke were sharp. Prickly, as
if it were bound in thorns.

When I'd swallowed all but the thinnest, most insubstantial thread, I felt a smile spread slowly from the
corners of my mouth to my cheeks, then into my eyes.
I heard only a ribbon of sound, so faint it could have
been my imagination. My shoulders slumped as an odd
peace filtered through me, settling into each limb. I'd
done it. I called up my wail when I needed it, and re-
stricted it on my own terms.

I opened my eyes, already grinning at Harmony. But
my grin froze, then shattered before my gaze had even
focused.

Harmony smiled back at me, curls framing her face,
her dimples piercing cheeks that should have been rosy
with good health and good cheer. But now they were
gray. As was everything else. A hazy, foglike filter had
slipped over my vision while I was modifying my wail,
like my eyes had been opened farther than should have
been possible.

The Nether-fog. A veil between our world and the Netherworld.

A female *bean sidhe*'s wail allows her—and any other *bean sidhes* near enough to hear her—to see through the fog into both the human world and that other, somehow *deeper* one simultaneously. Or to travel from one to the other.

My head turned, my eyes wide with horror. I wanted to learn about the Netherworld, but had no interest in going there!

"Kaylee? It's okay, Kaylee. Do you see it?" Harmony's words were smooth and warm like Nash's, but bore none of the supernatural calm his could carry. Harmony and I shared a skill set, and while Nash's voice could soothe and comfort human and *bean sidhe* alike, ours summoned darkness, and heralded pain and death.

Nash and I were two sides of the same weird coin, and I didn't like wailing without him.

My heart galloped within my chest, skipping some beats and rushing others, unable to find a steady rhythm. My palms dampened with sweat, and I rubbed them on the threadbare couch cushions, both to dry them and to anchor myself to the only reality I understood. The only truth I wanted any part of.

"Kaylee, look at me!" Harmony stroked my hand as she leaned to the side to place herself in my field of vision. "This is supposed to happen. I'm right here with you, and everything is fine."

No-no-no-no-no! But I couldn't speak as long as that last thread of sound still trailed from me. I could only glance around in panic at the fog layering Nash's house like a coat of dust too fine to settle. It hung in the air over Harmony's battered coffee table and old TV, darkening my world, my vision, and my heart.

My pulse raced, and each breath came faster than the last. I knew the pattern. First came the gloom, then came the creatures. I'd seen them before. Beings with too many or too few limbs. With joints that bent the wrong way, or didn't bend at all. Some had tails. Some didn't have heads. But the worst were the ones with no eyes, because I knew they were watching me. I just didn't know *how*....

Yet no creatures appeared. Harmony and I were alone in her house in the human world, and somehow alone in the Netherworld.

With that realization came the calm I craved. My tension eased, and my wail faded, thoughts of Emma's death melting into my memory to be used again when they were needed. Or better yet, forgotten.

The haze cleared slowly, until Harmony came into focus. Her hair looked more golden than ever, her eyes much brighter than I remembered in contrast to the

drab shades of gray that had covered her moments earlier. "You okay?" she asked, forehead pinched with
worry.

"Yeah. Sorry." I rubbed both hands over my face,
tucking my own limp brown strands behind my ears.
"I knew it was coming, but it still scared the crap out
of me. I don't think I'll ever get used to that."

"Yes you will." She smiled and stood, motioning for
me to follow her into the kitchen. "It gets easier with
practice."

That's what I was afraid of.

Harmony waved an arm at the round breakfast table,
and I pulled out a ladder-back chair with clear finish
chipping off the back and one missing rung while she
headed for the oven. The timer blinking above the stove
was counting back with thirty-eight seconds to go, and
it never failed to amaze me how Harmony always knew
when it was about to go off. That timer had never once
interrupted one of our lessons, and none of her treats
had ever come out over- or underdone.

Unlike the cookies I'd baked two nights earlier.

"There's soda in the fridge." She slid her hand into a
thick glove-shaped pot holder and pulled the oven door
open.

"How 'bout milk?" I like milk with my chocolate.

"Top shelf." She pulled a glass pan of brownies from

the oven and slid it onto a wire cooling rack on the counter. I took a short glass from the cabinet over the sink and filled it with milk, then sat at the table again while she poured one for herself.

"So, explain to me why I needed to learn to do that?" I sipped from my glass, suddenly grateful for cold, white milk, and all things normal and this-worldly.

Harmony shot me a sympathetic smile as she slid the carton onto the top shelf of the fridge, then swung the door shut. "It's mostly to help you learn to control your wail. If you can manipulate it on your own terms, you should be able to avoid screaming your head off in front of a room full of humans."

Because humans tend to lock up girls who can't stop screaming. Trust me.

"But other than that, it's helpful to be able to peek into the Netherworld when you need to. Though, I wouldn't suggest trying it unless you have to. The less you're noticed by Netherworlders, the easier your life will be."

She'd get no argument from me on that one. But I was curious on one point....

"So...why were we alone?"

"While you were wailing?" Harmony crossed the linoleum toward me and pulled out the chair next to mine while I nodded. "Well, first of all, we weren't really there. We were just peeking in. Like watching the bears at the zoo through that thick glass wall. You can see them and they can see you, but no one can cross the barrier."

"So the Netherworlders could see us?"

"If anyone had been there, yes." She sipped from her glass again.

"So how come no one was there?"

"Because this is a private residence. Those only exist on one plane or the other. Only large, public buildings with heavy traffic exist in both worlds."

"Like the school?" I was thinking of all the weird creatures I'd seen when I peeked into the Netherworld from the gym, the day Emma died. "Or the mall?" That one brought even worse memories...

"Yeah. Schools, offices, museums, stadiums... Anywhere there are lots of people most of the time."

I frowned and took another sip of my milk as a new worry occurred to me. "How would I actually go there?"

"You wouldn't." Harmony's blue eyes were suddenly dark and hard, as if the sky had clouded over. They didn't swirl, because she had more than eighty years' experience hiding her emotions, but I could tell she was worried. "Kaylee, you have no business in the Netherworld."

Let's hope you're right.

"I know." I smiled to set her at ease. "I just want to make sure I don't wind up there accidentally, practicing what I learned today."

She relaxed at my explanation, and the light flowed back into her eyes. "You won't. The difference between looking through the glass and stepping through it is all a matter of intent. You have to *want* to go there to be there."

"That's it?" I frowned as she stood and rummaged through a drawer, clanging silverware together in search of something. "Have desire, will travel?" It couldn't be that easy. Or that scary.

"Well, that and the soul song."

Of course. I felt the tension in my body ease, and I took another short sip of my milk, saving the rest to wash down my brownie.

Harmony finally pulled a knife from the drawer, followed by a long, thin metal spatula. She ran the knife across the glass dish, cutting the brownies into large, even squares.

"Harmony?"

"Hmm?" She slid the spatula under the first square and lifted it carefully out of the pan and onto a small paper plate. She liked baking but hated doing dishes.

"How can someone live without a soul?"

"What?" Harmony froze with a brownie crumb halfway to her mouth, the spatula still in her other hand. "Why are you…? What's going on, Kaylee?" Her eyes narrowed, and I felt guilty for making her worry.

I decided to tell her the truth. Part of it, anyway. "Nash and I saw Eden's concert last night in Dallas, remember?"

"Of course." Fear drained from her features again, and she scooped an extra-large brownie onto the second plate, then carried them both to the table, without forks. The Hudsons ate their brownies the proper way—with their fingers. My aunt would have thrown a fit, but I was enjoying being converted.

"I saw that on the news this morning." She set one plate in front of me, then sank into her chair with the other, smaller square. Her eyes brightened as the next piece of the puzzle slid into place. "Are you saying Eden died without her soul?"

I nodded, then chewed, swallowed, and washed the first rich bite down with a sip of milk before answering. "It was weird. She dropped dead right there on the stage, but I thought she'd just passed out, because there was no premonition. No death shroud. No urge to wail. But Tod said she was dead, and sure enough, a few seconds later, this weird, dark stuff floated up from her body. Too dark and heavy-looking to be a soul."

"Demon's Breath, probably." Harmony took another bite, licking a crumb from her lip before she chewed.

"That's what Tod said." I twisted my half-full glass of milk on the table. "That Eden sold her soul to a hellion."

She shrugged and brushed a ringlet back from her forehead. "That's the only explanation I can think of. A soul can't be taken from a living being. It can be stolen after a person's death—" or murder, as with Aunt Val's victims "—or it can be given up willingly by its owner. But then something else has to take its place, to keep the body alive. Usually, that something else is Demon's Breath."

"But I thought a person's soul is what determines his life span. If Eden's was gone, how did the reapers know when she was supposed to die?"

Harmony held up one finger as she swallowed, and I bit another huge, unladylike bite from my brownie. She wiped her lips on a paper towel, already shaking her head. "A person's soul doesn't determine how long he or she lives. The list does."

"So…where does the list come from? Who decides when everyone has to die?"

Harmony raised one brow, like she was impressed. "Now you're asking the good questions. Unfortunately,

I don't have an answer for that one. But maybe that's a good thing…."

I frowned, twisting my used napkin into a thin paper rope. "What do you mean?"

"No one actually knows who makes out the list. No one I know, anyway." She sipped from her cup before continuing. "Maybe the Fates traded in their thread and scissors for a pen and paper. Maybe the list comes from some automated printer in a secure room none of us will ever see. Maybe it comes straight from God. But there has to be a reason we don't know the specifics, and frankly, I'm pretty blissful about that particular nugget of ignorance."

"Me, too." I wasn't exactly eager to see whoever plotted my lifeline; I'd kind of drawn the short straw on that one. Though, it was very likely I'd live longer than I would have as a regular human.

"All we really know is that upsetting the balance between life and death is not an option. Somebody has to die for every entry on the list. Fortunately, there's a little wiggle room for special circumstances." Harmony hesitated, then met my eyes before continuing. "Which is how your mom was able to trade her death date for yours."

I cleared my throat and swallowed my last bite, trying to swallow my guilt along with it. I was supposed to die when I was three, but my mother took my place. I hadn't known the truth about her death until I discovered my *bean sidhe* heritage and my family was finally forced to tell me everything. Despite their insistence that what happened to my mom was not my fault, the fact was that if it weren't for me, she'd still be alive.

Guilt was inevitable. Right?

"Considering the sacrifice your mom made for you, I find it hard to understand how Eden—or anyone else for that matter—could possibly see her own soul as acceptable currency. As payment for something else."

I shrugged and dropped my wadded-up napkin on my empty plate. "I don't think she understood what she was getting into. Humans don't know about any of this."

"They're supposed to know, before they sign the contract. Hellion law requires full disclosure. But who knows if the poor fool actually read her contract before signing. What a waste." Harmony shook her head in disappointment and pushed the rest of her brownie toward me. "So much potential, squandered. For what, do you know?"

I shook my head, staring at her plate. I'd lost my appetite.

My best guess would be that Eden sold her soul for fame and fortune, but I didn't know for sure. All I knew for certain was that she was probably regretting that decision now, and that if we couldn't get Addison's soul back in four days, she would suffer the same fate.

I would not let that happen.

"So, what's with the fake name at the hotel? She's avoiding the press?" I tried to distract myself as I typed "hellion" into the search bar at the top of my laptop screen, then tapped the enter key. Links filled the screen faster than I could read the entries, and my vision started to blur with exhaustion. I hadn't slept very well the night before, thanks to nightmares of dead girls being tortured in the Netherworld, and had poured the last of my energy into my *bean sidhe* lesson that afternoon.

"I guess." Nash leaned back on my bed and I watched him in the mirror, my heart tripping faster when he put his hands behind his head and cords of muscle stood out beneath his short sleeves. Sometimes it still felt weird to be going out with a jock, but Nash Hudson wasn't your average football player. His *bean sidhe* bloodline, dead father, not-so-dead reaper brother, and familiarity with a world that would land most humans in a straitjacket meant that on the inside, Nash didn't fit in at school any more than I did.

He just hid it better.

And there were definite advantages to having a boyfriend as...aesthetically gifted as Nash. The downside was that I had trouble concentrating on anything else while he was around.

Focus, Kaylee... I took a deep breath and forced my thoughts back on track. "Isn't the whole fake name thing a little clichéd?"

He shrugged without dropping his arms. "So long as it works."

On-screen, the page had finished loading, and I skimmed the results. The first was about some kind of turbo engine for Mustangs, and the second was a link to a comic book Wiki. The rest of the links ran along those same lines. *So much for Internet research.*

"Tell me again why we're doing this?" Nash's normally hypnotic voice was pinched thin and sharp with reluctance. And maybe a little annoyance.

"Because Addison needs help and I believe in karma."

I glanced in the mirror again to find Nash watching me in amusement now.

"I meant dinner."

"Oh." I pushed my chair away from the desk and almost tipped over when one of the back wheels caught on the ratty carpet. Standing, I tugged my tee into place, then sank cross-legged onto the bed facing Nash. "Because my dad's trying really hard to make this whole single-parent thing work, and Uncle Brendon's the only one he has to talk to."

After my mom died, my father sent me to live with my aunt and uncle, to help hide me from the reaper-with-a-vendetta who'd traded my mother's life for mine. But we both knew my resemblance to her was at least as strong a motivator for my dad's absence from my life. Every time he looked at me, he saw her, and his heart broke a little more.

But after what Aunt Val had done, he'd come back, assuming it would be easier to protect me himself, now that I was in on the big secret of my species. And I was pretty sure he felt guilty for being gone so long. So, my dad had given up a good job in Ireland for crappy factory work in Texas, and together we were trying not to screw up the whole father-daughter thing too badly. So what if that meant a tiny rental house, no extra money, and weekly dinners with my uncle and mean-girl cousin?

Nash's knees touched mine and he took my hands in his, letting them lie in the hollow between our legs. "I know, but Sophie's turning into a real pain."

He was right about that.

Sophie didn't understand what had happened the night her mother died. My cousin had awakened from what we'd told her was a simple loss of consciousness due to shock—but was actually her own temporary demise—to find her mother dead on the floor, and me holding a heavy cast iron skillet like a baseball bat.

Though the coroner had said Aunt Val died of heart failure, Sophie remained convinced that I was somehow responsible for her mother's death. But I couldn't really blame her, considering how confusing and scary her life had recently become. My cousin had no idea that the rest of her family wasn't human, or that the world contained anything more dangerous than the ordinary criminals on the FBI's most-wanted list. But she knew there was something we weren't telling her, and she resented us all for that.

She knew better than to blame me openly, or to even throw a hostile word my way on family dinner nights, but at school it was open season on Kaylee. And Nash wasn't the only one who had noticed.

A metal clang rang out from the kitchen, and I laughed. I couldn't help it. My father wasn't much of a cook, but he was really trying.

"What's for dinner?" Nash's thumb stroked the back of my hand, sending shivers of anticipation through me.

"Lasagna and bagged salad."

"Sounds good." The browns and greens in his eyes swirled lazily, wickedly. "And I already know what I want for dessert…." He leaned forward and his lips met mine, softly at first. Then eagerly.

I tilted my head for a better angle and kissed him back, loving the feel of his lips on mine, his hand at the back of my neck. My fingers found his chest, trailing lightly over his shirt to feel the firmness beneath.

My heart raced, adrenaline pulsing through me in a steady, charged rhythm, leaving my limbs heavy, my body eager. My mouth opened beneath Nash's, and he moaned. The sound of his need skimmed lightly over my skin like a shadow given form, warming me as it slid down my neck, over my collarbones, and between my breasts to burn deep inside me.

He pulled me onto his lap and I crossed my ankles at his back, holding us tightly together while his lips moved over my neck. I could feel what he wanted through both layers of denim separating us, and my head swam with the knowledge that he was excited by *me*.

Nash Hudson could have had just about any girl he wanted—and he'd already had more than a few—but he was with me.

It's because you're a bean sidhe, some traitorous voice spoke up from deep inside me as I tangled my fingers in a handful of his thick brown hair. *You're a novelty. New prey to chase. But once he's truly caught you, the game will be over, and he'll move on to the next hunt.*

And I'd have no one to help me control my wail.

No. Nash wouldn't do that. He wouldn't help me help Addison if he was just trying to get my pants off. I wasn't that much of a catch, and there were easier ways to get laid, especially for him. And he hadn't even really pushed the issue.

Not that much, anyway.

Nash pulled my head down until our mouths met again, and I wrapped my arms around his neck and shoved my doubts aside. His hands found my hip, squeezing as our kiss intensified. Deepened. His fingers traveled up gradually as his lips slid down my chin and over my neck, singeing a path toward my shoulder. My head fell back, my mouth open, each breath slipping in and out silently as I concentrated on the pleasure of his skin on mine.

He pushed aside the neckline of my T-shirt, and his lips closed over the point of my shoulder, sucking gently. Nibbling just a little. My hand tightened around his biceps. Not stopping him. Not urging him. Just… waiting.

I inhaled softly as his other hand slid up my side, under my shirt. He kissed my shoulder again, his lips hot against my flesh, and his thumb brushed the underside of my right breast. My breath hitched, my heart pounding as infant flames of longing licked lower, deeper.

My skin felt flushed, my body pulsing with sudden awareness, impulsive craving….

"Don't stop on my account."

I jumped, and Nash leaned away from me so fast my head spun, my skin suddenly cold in his absence. "*Damn* it, Tod!" he snapped as I straightened my shirt, my cheeks flaming.

Avoiding the reaper's eyes, I climbed off Nash and pushed my bedroom door the rest of the way closed; my dad probably wouldn't hear Tod, but he could definitely hear the other half of the conversation. I glared at my uninvited guest. "If you don't learn to knock like regular people, I swear I'll…tell your boss you're abusing your reaper skills to pursue a life of voyeurism and debauchery."

Tod shot us a wry grin. "He already knows."

I huffed and sank onto the bed with Nash, relaxing into him as his arm went around my waist. "What's up? And make it fast. My dad's home." And as grateful as he was to Tod for helping save Sophie, my father wasn't very comfortable with the idea of me hanging out with a reaper, or—as he called them—one of death's minions.

And honestly, sometimes neither was I.

Tod rolled his eyes and glanced at the door, then his gaze slid back to me. "I just talked to Addy and she's arranged for some privacy tonight at eight-thirty, for an hour at the most. In her room at the Adolphus."

Eight-thirty? That only left an hour and a half for dinner and the drive into Dallas. We'd never make it.

"Uncle Brendon's going to be here with Sophie any minute, and I can't skip out early."

"Four days, Kaylee." The reaper's usual scowl deepened. "Addy only has four days."

I shrugged. "You're welcome to explain what we're doing to my entire family…."

Tod flinched, and that one movement told me just how much he respected the combined threat of my father and uncle standing together. *Bean sidhes* might not have any obvious offensive abilities, but together, my dad and uncle had almost three hundred years of experience. And they weren't exactly small men.

"Fine. Just get there as soon as you can."

"Do you have a plan, or are you just throwing us all into the deep end?" Nash's finger traced lazy figure eights on my lower back, and I wanted to lean into his touch. Or better yet, pick up where we'd left off.

Tod sank wearily into my desk chair, arms crossed over the back. "Well, obviously we need to know which hellion she sold her soul to."

"Yeah, good luck with that." I pointed at the computer screen behind him, and the reaper twisted in his seat to look. When he met my gaze again, a cocky smile had turned up one side of his mouth, and his blue eyes glinted in shadowed mirth.

"You thought you could figure that out online? Somehow I don't think hellions are much into social networking."

"You got a better plan?" Nash pulled me closer, and my heart beat a little faster in response to his.

"Yeah. I thought we'd ask her."

"You can do that on your own," Nash snapped.

Tod shook his head. "I need Kaylee. Addy likes her."

"And Addy always gets what she wants?"

I could practically hear the scowl in Nash's voice, and

I twisted to look at him in amusement. "Like you're one to talk!"

His brows rose, and his steamy gaze traveled south of my face. "I don't have everything I want. Yet." I flushed, and turned back to Tod in time to see his eyes roll. "Well, you guys aren't going without me." Nash stretched one leg out on my rumpled comforter. "But do you honestly think she'll know this hellion's name?"

Tod shrugged again. "I think it's worth a shot—"

Before he could finish, my door creaked open and my dad appeared in the gap. His gaze hardened when it landed on me and Nash, now reclined together on the bed, and I knew that if he had less control over his emotions, my father's irises would be churning furiously.

"Kaylee, I know I'm new at this, but I'm not *that* new. This door stays open when you two are alone in here."

I glanced at Tod, who smirked at me from my own desk chair. "We're not—" And that's when I realized my father couldn't see the reaper, and that I probably shouldn't remedy that. I'd rather my father think Nash and I were breaking the normal human rules than the weird *bean sidhe* ones. "Doing anything," I finished lamely.

"We were just talking, Mr. Cavanaugh." Nash didn't even glance at his brother, who was now making obscene gestures and rolling his eyes madly.

Unconvinced, my dad nodded curtly, then disappeared into the hall, just as the doorbell rang. "Kaylee, can you get that? I'm burning the bread."

"Eat fast." Tod leaned back to cross both arms over his chest as I stood. Then he was gone before I could reply. At least, I thought he was gone, but it was hard to tell with Tod.

Nash followed me to the door, behind which my cousin's voice rang out loud and clear. "…don't see why we can't do this at our house. There's barely room to turn around in their kitchen, and Uncle Aiden's place smells funny."

"It does not smell funny, and we hosted last week." Uncle Brendon sounded exhausted, but much more patient with his only daughter than I would have been. Especially considering how much he'd suffered from his wife's loss, in spite of what she'd cost us all. But Sophie seemed oblivious to her father's pain. "It's their turn."

I shot Nash a resigned smile, then pulled the door open, bracing myself for Sophie's acidic presence. "Hey, guys, come on in."

My cousin brushed past us into the house as if she hadn't heard my greeting, mumbling beneath her breath about how she'd rather spend a Sunday night. She left us to choke on a cloud of her perfume, overwhelming in our small, dark entry.

"I'm sorry about that." Uncle Brendon pushed the front door shut as he stepped inside. "She's…still suffering."

And making sure her misery has plenty of company.

Half an hour later, all five of us sat around the square card table in our eat-in kitchen, me straddling the corner between Nash and Sophie. There wasn't enough room to actually put the food on the table, so if anyone wanted seconds, he'd have to get up and refill his plate from the dishes on the counter. But that didn't seem to be much of a worry, considering that the rim of Sophie's plate was ringed with small bits of marinara-stained waxed paper, which my dad had forgotten to remove from the slices of cheese he'd layered into the lasagna.

If it hadn't embarrassed my father to no end, it would have been almost funny to watch her face twist with fresh horror each time she pulled a limp bit of paper from her food. Not that it mattered. She didn't eat enough to keep a squirrel alive, anyway, and had lost several pounds in the weeks since her mother's death.

There wasn't much conversation over dinner, but every now and then, my uncle would look across the table at his brother and chuckle as he pulled a piece of cheese paper from his pasta and folded it into his napkin, breaking the tension for another few moments. For which I was profoundly grateful.

Nash and I excused ourselves immediately after dinner, nodding at my father's reminder to be home by ten-thirty, and I drove, because Nash's mom had their car. I'd rarely driven in downtown Dallas and had never been to Addison's hotel, so I counted us lucky to get there in one piece.

The lobby of the Adolphus was full of dark, ornate furniture and fancy chandeliers, and I felt underdressed clomping through the lobby in jeans and sneakers. Fortunately, before I could work up the nerve to ask the snooty clerk behind an oversize desk which room "Lisa Hawthorne" was in, Tod appeared from around a corner, wearing respectably clean and intact jeans and an unwrinkled button-up shirt open over his usual dark tee. He jerked his head toward a cluster of elevators on one end of the lobby, and we followed him gratefully into the first one to open.

"She's pretty nervous, so go easy on her," Tod said, eyeing Nash as soon as the mirrored doors closed and the elevator slid into motion.

"She's not the only one." I ran one shaky hand over my ponytail, wondering if I should have worn my hair down. Or wiped my feet before walking through the lobby. But the overpriced hotel wasn't really the cause of my nerves.

I'd peeked into the Netherworld that afternoon, and wasn't anxious to do it again anytime soon. But as badly as the prospect of actually walking into that shadow-world scared me, my horror was much greater at the thought of condemning Addison Page to an eternity there. Even if she had signed away her own soul.

Tod was right. She didn't know what she was getting into. She couldn't have.

The elevator binged in warning and slowed to a smooth stop, then the doors slid open almost silently. Tod got off first, and Nash and I followed him down a thickly carpeted hallway past at least a dozen doors before he stopped in front of the very last one, nearest the emergency staircase.

"Hang on a minute," he said, then popped out of sight before we could protest, leaving me and Nash standing in the hall like idiots, hoping no one came out to ask if we'd lost our key. Or to call Security.

Who me? Paranoid?

Absolutely.

Several seconds later, the door opened from the inside, and for the second time in as many days, we walked into the private rooms of Addison Page, rock star. I had a fleeting moment of panicked certainty that once again, she wasn't expecting us. That Tod had made the whole meeting up. But Addison stood in the middle of the sitting room, watching us through red-rimmed eyes, and she didn't look surprised to see us. Thank goodness.

"Thanks for coming," she said as we made our way to a collection of couches gathered around yet another flat-screen television. "I know you guys probably think I don't deserve your help, and the truth is that I'm not sure I do."

Neither was I, but the fact that she had her own doubts made me want to help her for her own sake, beyond my need to make up for not being able to save the girls my aunt had damned to eternal torture.

"Yes you do." Tod guided her to a boldly patterned armchair with one hand on her lower back. She didn't pull away from him, and I was impressed all over again by her composure. I wouldn't have been so calm if I had an undead ex-boyfriend.

Or the staggering lack of a soul.

Nash sank onto the cream-colored couch and pulled me down with him, his lips firmly sealed against the dissenting opinion I read clearly on his face. He wasn't convinced that we had any business there. Or that Addison had any right to ask for our help.

Tod sat in the other chair, leaning forward with his

elbows on his knees. His gaze hadn't left Addy since we'd walked into the room, and I had a feeling it wouldn't anytime soon.

Addison wrung her hands together, twisting her fingers until I was sure one of them would break. "So… what's next? How can I help?"

"We need to know who—" Tod began, but Nash cut him off boldly.

"Addy, before we get started, you need to understand how dangerous this is. Not just for you, but for us." His voice was as hard and unrelenting as I'd ever heard it, and he squeezed my hand as he spoke. "We're putting our own lives in danger for you, and honestly, the only reason I'm here is for Kaylee. Because I don't want her to get hurt."

My heart jumped into my throat, and a smile formed on my face in spite of the solemn circumstances.

"I understand…." Addison said, but Nash interrupted again.

"I don't think you do. I don't think you *can*. We're *bean sidhes*." We both watched her face very carefully for a reaction, but got none. "Do you know anything about *bean sidhes?*"

"A little," she admitted, glancing briefly at the reaper. "Tod told me…some stuff." Her cheeks flushed, and I wondered what else Tod had told her.

"Good." Nash looked relieved to finally hear something he approved of. "Did he tell you that the Netherworld is a very dangerous place for *bean sidhes?* That we have no defenses against the things that live there? That we can't even pop out like he can, if something goes wrong?"

She nodded again, shyly. Guiltily. And I could see that Addison Page wasn't accustomed to asking for help. She looked…humiliated. As if the admission of her own powerlessness might break her.

And that alone told me she was stronger than she thought she was. Stronger than Tod thought she was.

Good. She'd have to be.

"Okay, then, the first thing we want to know…" He glanced at me for confirmation, and I nodded in spite of the suspicious glint shining in Tod's eyes. Nash and I had already discussed this. "Is how you got yourself into this mess. Why the hell would you sell your soul? I know I'm looking at your life from the outside, but I gotta say that from where we stand, it looks like you've got everything you could ever want."

Addison smiled wistfully, regretfully, as Tod glared at us. "I do now," she said, her famous, melodic voice so soft I could barely hear it. "But when they came to me with this deal, I had nothing but dreams and desperation. I know that sounds melodramatic, but it's the truth. They said they could make or break me, and they were right."

"Who?" I asked, speaking for the first time since we'd entered her room.

"Dekker Media."

A chill swept the length of my body, leaving me cold from the inside out.

Dekker Media was an entertainment *titan*. They had theme parks, production studios, television channels, and more large-scale marketing clout than any other company in the world. Dekker Media had its sticky fingers in every pie imaginable. Kids grew up watching their movies, listening to their CDs, playing with their toys, wearing their officially licensed shoes and clothes, and sleeping between sheets plastered with the faces of their squeaky-clean, family-friendly stars.

The company was pervasive. Ubiquitous. Obnoxious.

They signed most of their stars straight out of junior high, churning out one teenage cash cow after another.

"Wait, I don't understand," Nash said, having obviously regained his head before I had. "You sold your soul to Dekker Media?" He frowned at me briefly, then let his gaze slide toward his brother. "I thought she sold it to a hellion."

"She did." Tod's jaw bulged in barely repressed anger. "But the deal went through John Dekker himself."

Wow. I was stunned into silence for the second time in as many minutes.

John Dekker was the CEO and public face of Dekker Media, grandson of the legendary company founder, and more recognized by tweens around the world than the U.S. president.

"Okay, can you start from the beginning?" I leaned back on the couch, my head swimming from information overload.

Addison nodded, and once she got started, the words flowed quickly, and I had to listen carefully to keep up.

"It was two years ago, just after I turned sixteen. *The Private Life of Megan Ford* had just finished its first season and was up for renewal. John Dekker found me on the set on the first day of filming the second season and took me to his office. Alone. He said that the ratings were only okay so far, and that whether or not the show continued was up to me. It was my choice. But that if I wanted it badly enough, Megan Ford could be a huge hit. Make me famous. Make me *rich*."

"You sold your soul for fame and fortune?" Nash asked, contempt so thick in his voice I almost looked down to see if some had dripped on the carpet.

Addison flinched, but Tod spoke up, his own anger rivaling Nash's. "It wasn't like that. Don't you remember her family? Her dad was long gone and her mom was unemployed. Always strung out on one pill or another. They were living on Addy's income, and Dekker told her that if she didn't sign on the dotted line, that would all dry up. That he'd make sure she never worked again. He said her mother would go to jail for prescription drug fraud and neglect, and Addy and her little sister, Regan, would be split up in foster care."

Addison's hands shook in her lap, but she added nothing to Tod's speech. Nor did she deny any of it.

"He scared the shit out of her, Nash."

"Did you tell anyone?" I asked gently, trying not to upset her any more than she already was. "Your mom?" But I knew as soon as I said it that her mother would have been no help. "A friend?"

Addison nodded miserably. "I told Eden." She sniffled, obviously holding back sobs. "She'd done a guest spot on the show, and we'd become friends. She said I was lucky. That they only offered that deal to the best of us. The ones with real star potential. She said she'd signed two years ago and hadn't regretted it for a minute. And her first CD had just gone platinum. *Platinum!*" she repeated, glancing at Tod in desperation, begging him with her eyes to believe her. To understand her decision. "I could sign on to be a star, or I could put the entire crew out of work and let my family starve. I did it for them…."

I saw the struggle on Nash's face. He understood her choice. But he didn't want to.

However, I'd already moved on to the bigger picture.

They only offered that deal to the best of us. Addison's words haunted me, and their implication sent fresh chills down my spine to pool in my limbs as my teeth began to chatter.

They'd done it before. A lot. Dekker Media was making deals with demons—and letting its teenage stars pay the price.

7

"Wait, Dekker Media is blackmailing kids into selling their souls?" Nash looked as horrified as I felt.

"Honestly, I doubt we all had to be blackmailed." Addison leaned back in the hotel chair and ran her palms nervously over designer jeans–clad thighs.

Nash glanced across the coffee table from her to Tod. "But how does that benefit the company?"

"Greed, plain and simple. Right?" I looked to Addy for confirmation.

She shrugged and swallowed thickly, like her dinner was trying to come back up. "That's my guess. I mean, if we're rich and famous, so are the suits and pencil pushers, right?"

Nash frowned. "So what if their stars leave the corporation? Go mainstream, like Eden did?"

Addison crossed her arms over her chest, probably to keep her hands from fidgeting. "Eden went mainstream on-screen two years ago, but only after six years and three contracts with Dekker, during which she brought in cash faster than any other child star in history. But she's still on their record label, and so am I."

The singer inhaled deeply, as if her next words would be difficult to say. "When you sign with Dekker, even if you're not selling your soul, you're selling out. They get most of us before we hit puberty, and you become whatever they want you to be. They design your look, cast you in their shows, and put you in at least one made-for-TV movie a year. The movies themselves don't make much, but the merchandising brings in some serious cash." She sighed and began ticking points off on her fingers. "They pick the songs you'll record, schedule your appearances, and book your tours. They'll even choose your haircut unless your agent is a real shark. But most of the agents are in John Dekker's pocket, too, because they want clients who have guaranteed careers."

So. Creepy. Dekker Media was starting to sound scarier than the Netherworld.

"Okay, maybe I'm misunderstanding, but we're

talking about *the* Dekker Media, right? The child-friendly, shiny-happy sitcoms? With the cartoon squirrel and the squeaky-clean animated fairy tales? *That* Dekker Media is actually reaping the souls of its stars in exchange for commercial success?"

Addison's lip curled into a bitter smile. "Ironic, isn't it?"

I didn't know how to answer. Until they grew up and went mainstream, Dekker's stars didn't even bare their midriffs. Yet they were all soulless shells of humanity. Irony didn't even begin to cover it.

And I'd thought the whole *bean sidhe* wail thing was weird….

Tod shot a smile of support at Addison, and Nash rubbed his face with both hands. Acid churned in my stomach, threatening to devour me from the inside out, and the very air tasted bitter, heavy with the aftertaste of such sour words. But I had to ask…

"Addison, how long has this been going on? This soul trafficking?"

She shrugged and pulled a strand of white-blond hair over her shoulder, twisting the end of it as she spoke. "I don't know, but rumor has it a couple of their stars from the fifties sold out, back when they were still broadcasting in black and white. Who was the girl who did all those bonfire slasher movies after she left Dekker?"

"*Campfire Stalker* movies," Tod corrected.

"Yeah, those. That girl sold her soul. And she's getting old now...." Addison's voice trailed off, but the horror on her face was easy to read.

"Guys, this is much bigger than we thought." I crossed my arms over my chest, glancing from one somber, shocked face to the next. "Too big." The thought of tracking down one hellion with a second-hand soul was scary enough. But I had no idea how to go up against the Netherworld *and* Dekker Media over an arrangement they'd evidently had going for more than half a century.

All we could really do was take Addison to the Netherworld so she could enforce the out-clause.

"So, what's the deal with this out-clause? What happens if you ask for your soul back?"

"They take everything." Tod stood and waved one arm to indicate the hotel suite, and Addison's entire career, then crossed the room toward a small refrigerator against one wall. "Everything she's worked for will just be...gone."

"If she wasn't prepared for that, she shouldn't have sold her soul," Nash snapped, his irises a churning sea of brown and green. But I knew he wasn't so much mad at Addy as he was worried about us. In his opinion, risking two mostly innocent lives and one afterlife for a single compromised soul made little sense.

I was starting to agree with him. I wanted to help Addy, but not if she wasn't willing to help herself. What were fame and fortune compared to an eternity of torture? "That's kind of how the whole contract thing works, Addison. You fulfill it, or you have to pay back everything they've given you. But isn't your eternal soul worth it?"

She blinked at me, and her tears finally overflowed. "It's not about the money, or even the fame. There are days I'd like to trade my face in for one no one's ever seen." Addison swiped tears from her cheeks with both hands, smearing expertly applied eyeliner in the process, and I pushed a box of tissues across the table toward her.

"So, what is it about?"

She took a deep breath. "If I demand my soul back, they'll take back everything I ever got as a result of signing that contract—and everything anyone else ever got from it through me. They'll ruin me, but the fallout will hit my agent, my lawyer, my publicist, and everyone who ever worked for me. It'll devastate my whole family." She sniffled, but now there was a sharp edge of anger in her voice. "My mom. Regan. My dad, and whatever twenty-year-old he's shacked up with this week. And I'm not just talking about money. We've been poor, and we can be poor again. I'm talking debt, disgrace, and public humiliation, a thousand times worse than any of them would have suffered if I'd turned down the original offer."

Nash's eyes narrowed as Tod kicked the fridge shut and returned with four cans of diet Coke, evidently all Addy kept on hand. "They can't do that. Can they?"

Addison laughed bitterly, and accepted the can Tod handed her. "You remember Whitney Lance? Lindy Cohen? Between the two of them, they have three divorces, seven arrests, five stints in rehab, and two children taken away by the courts. And it gets much worse. Others have had nude photo scandals, public breakdowns, and weeks spent in the psychiatric ward. Carolina Burke served two years for tax evasion, and Denison Clark was arrested for drunk driving two months before his twenty-first birthday. Then again for statutory rape six months later."

"Yeah, but they all actually did those things, right?" Nash popped open his can, looking less sympathetic by the moment. "Please tell me you don't have an arrest record or a love child hidden away somewhere."

"Of course not." Addy's eyes flashed in anger, and I was glad to see it. If she couldn't stand up to us, how could she possibly have enough nerve to demand her soul back from a hellion?

"Well, if you haven't given them any rope, how are they supposed to hang you?"

"I'm not perfect, Nash!" Addison used the arms of her chair to shove herself to her feet and stood staring down at him. "Don't tell me you've never had a drink. Or that you're a virgin."

Nash's face hardened, but he remained silent.

"My contract keeps me bubble wrapped, but if I get my soul back, not only will they strip the padding, they'll start throwing knives at me. They'll twist every decision I make and hurl it back at me. Every drink I take will be a public binge. Every relationship I get into will be a disaster played out in full color on newsstands all over the world. Exes will sell stories and pictures to magazines." She was pacing now, words falling from her lips almost faster than I could understand them. "The paparazzi will get shots of my mom all strung out. Hell, she'll probably go to prison for buying narcotics online, or something like that. My dad's DUIs will catch up with him, and without me to bail him out when he gets in over his head, his creditors will eat him alive. And I don't even want to know what'll happen to Regan. She just scored a role in a new tween drama. Her career will be over before it begins."

Addison fell into the chair again and practically melted into the upholstery. "They'll drive me crazy, and that will only fuel the media frenzy."

I leaned back, trying to absorb it all. Trying to imagine my own life under the microscope, my every indiscretion on display. "Okay, yes, it sounds bad. But your parents dug their own holes, and you can't hold yourself responsible when they fall in." I popped open my own can and took a sip, still thinking. "Are poverty and embarrassment really worse than eternal torture?"

Addy shook her head halfheartedly. "No, and I know I probably deserve whatever I get. But Regan doesn't, and neither does anyone else I wind up hurting." She met my gaze, her pale blue eyes swimming in tears again. "Remember last year, when Thad Evans flipped his car? He killed two people and messed up his own face for good when he went through the windshield. Then he lost nearly everything he owned in lawsuits from the dead kids' parents, and the rest of it to crooked accountants and lawyers. And what about—"

"Whoa, wait a minute." I rubbed my temples with both hands, fighting off a headache from information overload as everything she'd told us finally began to sink in. "Are you saying that all the Dekker stars with wholesome images and squeaky-clean backgrounds are actually soulless human husks, and Hollywood's bad boys and girls are really the good guys, because they got their souls back?"

She stared down into her can. "I wouldn't exactly call them good guys for taking the out-clause."

"What does that mean?" Nash pulled a throw pillow from behind his back, then dropped it on the floor beside the couch.

Addison glanced at Tod instead of answering. The reaper sighed and leaned forward with his elbows on his knees, and his focus shifted from Nash to me, then back to Nash. "There's a little complication with the out-clause."

My stomach churned. Something told me his definition of a "little complication" and mine wouldn't have much in common.

"Addy doesn't actually have a copy of her contract…."

"I was barely sixteen," Addison interrupted, her cheeks flaming in embarrassment. "It never occurred to me to ask for a copy to keep."

Nash scowled at her, hazel eyes swirling rapidly with mounting anger. "Or to actually read the damned thing before you signed it, I'm guessing."

"Wait, isn't sixteen too young to sign a contract without your mom's permission?" I asked, hoping I'd just discovered a brilliant legal loophole.

Tod's blue-eyed gaze seemed to darken. "The Netherworld considers humans adult once they hit puberty."

I frowned. "That's messed up."

He shrugged. "It's the Netherworld. And she had no idea she was entitled to a copy of her contract, and hellions aren't known for explaining your rights up front." He deliberately shifted his focus to me. "Anyway, I asked around a little bit today…"

The sick look on his face told me I didn't want to know who he'd spoken to, or what he'd had to do for the information.

"…and if Addy's contract reads like all the rest of them do—and I'm sure it does—her out-clause requires an exchange."

"What?" I blinked, hoping I'd heard him wrong, or was misunderstanding something. "An exchange like my mom made? A life for a life?" The horror crawling through me had no equal. I rubbed my arms, trying to keep goose bumps at bay, but they rose, anyway.

"A soul for a soul," Tod corrected, staring at the floor for a second before meeting my gaze again. "But basically, yes. Addy can only get her soul back by trading it for another one."

"Wait…" Nash rubbed his forehead, like that might help the new information sink in. "Souls can't be stolen.

They can only be taken when someone dies, or given up freely by their owner."

I searched Addison's face, struggling with my own mounting nausea. "So, all those people you mentioned? They all had to kill someone to get their souls back?"

"Or recruit someone," Tod said, twisting the tab on his can, as if unbothered by the new development.

"And you call that a *little* complication?"

Tod shrugged and glanced at Nash as if he wanted a second opinion. "I know we're short on time, and I'd suggest steering clear of murder just to keep things simple, but I'm sure Addy knows someone looking for a quick career boost—"

"No!" she and I shouted in unison, shooting twin looks of horror at the reaper. "I can't take the out-clause, Tod," Addison continued. "Even if I were willing to throw my family to the wolves, I can't put someone else in my position."

"Would you rather die without your soul?" He looked irritated with her for the first time that I'd seen. Was he really ready to damn someone else to the Netherworld to save Addison?

Yes. I could see that in his eyes, in how they lit up every time she spoke. In the way his gaze never left her for long. He'd literally do anything for her, and that knowledge scared me almost as badly as the thought of traveling to the Netherworld.

"No," she answered finally, spinning her can slowly on the coffee table. "That's why I need your help. I need to get my soul back without using the out-clause."

"Damn it!" Nash slammed his empty can down on the coffee table, his irises flashing with a confusion of angry colors.

"She's right," I said softly. Then I pinned Tod with my gaze. "I won't help you lead another lamb to the slaughter. If we do this, we do it without the exchange."

Tod scowled, and again his willingness to take the easy route chilled me. But then he glanced at the raw desperation on Addison's face and nodded.

"Nash?" I took his hand and folded my fingers around his. "I understand if you want to back out."

He exhaled heavily. "Like I can let you do this alone. I'm in."

My relief was a bitter mercy. I didn't want to do this any more than he did. But I wanted to do it without him even less.

"So…how do we start?" Addison glanced from me to Nash, then to Tod. "What can I do?"

I took a deep breath, then gulped from my can. "First, we need to know who this hellion is. It is a he, right?" I asked, as it occurred to me that I'd been thinking of the hellion as male.

"Yes, it's a…um…guy demon." She flushed and shook her head. "But I don't know his name. I didn't even know for sure that they had names."

"But you did actually meet him, right?" Frustration flavored my words, and we could all hear it.

"She did." Tod answered for her, clenching his hands into tense fists in his lap. "The transfer process is… hands-on."

Wow. So many things that *could mean…*

"Good. Tell us everything you remember." I rubbed my damp palms on my jeans, half dreading whatever we were about to hear. But if I was *half* dreading it, Addison was all the way there. She glanced at Tod, reluctance obvious in the lips she'd pressed together and the panic swimming in her eyes.

"It's okay." He leaned forward to rub her bare arm. "We need to know what you know." But Addison's hands began to shake, in spite of his reassurance.

I elbowed Nash and glanced at Addy. He rolled his eyes, then nodded curtly. "Just tell us what you remember." In spite of his reluctance to coddle her, his voice radiated safety and comfort, flowing over us all like a warm, familiar blanket. "Close your eyes, if you need to. Pretend we're not here." After a moment,

Addy nodded and leaned back in her chair, her eyes closed. "Start from when you signed the contract," Nash soothed. "Where were you?"

"In John Dekker's office. He had the curtains closed and the air cranked. I was freezing."

"Okay, good…" Nash said, and I glanced at my watch. Addison's hour of privacy would be up in about twenty minutes and I was not up for another high-pressure getaway. "So you signed the contract. Then what happened?"

Do you sign a demon contract with ink, or with blood? I couldn't help but wonder.

"Dekker took the contract into another room. When he came back, he had a woman with him. She was tall and pretty, but she looked at me weird. Like she was hungry and I was dinner."

I shifted uncomfortably on the couch until Nash took my hand again, squeezing gently. The feel of his skin against mine did almost as much as his voice to calm me. "What did the woman do?" he asked.

Addy cleared her throat and continued, eyes still pinched closed. "She held my hands and I started to feel dizzy. I closed my eyes and when I opened them—" she opened her eyes to look at us then, as if acting out her memory "—Dekker's office was gone."

Both brothers met my gaze, confirming my suspicion. Dekker had a rogue reaper in his pocket.

"Where were you?" I asked. I couldn't help it. I'd peeked into the Netherworld several times, but had never actually been there.

"I don't know." Her eyes went distant as she sank back into her own memory. "We were standing on a white marble floor in a room so big I couldn't see the walls, but I could tell from the echo that there *were* walls. And there was this weird gray haze over everything for a minute or so. Then that cleared all at once, like it was never there. But I know I saw it...."

Nash glanced at Tod, and something unspoken seemed to pass between them. I elbowed Nash, hoping for an explanation, but he only held up one finger, asking me to wait. I nodded reluctantly, then sipped silently from my can as he continued. "What happened next, once the haze cleared?"

"Nothing, at first." Addy's eyes regained focus, and her gaze held mine for a moment before sliding to Tod. "Then I heard footsteps on the marble, and saw someone walking toward us from behind the woman."

"That was the hellion?" Tod asked, his words clipped in anger. Or was that fear? "What did he look like? Tell us everything you can think of."

Addy closed her eyes again in concentration. "He

looked pretty normal. Like any businessman. He wore a plain black suit and had brown hair. He didn't look very scary, so I started to relax. But then I saw his eyes. They had no color. At all." Her eyes opened then, glazed with fear so fresh I could almost taste it. "They were just solid black balls stuck in his head, with no pupils or irises. It was…weird. I couldn't tell if they were moving, and didn't know whether or not he was looking at me."

Tod and Nash looked at each other again, then back at Addy. "What did he do?"

"He kissed me." Addison's voice broke on the last word, and she began to tremble all over. When Tod stood and crossed between her chair and the couch, her eyes caught his movement and were drawn back into focus.

"Are you okay?" I asked as Tod slid the closet door into the wall and pulled a blanket from the bottom shelf.

"Yeah." She smiled in thanks when Tod draped the blanket over her lap and tucked it around her sides. "I just don't want to think about what I did. About what I let him do."

I nodded sympathetically, and Nash cleared his throat. "Okay, so he kissed you…?"

"Yeah, only it wasn't really a kiss." Addison leaned

forward to sip from her can, then set it on the table and pulled the blanker tighter around herself. "His mouth opened, and he…sucked on me."

"He sucked on you?" I repeated, confused by her phrasing. "Isn't that kind of what a kiss is?" *Unless* I've *been doing it all wrong…*

Her teeth began to chatter, and it took obvious effort for her to speak clearly. "He sucked on me like I was a human Popsicle, and it felt like I'd swallowed a hurricane. Like he'd stirred something up, and I could feel it whipping around inside me. Then it just went… through my lips and into him."

Wow. Hellions suck. Literally.

"When it was over, I was cold on the inside. I was shaking so badly I could hardly stand. I felt so empty I thought my body would collapse in on itself, like I was a vacuum that couldn't be filled. I knew then that I'd made a mistake. But it was too late."

Addy leaned forward to pick up her can again, but it shook violently in her hands and sloshed soda over the sides. She set it down in disgust and pressed her hands together between her knees, trying in vain to stop shivering. "The man—the hellion—just stepped back and licked his lips, like I tasted good. He smiled at me, and I felt dirty. Like I could scrub for hours and never get rid of his filth." Her hands rubbed at her jeans again, pressing so hard her fingers went white. "Then he leaned down and kissed me again, only this time he exhaled into my mouth, and his breath felt thick and heavy."

She paused and closed her eyes, rubbing her face roughly as if to wipe the memory from her mind. But it wouldn't go. I knew that from experience. The worst memories stick with us, while the nice ones always seem to slip through our fingers.

"I'd thought I was cold before, but that was nothing compared to being filled with his breath. Filled with *him.* The demon took part of me and left part of himself in its place. I could feel him rolling through me. Exploring me from the inside, so cold he burned every part of me he touched. The first few times I exhaled, my breath was white, like in the middle of winter. My teeth chattered for two days afterward. But the worst was the chill." She shuddered and clutched the blanket tighter. "That awful, hollow cold, swallowing me from the inside out…"

"When did that go away?" I asked, my voice so soft and horrified I barely heard it.

Addison looked at me and smiled softly, her expression empty, and all the creepier for that fact. Then she reached up with one hand and pulled her left eyelid up.

With her free hand, she pinched the front of her eye, and something fell out onto her palm.

"When did the chill fade?" She blinked then, and when she looked at me, I saw that without her contact lens, her left eye was solid white, with no pupil and no iris. "It never did."

"WHOA." Nash leaned closer for a better view, as my heart leaped into my throat. And if I weren't busy being horrified by Addison's featureless eye, I might have been surprised by his fearless curiosity. "The demon did that to your eye?"

Addison nodded. "Both of them." She held out her hand so we could see the small, curved, plastic disk cradled in her palm. It was too big to be a regular contact lens, and she must have seen my confusion. "Demon technology. Dekker provides them, to make us look normal."

My pulse still racing uneasily, I leaned over for a better look and noticed that the lens was detailed with the specifics of a human eye. Addison's eerie pale blue iris was right there in her palm, surrounding a pinpoint black pupil.

"The pupils even dilate and constrict, depending on the amount of light in the room." She smiled bitterly and blinked with a creepy, mismatched set of eyes. "Don'tcha just *love* foreign technology?"

I had no answer for that, and hoped she was being ironic. I wasn't particularly fond of technology that allowed elements of the Netherworld to hide in our world. But I did have questions. "Why did he do that? Wouldn't it be in the hellion's best interest to avoid making you stand out?"

"He had no choice." Tod scowled. "It's a side effect of the process. You know how they say the eyes are the windows to the soul?" he asked, and I swallowed thickly before nodding. I didn't like where this was headed. "Evidently they mean that literally. Once the soul is gone, there's nothing to see through the windows."

Nash whistled softly. "That has to be the weirdest thing I've ever seen." And that meant a lot coming from a *bean sidhe*.

"You want me to put the contact back in, don't you?" Addison cocked her head and gave him a small, eerie smile.

"That'd be great, thanks." Nash nodded decisively.

Addy stood and crossed into the attached bathroom. She was back in under a minute, and her eye looked normal. Only it also still looked weird, probably because I now knew what the contacts hid.

"So, when she gets her soul back, her eyes will go back to normal?" Nash aimed his question at his brother, rather than Addison, and I realized he was avoiding looking at her. Her eyes freaked me out, too, but I couldn't help being amused that Nash was more comfortable dealing with a grim reaper—a living dead boy who killed people and harvested human souls—than with an otherwise normal human girl who'd lost hers.

"They should."

"Okay, wait a minute. I've seen several dead people—" not a statement I could have imagined saying a few months earlier "—and none of them looked like that, even after the reaper took their souls."

Tod nodded, Addy's hand held between both of his. "When your heart and brain stop working, your eyes stop working. They reflect the state the soul was in when the person died. It's kind of like when a clock battery runs down. The hour and minute hands don't disappear, but they don't keep ticking, either. They freeze on the last minute they measured."

"Okay, that makes sense." In a really weird way. But

I didn't plan to dwell on it. I was ready to give Addison her privacy and go work on her problem somewhere her empty soul-windows didn't stare at me from behind their eerie human facades. But first we needed the information we'd actually come for. "Addison, did you notice anything about the hellion that might help us identify him? A crooked nose or a dimpled chin? Bad teeth?"

But even as I asked, I realized her answer probably wouldn't help, even if she had noticed something. I didn't know much about hellions, but I did know they could assume more than one form, so any description she gave us might not fit the hellion a moment after she'd met him.

She shook her head slowly. "No. Other than the eyes, he looked normal. Brown hair. Average height. Normal clothes. And I didn't see any birthmarks or anything."

"And you sure you didn't hear the hellion's name?" Nash asked.

"If I had, I don't think I could have forgotten it."

"What about your contract?" I asked, struck by a sudden bolt of brilliance. "He signed, too, didn't he? Did you see what he wrote?"

She shook her head miserably. "They must have done that after I left. The spot for his name was still blank when I signed."

My hand tightened around Nash's; my frustration was getting harder to control. "Okay, then, think carefully. Did he say anything to you? Or to the woman who took you to him?" No need to tell her the woman was a reaper. I wasn't sure how much she knew about Tod, or the Netherworld in general.

"Um…" Addy closed her eyes in concentration, but opened them after only a few seconds. "No. He never spoke. I never even heard his voice."

"What about the woman?" Nash's foot bounced on the carpet, and his knee bumped the coffee table over and over. He was obviously as eager to go as I was. "Did she say anything to either of you?"

"No." Addy didn't hesitate that time. "No one spoke while we were in…that place." Her nose wrinkled in disgust, or maybe in fear.

"What about when you got back?" I laid my hand on Nash's knee to make it stop bouncing. "Did she say anything when you got back to Dekker's office?"

"Yes!" Addy's weird, fake eyes widened, and I noticed absently that the pupils *did* dilate with varying levels of light. That would have been cool, if it weren't so strange. "When we got back, Dekker was still there. On her way out of the room, the woman kind of trailed her hand up his arm and over his shoulder, smiling at him like he was edible. She said, 'Your avarice is secure for another year.' Then she just walked out the door."

Avarice… I could practically hear the gears in Tod's head grinding, as he searched his memory, but if he came up with anything, I couldn't tell.

"Does that mean anything to you?" Addison studied the reaper's face in obvious hope. "Avarice means greed, right?"

"Yeah," I said when Tod didn't answer. I ran my thumb over Nash's knuckles, where his fingers were still wrapped in mine.

"So, does that tell you who the hellion is?"

"No." Though, I hated to admit it. "But with a little research it might." I stood, signaling to the guys that I was ready to go. Immediately. "Tod, can you try to get a copy of Addy's contract? Surely Dekker has it in a file somewhere." That seemed to me to be the easiest way to identify the hellion, considering that Tod could pop into and out of places at will.

He nodded, but his face betrayed little hope.

"Good." I turned back to Addy and scrounged up an encouraging smile. "We'll let you know what we find out."

I shoved the front door open and pocketed my keys, glancing into first the living room, then the kitchen to make sure Nash and I were alone. My dad worked an extra half shift most Mondays, so he shouldn't be home until after nine, which would give me and Nash several hours alone together.

But I couldn't get used to having the house to myself—Aunt Val had almost always been home—so I shouted for him just in case, as Nash closed the door behind me. "Dad?"

No response, but I dropped my backpack in his recliner, then checked his bedroom to be sure. He'd kill me if he found out I was messing in reaper business. Again. Not to mention the hellions.

My dad's room was empty, and by the time I got back to the kitchen, Nash had shed his jacket and pulled two cans of soda from the fridge. I shrugged out of my coat and tossed it over the back of an armchair, barely glancing at the ripped upholstery.

It would have cost too much for my dad to bring his furniture over from Ireland, so we'd been slowly furnishing our new-to-us home as we could afford to. Fortunately the rental house was tiny, so we didn't need much. And Uncle Brendon had insisted I keep everything I'd used at his house, so my bedroom looked much the same here, except for the plain white walls and little available floor space.

I didn't care about any of that. All that mattered was

that Sophie wasn't around to stick her nose in my business. Except on Sunday nights. And even then, she usually ignored me completely.

"You hungry?" I opened an overhead cabinet and pulled out a flat, folded bag of popcorn.

"Starving," Nash said, so I stuck it in the microwave and set the timer. While the microwave hummed, I popped open my can and stood with my back against the countertop, watching the view as Nash rooted through the fridge. Evidently two and a half minutes was too long to wait for a snack.

But then, with the state football play-offs coming up, Coach Rundell had been working him extra hard for the past couple of weeks. No wonder Nash was always hungry.

"So, any ideas?" I asked as the first pop echoed from the microwave. Between conflicting schedules at school, his football practice, and my shift at the Cinemark, we'd barely had a chance to talk all day.

Nash stood with a jar of salsa in one hand, and I tossed him a half-empty bag of corn chips from the countertop. "Not even one." He rounded the peninsula and sank into a chair at the folding card table currently furnishing our eat-in kitchen. "Find anything online?"

"Role-playing games and band lyrics," I said, pulling

open the grimy door when the microwave buzzed. Obviously, the Netherworld had yet to extend its influence to the Internet. Which was probably fortunate, now that I thought about it.

I dumped the popcorn into the largest bowl in the cabinet and shook a small bottle of nacho-cheese-flavored seasoning over it, then grabbed my soda on the way to the table. "So…what do you know about hellions?"

"Nothing more than what Addy told us last night." Nash dipped a corn chip into the wide-mouthed jar, and it came out loaded with chunky hot salsa.

"After seeing her eyes, I never want to lay mine on a hellion. Ever." I crunched on several pieces of popcorn. "But it doesn't look like we'll have much of a choice."

"I could kill Tod for getting us into this."

"It's a little late for that." I wrinkled my nose in distaste when he dipped a piece of popcorn into the salsa jar, then tossed it into his mouth.

"Weird." Nash cocked his head to one side, chewing as he considered the odd combination. "But good-weird."

"You want something to put that in?" I stood to grab a bowl before he could answer. "When's Tod supposed to be here?"

He glanced at his watch. "He's taking his break in

about fifteen minutes. But knowing my brother, he's already here somewhere, spying on us."

I set the bowl on the table and poured salsa into it. "He needs a life of his own. A girlfriend. Addison seems pretty interested in him...." I ventured, leaning over his shoulder to dip a popcorn kernel into the sauce. I hesitated, then finally closed my eyes and stuck it in my mouth.

Eww! You'd think nacho seasoning and salsa would go well together, but they don't. At least, not on popcorn.

Nash laughed at me while I washed the taste from my mouth with a gulp from my can. "The last thing Tod needs is a soulless human husk of a girlfriend. Especially a famous one. He's legally deceased, and she's followed around all day by photographers. I can see the headline—*Addison Page dates dead boy!*"

"Okay, so it's not an obvious paring." I shrugged and grabbed another handful of regular popcorn. "But it's not like you and I are exactly simple." Not with his mom teaching me *bean sidhe* stuff, and my dad watching his every move. Though, there was the little matter of our mutual species....

"I like a challenge." Nash stood, his irises swirling lazily. Hungrily.

"Oh, yeah?" I smiled up at him and retreated slowly

until my hip hit the countertop, my insides smoking from the heat of his gaze.

"Yeah…" Nash stepped close enough that I could feel the warmth of his chest through both of our shirts. But he didn't touch me. His head dipped toward my neck, and I inhaled sharply when his breath brushed my collarbone.

I tilted my head back. My heart slammed against my ribs, and I held my breath, waiting to feel his lips on me. They would be soft, and hot. I knew it. I wanted it. But it didn't happen.

His head rose gradually, his breath traveling up my neck unbearably slowly. My pulse raced faster with each hot, damp puff against my skin. "Nash…" My arms rose, and my fingers hovered millimeters from his shirt when his warm hands wrapped around my wrists. Holding me. Stopping me.

"Mmm?" His breath brushed my ear then, and shivers shot up my spine, lingering in pleasant places all over my body.

"Let me touch you." It came out as a moan, and part of me was mortified by the need in my voice. But he liked it. I could tell, and that made it okay.

"Not yet," he murmured, his words indistinct, a groan granted the bare minimum of consonants. The sound buffeted my earlobe. Scalding me.

"Now," I whispered. I couldn't breathe. Not until I could touch him. Or he touched me. "Now. Please, Nash."

"Are you sure?" His words surged over me like a wave of heat, pulsing with barely controlled desire. Power. Compulsion. Considering his particular talents, he could probably have talked me into anything he wanted me to do, and that knowledge scared me and thrilled me at the same time. But he wouldn't do it. He wanted me to want him on my own.

Oh, and I did. I wanted him so badly every part of me ached, some places worse than others.

Nash pulled back enough so that I could see the brown of his eyes, churning in a sea of green. And still his breath brushed my chin, sending a wave of sensation over me, so delicate I froze to keep from shattering it.

Then I nodded. I was *totally* sure.

Nash let go of my wrists, and one hand slid over my skin to the back of my neck, cradling my skull. He tilted my head to one side and his lips met mine, just as hot and soft as I'd known they'd be.

I opened my mouth for him, drawing him in farther. Deeper. As much as I could take, and still I wanted more. My hands skimmed his chest, traveling boldly over each plane, each ridge, and soon that wasn't enough, either, so I tugged his shirt up, eager for the feel of his flesh beneath my fingers.

Nash's free hand found my waist, squeezing. His fingers slid beneath the waistband of my jeans, gripping my hip, scalding me with each touch. I moaned into his mouth when his fingers tightened, and he kissed me harder, teasing me.

My hands wrapped around his waist, traveling up the broad expanse of his back, smooth and hard, and…

"Give it a rest, already," Tod snapped from somewhere behind his brother. "It already smells like sex in here, and you're both still dressed. You have no idea how messed up that is."

Nash stiffened and pulled away from me. Then his forehead fell against my shoulder, and he growled in warning at his brother, as my hands slid down his back and out of his shirt. Nash breathed heavily against my neck as he pulled his fingers slowly from my waistband. He wanted more. Was ready for more.

I could feel his readiness against my hip.

I couldn't make my heart stop pounding. Couldn't control my ragged breathing. Couldn't cool my burning cheeks.

Nash finally stepped away from me, and he was still breathing heavily, too. He shoved his hands into his pockets and collapsed into his chair.

"You're lucky no one else walked in on you," Tod continued, snatching a chip from the bag, completely oblivious to our discomfort, as usual. "If I were her dad, you'd be hobbling home with your balls in hand tonight, little brother."

"Shut up, Tod!" I snapped, tugging my jeans into place below my navel, both delighted and mortified to realize I could still feel the warmth of Nash's bare hand on my hip. "Or you're not going to be in any shape to help Addison!"

"Speaking of which…" Tod dipped his chip into the salsa, then crunched as he spoke. "I'd appreciate it if you two could keep your sticky fingers out of my personal life…."

"What life?" Nash mumbled angrily. "Just sit down so we can get this over with. Kaylee's dad will be home by nine, and we'd like at least a couple of hours alone before then."

Tod smirked. "You think she's ready for any more time alone with you?"

"Not your business, Tod. I'll decide what I'm ready for." I dropped into the chair across from him. "Your business is finding the hellion who has Addy's soul, and figuring out how to get it back from him. Did you find her contract?"

Tod scowled in defeat. "No. It took me three hours

of digging and snooping this morning just to find out that all copies of demon paperwork are kept in the Netherworld."

"So, she never really had a shot at enacting her out-clause." I shoved the bowl of salsa across the table, suddenly too angry to snack. "How did the others do it?"

"They probably actually read their contracts," Nash snapped.

"Or else they went through Dekker again. I'm guessing he doesn't care if they renege, so long as they provide a replacement soul." Tod rocked back and forth on the uneven legs of his folding chair.

"Lovely," I spat, closing my eyes briefly in disgust. "Any idea how to ID the hellion on our own?"

"No." The reaper sighed in frustration and grabbed a handful of popcorn. "I've never actually met a hellion, and so far as I know, there's no demon directory to refer to. Not that we have a name to look up."

"But hellions have specialties, right?" Nash asked. "Like, there's a demon of pain, and a demon of lust…"

"…and a demon of joy, and a demon of hope, and even a demon of love," Tod finished, gesturing with a corn chip. "There's a hellion for every emotion and weakness known to man. More than one. There are hundreds of hellions in the Netherworld. Maybe thousands. Knowing what Addy's demon specializes in won't be much help without something more specific."

"But it's a starting place, right?" I twisted my can on the table. "It's more than we knew yesterday."

Tod nodded slowly. "For what little good it does us."

"Wait…" My thoughts had stalled on something he'd said, like a thorn caught on a loose thread. "How can there be a hellion of love? Or of hope? I thought hellions fed on pain and suffering. And chaos. How can they possibly feed on emotions that make people happy?"

Nash smiled at me, but it was a sweet, pitying smile, like he was humoring me. As if I were too naive for words. But it was Tod who answered, as usual more than willing to enlighten me on the darker side of life.

"A hellion can wring pain and chaos from any emotion, Kaylee. If you want love, he gives you unrequited love. Pangs of it so torturous you go insane and die. If you ask for hope, he makes it vain hope, hope so fruitless that after grasping at it, clutching it, you eventually go insane and die. And if you beg for faith, you get blind faith. Faith you cling to, and build upon, until the day you discover that it's unfounded, and you—"

"I get it," I interrupted, a chip halfway to my mouth. "You go insane and die. Hellions are the sum of all things cruel and evil. Thanks for clarifying."

Nash chuckled, and I couldn't hold back a grin.

"You two are cracked," Tod snapped.

My smile widened. "Says the undead man in love with the soulless pop star."

Tod scowled, and I thought I saw his cheeks flush. Which struck me as kind of weird for a man who'd died two years ago. "I'm not in love with her."

"So you pulled us into a potentially deadly scheme to save the soul of some girl you don't even care about?"

His scowl deepened, and Tod scooted his folding chair across the faded linoleum. "Fine. You don't want to help? I'll do it myself." He stood. "So what if I get killed in the process? Permanently, this time."

I rolled my eyes. "Sit down, reaper, we're going to help." I just couldn't resist getting back at him for constantly invading our privacy. "But we're suffering from a conspicuous lack of ideas, here. We need someone who knows more about hellions. Or at least about the Netherworld in general."

"Hello? *Reaper* here." Exasperated, Tod laid one hand flat on the tabletop. "I know about the Netherworld."

"Not enough, apparently." Nash tossed another piece of popcorn into his mouth, ignoring Tod's annoyed under-his-breath muttering. "We need to talk to someone who's been around longer." He eyed me solemnly. "Kaylee, we need to talk to your dad."

"No." I shook my head firmly. "No way. If I even mention the word *hellion* he'll lock me in my room and swallow the key."

"He's the oldest non-human I know, and you don't have to tell him what we're doing." Nash shrugged, as if my decision should have been a no-brainer. "Just tell him you're curious. Or come up with something that won't make him worry. Besides, he promised not to keep any more secrets from you."

"Yeah, but he never promised to give me the inside scoop on demons." I looked him straight in the eye to convey my final word on the subject. "If I ask my dad about hellions, this whole thing is over." Then I smiled as an alternate solution came to mind. "Why don't you ask your mom?"

Nash frowned, and Tod's expression echoed the sentiment. "Because not only would she freak out, she'd call your dad so they could freak out in stereo."

"So we're back where we started." My shoulders slumped, and I dipped a chip into the bowl of salsa. "We need someone old enough to have lots of experience in the Netherworld, but who won't care what we're up to."

Tod sat up straight in his chair, as if the lightbulb over his head had just blinked to life. "Libby. We need to talk to Libby."

9

"HOW MUCH TROUBLE are you going to be in if we get caught?" Nash asked, concern lining the edges of his perfect, practically edible mouth. A tall, skinny guy in a letter jacket rushed past us in the hallway, carrying a huge black tuba case. He narrowly missed smashing my shoulder with it, and when Nash tugged me out of the way, the tubaist ran into the lockers instead with a horrible metal-crunching crash.

"You mean if we get caught here…" In the human world. "Or there?" I whispered, unwilling to say "the Netherworld" in public. Especially at school, with the tuba player still regaining his balance a few feet away.

"Either one." Nash veered away from the dark green

lockers and I followed him, ducking into an alcove near the first-floor restrooms.

"Well, I doubt Coach Rundell will even notice I'm not there." I had American History last period, and with the football play-offs coming up, the coach had been too busy studying his playbook to come up with actual lesson plans, so we'd been watching installments of a documentary about the Civil War for the past week and a half. "But if he does, and they call my dad…" I'd have to be home before dusk for the remainder of my adolescence.

My father was trying really hard to be a good dad, and he wasn't doing too bad a job, considering he'd been absent for the past thirteen years of my life. But he was going overboard on a few vital issues. Like quality family time—thus, our Sunday night dinners—and his need to know where I was at all times.

That was appropriate the last time we'd shared a home—back when I was three. But at sixteen, I needed a little more freedom, and a lot less nosiness.

"And if we get caught *there*…" I shrugged. "All bets are off."

Nash swallowed thickly. "With any luck, we won't have to actually cross over. Yet." But we both heard the uncertainty in his pause. "Where does your dad think you're going?"

"Downtown with me," Emma said. Startled, I spun to find my best friend leaning against a bright purple chess club flyer taped to the wall behind us. "After work, we're grabbing pizza and going birthday shopping for my mom." Emma winked one deep chocolate-colored eye at me and smiled to show even, white teeth. She was pretty enough to be spectacularly popular, but smart enough not to give a damn, and I loved her for it.

I'd convinced a lovesick coworker at the Cinemark to switch my Tuesday shift for his Friday shift just by mentioning that he'd spend all four hours alone with Emma in the ticket booth. As soon as I said her name, he'd offered to trade entire schedules.

"I said I'd have her home by ten-thirty, so don't be late," Emma teased Nash.

He grinned and pulled me closer, and I wanted to melt into him. "No problem." But I couldn't help mentally crossing my fingers. Tod had done some digging and found out that Libby would be pulling in another dose of Demon's Breath that night in Abilene. But Abilene was a six-hour round-trip. Counting rest stops, dinner, and however long it took to actually convince her to help us, it was bound to be a long night.

"So, where are you really going?" Em tucked a strand of long, straight blond hair behind one ear and eyed us both with a knowing grin. "Or do I even want to know?"

"Probably not. It's not what you think." I sighed, wishing it was what she thought. Wishing *hard*.

Her grin melted into a look of concern to match Nash's, and she tugged her backpack higher on her shoulder. "*Bean sidhe* business?" she whispered, glancing around dramatically for potential eavesdroppers.

"Yeah." We'd had to fill Emma in on some basic Netherworld stuff when Nash and I had reinstated her soul, thus saving her life. And accidentally ending another, a fact which haunted me constantly. But Emma didn't know about Tod, or that reapers even existed, and I wasn't going to tell her anything that could bring her to the attention of any dangerous Netherworld elements. I hadn't saved her just to let her go again. Ever.

Which is why I felt guilty asking her to cover for me. Unfortunately, I had no other options, since Nash would be with me. *I really needed to find more friends....*

"You're not missing French, are you?" Panic peeked around the edges of Emma's expression, and I laughed.

"No, just history." Emma's memory for foreign vocabulary was as fragile as mine for dates and numbers. I helped her out in French, and she returned the favor the next hour, in history. It was a good system, and we weren't really cheating. We were just…helping.

I'd probably never need to know when the War of 1812 ended, anyway. Right?

"Then come on, we're gonna be late."

Grinning, Nash leaned forward and kissed me, but Emma dragged me back by one arm before I got much more than a taste of him. Nash winked and took off in the opposite direction. I watched him for several seconds, until Emma hissed my name, and I followed her, still looking over my shoulder.

When I finally turned, I gasped to find myself less than four inches from Sophie's overglossed sneer. "You almost flattened me," she snapped, icy green eyes glittering with anger that went deeper than resentment of my intrusion into her social circle.

"Sorry," I mumbled, thrown off by the unexpected confrontation. It was easier to stay mad at her before, when her general bitchiness was superficial in nature. But now that pain and grief peeked out at me from behind the armor of her arrogance, I found it much more difficult to do anything but pity her.

Even if she did blame me for her mother's death.

When my pride wouldn't allow me to step out of her path—well, pride and Emma's tight grip on my arm, refusing to let me back down—Sophie sidestepped me with a look so pompous it might have seared the soul of someone with a lesser spirit. But I could only return her look with pity, which fueled her anger even more.

"Your cousin is *such* a freak," Sophie's best friend, Laura Bell, said at her side.

Sophie rolled her eyes at me as she turned to march off down the hall. "You have no idea…."

"Just ignore them," Emma insisted, as I followed her around the corner and through the first door on the left, just as the bell rang. "Laura's jealous of you and Nash." Because she'd had him first, a fact she reminded me of at every possible opportunity. "And Sophie's always been a bitch."

I slid into my fifth-row seat as Madame Brown—who'd probably never even been to France—cleared her throat at the front of the class. "She lost her mom, Em."

"So did you!" Emma hissed, flipping open her textbook in search of the homework she kept folded between the pages. When she'd actually done it. "And you don't practice 'bitchy' like it's a lost art."

Before I could remind her that I'd had thirteen years to get over my mother's death, Madame Brown eyed Emma from the front of the class, a black dry-erase marker poised and ready in one hand. "Mademoiselle

Marshall?" she said, thin black brows arched dramatically. *"Avez-vous quelque chose pour dire?"*

"Uh…" Emma's cheeks went scarlet, and she flipped frantically through more pages in her book, muttering under her breath. *"Dire…dire…"*

"Something to say," I whispered, without moving my lips. I was getting really good at that. "'Do you have something to say?'"

"Oh. *Non, Madame,*" she said finally, loud enough for the entire class to hear.

"Bon." Madame Brown turned back to the white board.

Emma slumped in her chair in relief, smiling at me in thanks. "How do you say, 'I hate this class?' in French?"

"Should we wait for him?" I tapped my fingers on the steering wheel, and glanced at the clock on my cell phone for the thousandth time in the last five minutes. "Maybe he got stuck at work." As a rookie reaper, Tod worked from noon to midnight every day at a local hospital, ending the lives of the patients on his list, then taking their souls to be recycled. It was a creepy line of work, in my opinion, but creepy seemed to suit Tod.

"Nah, he traded shifts with one of the other death-dealers. Tod will show up whenever and wherever he wants." Nash bent at the waist to see me through the open passenger side door of my car, and behind him, digital numbers scrolled upward across the front of the gas meter as the price rose with each fraction of a gallon he pumped. "Calm down. It'll be fine."

I forced a smile and clutched my hands together in my lap. But the moment my hands stilled, my foot began tapping uncontrollably on the floorboard. I'd never skipped a class before, and knowing my luck, getting caught seemed inevitable. But so long as we didn't get caught until after we'd returned Addison's soul, I was willing to face the consequences.

Nash tore his receipt from the paper slot on the pump and slid it into his back pocket, then dropped into the passenger seat and pulled the door shut. "Let's go!"

I'd only had my license for about six months and had never driven farther than Fort Worth. Fortunately, once we got out of the Metroplex, Abilene was a straight shot along I-20, and with Nash navigating, the most complicated part of the road trip was deciding where to stop for dinner.

At least, until Tod popped into my backseat with no warning, as I was bending for a sip of my watered-down soda. His bright blue eyes suddenly staring back at me in my rearview mirror startled me so badly I stuck the straw up my nose instead of into my mouth. "Ow!" I clutched my nose and dropped my cup in my lap, but Nash grabbed it before it could spill. His free hand went to the wheel, in case I dropped that, too.

Fortunately, one good swerve put us back between the lines on the highway, even as my heart thumped painfully after a near miss with the guardrail.

"Damn it, Tod!" Nash shouted into my ear, and I flinched even though I'd known it was coming. Those were the three words he yelled the most.

When I'd recovered from the shock—to both my nose and my heart—I glared at Tod in the rearview mirror. "What took you so long?"

"I was with Addy." He stared out the rear passenger's side window, but even at that angle, I could see tension in the tight line of his square jaw. "She's a wreck, and I hate to leave her alone with her handlers. Damned parasites are worse than Netherworld leeches, sucking her dry one radio ad or guest spot at a time. I'll catch up with her after we talk to Libby."

"What's she doing in Abilene?"

"Collecting Demon's Breath from some eighty-year-old oil tycoon." Tod didn't look at me until I cleared my throat for his attention, as I flicked on my blinker and changed lanes to make room for a cop stopped behind a station wagon on the side of the road.

"Where exactly is this oil tycoon supposed to die?"

I envisioned a sickroom in a huge old house decorated with doilies and dust-covered photographs of laughing grandchildren. Where there would be nowhere for us to hide, if we could even get in.

Maybe we should have let Tod go alone….

"He's in a nursing home. I know the reaper on duty tonight, and he's planning to take an extra-long coffee break. I think Libby kind of freaks him out."

I had the feeling we should have been freaked out by her, too, and the fact that we weren't was starting to scare me a little.

An hour later, I followed Nash's directions into the parking lot of the Southern Oaks nursing home, just as the sun sank below the roof of the low, orange-brick building. We were running late, so we jogged across the asphalt, the early November air stinging our lungs, and through the double front doors, where we paused to catch our breath to keep from making the staff suspicious.

Except for Tod. He'd blinked straight from the car into the nursing home as soon as we got to Abilene, so he could watch Libby work again. And to keep her from leaving before we caught up with her. He could have come alone, but Tod seemed to think Libby liked me—she'd actually acknowledged my presence in the concert hall—and would be more likely to answer our questions if they came from me.

I was skeptical, but willing to give it a shot to help Addison.

We'd just passed the front office, nodding politely at the nurse on duty, when Tod appeared behind us. The nurse didn't even blink at his sudden appearance—she obviously couldn't see him.

"Henry White." Tod waved us forward with one hand. "Room 124. Hurry, it's almost time."

But even knowing I wouldn't have to wail, I was less than eager to watch some poor old man die. I'd seen quite enough of death in what little of my life I'd lived so far. Unfortunately, even with me dragging my feet, we got there just in time for the show.

Libby stood in one dark corner, dressed in another variation of black-on-black leather, looking psychotic-scary in deep blue and gold eye shadow. Sweat stood out on her forehead, an obvious sign of the effort it took to suck in the dark substance leaking slowly, thickly from the wrinkled man lying limp on the bed.

Henry White was alone in his room, except for us and the monitor near his head, leaking a steady, high-pitched tone, which speared my brain almost as sharply as my own wail would have. I rubbed my temples, both surprised and sad that White's only deathbed visitors were two *bean sidhes* and two reapers, one of which had come to kill him. Where were his kids? Grandchildren? Or even the poor man's accountant, or money-grubbing lawyer? Surely he'd meant enough to someone to warrant a little company when death came a-knockin'.

Even as that last thought passed through my head, footsteps rushed down the hall. A heavyset nurse appeared in the doorway, wearing bright purple scrubs. She glanced my way and smiled sympathetically as she brushed past me to press a button on the monitor. "Are you family?" she asked, as the annoying beep ended and welcome silence descended.

"No." I glanced from her to Henry White's still form, then to the corner, where Libby was slurping up the last of the Demon's Breath like some kind of putrid, ethereal sludge.

"We're…visitors," Nash finished, threading his fingers through mine when my hand began to tremble. Tod watched Libby in fascination, practically drooling as she wiped her mouth with one delicate, black-gloved finger. But I was so creeped out, chill bumps had burst to life all over my body.

If she burped up black smoke, I was out of there, no matter what she could tell us.

Clutching Nash's hand, I backed toward the wall. I kept hoping the shock would wear off. That death would eventually become routine for me. But it hadn't, and on second thought, I decided that was probably a very good thing. If death ever ceased to bother me, it would be because I'd seen entirely too much of it.

The nurse continued taking Henry White's pulse, though it was obvious by that point that he was already gone. "Well, then, you'll have to go," she said, without looking up from her work.

I was happy to oblige. "Why didn't she give him CPR?" I asked Nash on the way out of the room. We all knew she couldn't bring him back, but she didn't even try.

"Honey, he signed a DNR years ago," she said, watching me with more of that weird, detached sympathy behind her eyes. She probably would have made a good reaper.

I glanced back at her from the hall. "DNR?"

"Do not resuscitate. He signed a form asking not to be brought back when his heart gave out. He was ready to go."

Her words sent fresh chills down my spine. I had no doubt that if Henry White had known what his afterlife would consist of, he'd never have signed that paper. Or his demon contract.

Tod and Libby trailed us into the hall, though no one

else could see or hear them. "Are you following me?" she asked Tod.

"Um, yeah. Kind of," Tod said, and I turned to find him grinning up at Libby. "I'm, um, seriously interested in doing this. Collecting Demon's Breath instead of souls. When I found out you were going to be here, I couldn't resist coming to ask you a few more questions."

"This job is not for children." Libby's eyes flashed fiercely. Her grim smile looked more like a snarl. "You have five minutes."

Tod exhaled in relief, and the reapers followed us into the frigid parking lot, while Nash and I pretended to be alone, a skill I was getting pretty good at. Behind the nursing home, Libby sat on the hood of my car and lit a cigarette, watching Tod expectantly, and I wondered if passersby would be able to see the smoke she exhaled.

"Is that…" Tod's words puffed from his mouth on a white cloud. "Does that help you hold the Demon's breath?"

"This?" She held the cigarette up, flicking ash onto the asphalt. Tod nodded, and she shook her head slowly. "It just tastes good."

Tod flushed beneath the light overhead. As uncomfortable as I was hanging out with a reaper who'd been old when the New World was discovered, it was almost worth it to see Tod too embarrassed for words.

Almost.

"Three minutes," Libby prodded, without even a glance at her watch. "When I have finished with this—" she held up the cigarette again "—I will be finished with you."

"Right." Tod glanced at first me, then Nash, but we only stared back at him. This was his show; the reaper had yet to acknowledge either of us existed. "Um… does all Demon's Breath taste the same, or does it vary from hellion to hellion? You know, like 31 flavors?"

Libby's eyes narrowed as she watched him, and I was sure she'd ask a question of her own, and our little road trip would end in disaster. But after a moment's hesitation—just long enough to blow smoke into his face— she answered. "It all tastes the same. Foul. It would probably kill you, so do not consider trying it."

"I won't." But Tod didn't look anywhere near as put off by the idea as I thought he should be. "So…you can't tell what hellion this particular breath…came from?"

"No." She inhaled from her cigarette and crossed her opposite arm over her chest. "Nor do I care."

Tod exhaled in frustration and glanced at us again, but I could only shrug. I had no idea where to go from there. "When they give you your list, does it say what hellion owns the target's soul?"

"No." Libby dropped her half-smoked cigarette and ground it beneath her boot, and I was sure she'd simply disappear without another word. Instead, she turned to face us. All three of us. And I literally squirmed beneath her gaze. "Why are you following me, asking about hellions? Demon's Breath is nothing for children to play with."

I wanted to insist that we weren't children, but I kept my mouth shut because arguing with Libby probably wasn't the best way to get information out of her. And because compared to her, even poor old Mr. Henry was a child.

"I'm just curious…." Tod began. But his mouth snapped shut at one angry glance from the older reaper, who could clearly smell his lie. "We… We're trying to help a friend."

"Who?" Libby pushed off of my car and crossed both arms this time, glaring down at us.

Nash and Tod exchanged glances but remained silent, so I answered. Silence obviously wasn't getting us anywhere. But the truth might.

"We're trying to help Addison Page get her soul back."

"That cannot be done," Libby said, without missing

a beat. Any surprise she may have felt was instantly swallowed by her perpetual scowl. "And you will die trying. But she can reclaim it herself. Her contract has an out-clause. They all do."

"We know." I sighed and let my shoulders slump, hoping she couldn't tell from my posture that I was about to tell a half truth—I was afraid she wouldn't help us if she knew what we were really planning. "But she doesn't know the hellion's name. She can't enact the out-clause if she can't find him, and she only knows he's a hellion of avarice."

"I do not have direct contact with hellions." Libby scowled. "Stupid humans." She closed her eyes briefly before meeting mine again. "She does not have a copy of her contract?"

"No, and we couldn't come up with a copy, either."

"Those bastards never play fair," Libby muttered. "But there is nothing you can do about it. Go home." She turned then, as if to walk away, but I knew it wasn't over. If she were truly done with us, she would simply have disappeared.

"Please." I started after her and she whirled around, long leather coat flaring out behind her. Libby's surprised, angry gaze found me immediately, and I made myself speak, in spite of the nerves tightening my throat. "Anything you could tell us might help."

"I do not know who has her soul, and I will not ask for you. That is beyond what is safe, even for me."

"Fine. I understand. But…" I closed my eyes, thinking quickly. "What else can you tell us about your job? Where do you take the Demon's Breath after you collect it?"

One corner of her mouth twitched, like she was holding back a smile, and I was suddenly sure she was proud of me. As if I were on the right track, and she secretly wanted me to follow it.

"There are disposal centers in the Nether. The closest is near Dallas. In the large stadium."

"Texas Stadium? The old one, right?" I asked, still thinking, and she nodded. "Would anyone there help us?"

Libby's mouth quirked again. "No. Definitely not."

But then, she hadn't planned to help us, either. "Thank you." I exhaled slowly, sure we were headed in the right direction. "Thank you so much."

"Child," she called, as I turned toward my car, key already in hand. When I glanced up at her, something unfamiliar passed over her face. Concern? Or maybe amusement? Figures that I'd amuse a reaper. "Demon's Breath is very powerful, and it attracts both the desperate and the dangerous. Watch out for fiends."

I nodded, trying not to reveal fear in my posture.

But as I started my engine, Nash buckling himself into the seat next to me, I couldn't stop my hands from shaking.

I had no idea what a fiend was, but something told me I would soon find out.

10

"I CAN'T BELIEVE you did that!" Nash said, and I glanced away from the dark highway long enough to see him grinning from ear to ear in the passenger seat, his irises swirling in the deep shadows. He looked…excited.

"Did what?" A car passed us going the opposite direction, and when it was gone, I flicked my brights back on.

"He can't believe you asked a several-thousand-year-old reaper for help getting a human's soul back," Tod answered from the backseat. He had both arms crossed over his usual dark T-shirt, but I knew by the tilt of his fuzzy chin and the shine in his eyes in the rearview

mirror that he was pleased. Maybe even a little impressed.

I shrugged and stifled a giddy smile as I turned back
to the road. *It was a bit of a rush.* "I figured it couldn't
hurt to ask…"

"But it could have." Nash aimed the heater vents
toward the center of the car and closed the broken one,
which wouldn't twist. "You keep forgetting that most
reapers don't like *bean sidhes.* And vice versa."

"Maybe I keep forgetting that because the first *bean
sidhe* and reaper I met are brothers. Neither of whom
seems to hate me."

Still half grinning, Nash twisted to look at Tod.
"Maybe we should have introduced her to Levi first."

"There's still time," Tod said, and that time he actually smiled. A little.

Levi was Tod's boss, the oldest and most experienced
reaper in Texas. Except for Libby, who worked all over
the southern U.S., whenever and wherever she was
needed. But evidently Levi was enough of a threat to
keep several hundred other reapers in line.

"So, what's the plan?" I turned down the heat now
that my goose bumps were gone. "I have to be home
by ten-thirty, so we can't look for this disposal station
tonight. So…tomorrow after school?"

Nash nodded and flipped another vent closed, but

Tod's frown deepened in the rearview mirror. "Are you seriously saying your curfew is more important than Addison's soul?"

"You're in no position to complain." Nash twisted in his seat to face us both, gripping the back of my seat. "Kaylee and I don't owe either you or Addy a damn thing, and if you don't lay off, we'll both just walk."

Only they both knew I'd never do that. I'd said I was in, and I meant it. But…

"If I get home late, I get grounded, and I won't be much help to Addy while I'm stuck in my room." I eyed Tod in the mirror and flicked off my brights as another car approached in the opposite lane. "She's not supposed to die until Thursday, so we still have all day tomorrow, at least, right?"

Instead of answering, Tod scowled, and his curls shone brightly in the glare from the passing car's head-lights. "Can't you sneak out after your dad goes to bed?"

I nodded and flicked my brights back on. "Probably. But if I get caught, we're right back where we started, only getting caught sneaking out is much worse than being late for curfew in the first place. I could be late because of traffic, car trouble, or the built-in delay of hanging out with Emma. But sneaking out implies that I'm up to something my dad won't like." Which was true, but not in the way my father would be thinking. "And then he'll start checking up on me all the time. He's new at this, and way overzealous."

Nash and Tod had it easy. They were both legal—Nash had turned eighteen in late August—and thus mostly free from curfews and other unreasonable parental restrictions. Especially Tod, who was not only of age, but technically dead.

It's hard to ground someone who doesn't even officially exist. And can walk through walls.

"Whatever." He ran one hand through his mop of curls. "Can't you skip school tomorrow?"

"Love to," I said, and Tod's eyes brightened. Until I continued. "But I can't. I skipped last period today for this little road trip, and if I miss again, the school will call my dad."

"High school's a pain in the ass," Tod snapped, and I almost laughed out loud at the absurdity of such an understatement. "I'll be glad when you turn eighteen."

That time I did laugh. "Me, too."

"That makes three of us." The heat in Nash's eyes said his agreement had nothing to do with helping either Tod or Addison, and everything to do with uninterrupted privacy. At least where my father was concerned.

Something told me getting rid of Tod would be a little more difficult.

My phone rang as I took a long, gradual curve in the highway, and Nash helped me hold the wheel while I dug my cell from my pocket. I didn't recognize the number, which meant my father probably hadn't figured anything out yet.

I flipped my phone open and held it to my ear with my right hand, while I steered with my left. "Hello?"

"Kaylee?" It was Addison, and she sounded stuffy, like she had a cold. Or like she'd been crying.

"Addy, what's wrong?" I asked, and Tod's image in the rearview mirror lurched when he leaned forward. His arm brushed the back of my shoulder as he hovered near my phone to listen in.

"Tod doesn't have a phone, so he gave me your number," Addison began, sniffling into my ear. "I hope that's okay." She sniffed again, and I wanted to tell her to blow her nose.

"It's fine. What's wrong?" I asked again, as Tod's breath warmed the back of my neck, stirring my ponytail. How weird that he was alive enough to breathe hot air, but not to carry a cell phone. Maybe it was hard to get an account in a dead man's name....

"It's Regan." Addison sobbed haltingly while I twisted the wheel to the left to keep us on the road when it curved. Suddenly it felt like I was trying to do a dozen things at once. And failing.

"What's wrong with Regan?" Tod asked over my shoulder, and she must have heard him.

"John Dekker offered her the contract, and she said yes!" Her voice rose in disbelief on the last word, and it echoed like a siren going off in my head. For a moment I wondered how certain we were of Addison's humanity. "He's on his way here now. He always brings the contract personally—he doesn't trust anyone else with it."

My heart beat so hard my chest felt bruised. John Dekker was coming to Texas, and he was bringing a soul-sucking demon with him.

The road swam before me as my horror and confusion crested in a startling wave of disorientation. Nash grabbed the wheel again, though I hadn't let go of it, and I took a deep breath, forcing my thoughts apart. Each to its own distinct corner of my mind. That was the only way I could concentrate on one at a time.

I tightened my grip on the wheel, eased up on the gas, and focused on the road, nodding absently to tell Nash I was fine. Until a semi blasted past on our right, nearly blowing us off the highway.

Maybe I should pull over....

"Wait, your sister sold her soul?" I said, hitting the

speakerphone button as I glanced over my shoulder to make sure there was nothing in the other lane. But the entire highway was blocked by Tod's face, crinkled with fear—an odd expression to find on a reaper.

"Move!" I mouthed, handing the phone to Nash, and Tod immediately dropped back into the rear passenger seat. I swerved too quickly into the right lane— blessedly empty—then onto the shoulder of the road.

"She hasn't actually signed the contract yet," Addison continued, oblivious to my driving woes. "But she will as soon as Dekker gets here. You guys have to help me. Please. She won't listen to me, but she can't argue with you. She knows Tod's dead. You all have to come tell her what you told me. What will happen to her when she dies."

"Why won't she listen to you?" I shoved the gearshift into Park, and Nash stabbed a button on the dash to turn on the hazard lights.

"She thinks I'm trying to hold her back." Addy sobbed again and springs creaked as she sat on something. It sounded like a bed, rather than a chair. "She said she was tired of 'singing in my shadow.'"

Nash spoke loudly, to make sure she could hear. "Addy, where's your mom?"

Addison sniffled again, sounding much younger than eighteen. I guess true terror does that. "She went out, and she's not answering her phone." She didn't elaborate, but I recognized the embarrassed, disgusted tone in her voice. Her mom was strung out again, and gone when she was needed most.

"Does she know what your sister's about to do?" Nash continued.

Addison sobbed miserably. "Yeah, but she doesn't understand. I tried to tell her Regan was selling her soul, but she thought I was speaking in metaphors." She sniffled again. "I doubt she'd care, anyway. She'd just see dollar signs."

I already hated Mrs. Page, though I'd never met her.

Tod leaned forward with his arms folded across the back of Nash's seat this time. "Where's Regan now?"

"We're both at home," Addy said. "My mom's house in Hurst. Do you remember how to get here?"

Tod nodded, then realized she couldn't hear him. "Yeah." But then he faltered, obviously at a loss for how we could help.

But I had an idea—a stroke of genius, really—that sent adrenaline racing through my veins fast enough to leave me light-headed. "After she signs the contract, Dekker has to take her to the Netherworld like they did with you, right?" My small car rocked violently as another huge truck blasted past us on the highway, without bothering to move into the far lane.

Addison cleared her throat, and more springs groaned. "Yeah, but we can't let that happen. We have to stop her from signing."

"I know." I held up one finger to tell Nash and Tod to wait—that I really was going somewhere with this. "But my point is that in order to take her to the Netherworld, Dekker has to bring along that reaper, right? The lady who took you to the hellion?"

"Yeah, I guess…"

"And, Tod…" I twisted in the driver's seat to face him, though the steering wheel bruised my side. "Using your soul-wrangling abilities for anything other than reaping from the approved list is illegal for a reaper, right? Including taking humans to the Netherworld to facilitate the removal of their souls?" He nodded, and I continued. "Would you call that a firing offense?"

"Definitely." His eyes lit up, as my point became clear.

"And would your boss be interested in the chance to fire such a reaper?"

His brows arched. "It would make his decade."

"That's what I thought." I faced forward again to spare my ribs, just as the first drops of rain went splat on the windshield. "And without his pet reaper, Dekker has no way to get Regan to the Netherworld. Right?" My excitement grew as Tod and Nash both nodded eagerly. We had a chance to save Regan from making a huge mistake *and* bring justice to the rogue reaper involved. Plus, if I could peek into the Netherworld, I could at least get a good look at the hellion we needed to identify. "So, what do you think? Will it work?"

Nash grinned from ear to ear and made a gruff happy noise deep in his throat. "I think it might."

"So, wait, you have a plan?" Addy squeaked over the line.

"Yeah, I think we do." I twisted my key in the ignition, and the car rumbled to life, more like an ailing house cat than a purring tiger, but so long as my poor car moved, I wasn't going to complain.

"What should I do?"

I rebuckled my seat belt and flicked the switch to start my windshield wipers. "Stall them until we get there." The passenger side wiper stuttered across the glass once, then died without so much as a whimper. Fortunately, I didn't need to see through that side. "Say whatever you have to say. But don't let her sign that contract, and do *not* let the reaper take Regan to the Netherworld."

"Okay, I'll try." But she sounded less than confident.

"Try hard, Addy." I punched the button to make the hazard lights stop blinking and glanced over my left shoulder before pulling into traffic again. "You only have one sister, right? And she only has one soul."

"Yeah, okay." She sniffled again, but this time determination echoed in her voice like a vow sworn in a cavern. "I'll keep her here if I have to chain her to the kitchen cabinets."

"I hope you're kidding, but in case you're not, that won't work. Neither your cabinets nor your chain exist in the Netherworld, because they're in a private residence." *Huh. Look at that.* I'd actually learned something in how-to-be-a-*bean-sidhe* lessons…

"Yes, but the concept has some real potential," Tod muttered from behind me, and I glanced in the mirror to see him grinning lasciviously.

"I'll come up with something," Addison said. She obviously hadn't heard the reaper's last comment.

"Good. We'll be there as soon as we can." I nodded at Nash, and he closed my phone, but held on to it, so I wouldn't have to dig for it if it rang again. Then I stomped on the gas, and nearly had a heart attack when my poor little car hydroplaned a good ten feet before finding traction again.

"I'd rather be late-but-whole than punctual-but-dead," Nash suggested, teasing me much more calmly than I could have managed if he'd nearly killed me.

"I'm gonna find Levi and meet you guys there," Tod said, and I frowned when I realized the fear shining in his eyes probably had as much to do with my driving and the possibility of his own second death than with being late to Regan's soul harvest.

Was that some kind of residual human fear, or could a car crash actually hurt a reaper, if he didn't blink out in time? And for the first time, I wondered exactly how dead Tod was....

"Wait!" I shouted, and Nash reached for the wheel again when I stretched my neck to catch his brother's gaze in the rearview mirror. Tod arched one brow at me. I'd caught him right before he would have disappeared. "Reapers don't have death dates, because they're already dead, right?" I asked, and Tod nodded. "So... do you guys still have souls?"

He scowled. "Do my eyes look empty to you?"

I breathed a little easier, knowing the dead boy in my backseat wasn't soulless—even if his conscience wasn't exactly bright and shiny. "So, what happens to a reaper's soul once it's confiscated?" I asked, watching his face for any unspoken reaction. Because a fired reaper was a dead reaper. Permanently dead.

"It's recycled, just like a human's," Tod said, and I

could see the gears grinding behind his eyes, as he tried to follow my thought process. His brother's expression was eerily similar, only without that edge of suspicion. Nash might not have known exactly what I was up to, but he trusted me completely.

I wasn't sure whether that made him sweet or naive.

"So…who collects it?" I asked, not surprised to see my brow crinkle in the mirror. "Can just any reaper kill a fellow reaper and take her soul?"

Tod shrugged, and suddenly looked completely invested in the conversation—a relative rarity for him. "In theory, yes. But that would be a really good way to piss off your coworkers. So we usually leave that to managers and Dark reapers, like Libby."

The rain had started to slow, so I dared a little more pressure on the gas pedal. "Does it work the same way it does with humans?"

"As far as I know. Though, reaper souls are much rarer than human souls, so I've never actually seen it done."

"What are you getting at, Kaylee?" Nash asked, as I put my blinker on to pass an old pickup in the right lane.

"I was just curious," I said, not yet willing to mention the kernel of an idea sprouting slowly in my head.

"Do you know how to get to Addison's mom's house?"
I asked Nash, and when he nodded, I eyed Tod in the
mirror. "Go find Levi. We'll meet you there as soon as
we can."

He nodded, then disappeared.

I drove as fast as I could without risking an accident or police intervention, and when we got to Hurst,
Nash gave me directions to her neighborhood. Which
is where we got lost. The roads in Addison's subdivision
wound around in interconnected circles and cul-de-
sacs, several of which seemed to share variations of the
same name. And all the houses looked the same, especially in the dark.

My ten-thirty curfew came and went while we wandered the neighborhood, trying to call Addy the whole
time, but she never answered her phone. Finally, Nash
suggested I let him drive while I took a peek into the
Netherworld to see if I could give him a general direction from there. Reluctantly—very reluctantly—I
agreed.

In the passenger seat of my own car, as a late-night
mist still sprayed my windshield, I called up the memory
of Emma's death, forcing myself to relive it one more
time. I told myself I was doing a good thing. Trying to
save the soul of a thirteen-year-old girl who had no idea

what she was getting herself into, rather than simply exploring my own abilities.

It didn't help.

Summoning my own wail was still one of the most difficult things I'd ever had to do, probably because I didn't really want to remember how Emma had looked when she'd died. How her face had gone blank, her eyes staring up at the gym ceiling as if she could see straight through it and into the heavens. *Though, she actually saw nothing at all….*

That did it. The wail began deep in my chest, fighting to break free from my throat, but I held it back. Swallowed most of it, as Harmony had taught me. What came out was a soft, high-pitched keening, which buzzed in my ears and seemed to resonate in my fillings. And finally a thin gray haze formed over everything, in spite of the fact that there was very little light to filter through it. To reflect off of it.

Since I was just peeking into the Netherworld, rather than going there, my vision seemed to split as one reality layered itself over the other. It was a bit like watching a 3-D movie without the proper cardboard glasses. The images didn't quite line up.

And the Netherworld—rather than being lit by what paltry moonlight shone in the human plane—was illuminated by a ubiquitous white glow from above, similar to the way the lights of a city in the distance reflect off low-lying clouds in the dark. This light was indistinct and somehow cold, and seemed to blur the world before me, rather than to truly lighten it.

However that was par for the course, at least as far as I could tell. I'd never been able to see very far in the Netherworld, which gave me the impression that if I took one step too many, I'd fall into some huge, gaping pit, or step off the edge of the world. That thought, and the cool, hazy light, made me want to step very carefully. Or to close my eyes and shake my head until the Netherworld disappeared altogether.

But I resisted the urge to deny the Netherworld, though every survival instinct I had groaned within me. I'd never find Regan and Addy in time if I didn't look in both worlds.

"What do you see?" Nash asked. Because he could hear my keening, he would have been able to see into the Netherworld with me, if he'd wanted. But someone had to drive.

I couldn't answer him—not while I was holding back my wail. So I shrugged, and squinted into the distance, turning slowly in my seat. At first there was nothing but the usual gray fog, paler toward the sky, and the eerie impression of movement just outside my field of vision.

As Harmony had explained, human private residences didn't exist in the Netherworld, so when I peeked into it, Addy's neighborhood was suddenly overlaid with a second, similar series of gravel streets and walkways, which ended in nothing. And some darkly intuitive part of my mind insisted that the gravel was really crushed bone. Though, from what sort of creature I couldn't begin to imagine….

I wondered what I'd see if I were actually in the Netherworld. What would the homes look like? Could I go in one? Would I want to?

"Well?" The urgency in Nash's voice reminded me of the ticking clock. I squinted into the fog again and this time made out a series of darker-than-normal shapes in the ever-present gray spliced into our world. Shapes that weren't moving. Or at least, weren't moving *away*.

I pointed to my right, and was surprised when my hand smashed into the glass of my own window. Though I still sat bodily in the human world, my senses were so intensely focused on that other world that I'd become oblivious to my physical surroundings. The car didn't exist in the Netherworld, where I seemed to float over the road alone, in an invisible chair.

Weird.

Nash turned the wheel in the direction I'd pointed,

and vertigo washed over me as I moved along with a vehicle I could only see and feel on one plane. In one reality.

Double weird. Evidently I get carsick in the Nether-reality.

As we drew closer, the shapes became a little more distinct. Two tall forms, and one small. Small, like a little girl. A young teenager, maybe.

Crap. Regan had already crossed over.

A little more of my wail slipped out, and I was surprised all over again when the echo of my voice bounced around in the car, rather than rolling out to points unknown. Nash followed my finger, and I had to slap a hand over my mouth to keep from vomiting when the car tilted up suddenly, and he slammed my gearshift into Park. We were in a sharply sloping drive-way, only feet from those three dark figures now.

The driver's side door opened, and cold air swirled around me. A moment later, my door opened, and Nash helped me out of the car by one arm. Icy mist settled on me, rendering me instantly damp and cold, and distantly I wished I'd worn a jacket.

Nash's lips brushed my ear. "Let it go…" His words slid over me like warm satin gliding over my skin. I felt myself relax, even as the largest of those gray figures turned to walk away. "We're here now, so just let it go."

I let the wail fade, and the grayness melted from my vision, leaving me with a scratchy throat and haunting images lingering behind my eyes. And a crystal-clear view of a large brick house with a stone facade around a bright red front door, illuminated by a series of flood-lights.

Parked on the street in front of the house was a plain black limousine—if a limo can ever be consid-ered plain—with the engine still running, the driver half asleep behind the wheel. That would have been a remarkable sight on my street, but in Addy's neighbor-hood, it was probably commonplace.

Nash dashed toward the house, and I sprinted after him, without taking time to truly reorient myself in the human world. I tripped over the front step, but he caught me with one hand, already twisting the knob with the other.

It opened easily. Dekker and the reaper obviously weren't expecting company. Fortunately, Addison was.

We rushed through the tiled foyer into a large, plush living room, where John Dekker held Addison Page by her upper arm, his other hand gripping an expanding file folder closed with a built-in rubber band.

Was that Regan's contract? Excitement surged through me like an electrical charge. Could the hellion's name really be so close?

An instant later, two female figures appeared in the center of the floor, holding hands.

The taller form I assumed to be the rogue reaper. The other was Regan Page. I recognized her from the ads for her new tween drama. Except that on TV, she had crystalline blue eyes only a couple of shades darker than her sister's.

Now her eyes were solid white orbs, shot through with tiny red veins, as if the whites had absorbed her pupils and irises.

Despair crashed through me, heavy and almost too thick to breathe through. My hand tightened around Nash's. We were too late. She'd sold her soul, and the brief, dark-'n'-blurry glimpse I'd gotten of the hellion who took it wasn't enough to let me identify him, much less find him.

I'd failed—again—and another girl had lost her soul.

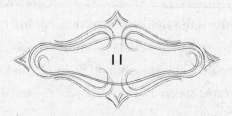

11

"Regan…" Addison moaned, staring into her sister's featureless eyes, slowly shaking her head. Her own eerie, fake-blue eyes filled with tears and her hands began to tremble.

"You made the right choice," Dekker told Regan, flashing that famous, million-dollar smile. The caps that launched a thousand amusement park rides. His grandfather would have been proud. "You'll be rich and famous for the rest of your life."

Sudden anger flamed behind the icy blue rings of Addy's contact lenses, blazing through her weaker emotions like kindling. She ripped her arm from Dekker's grasp and pulled Regan away from the reaper. "Is the hellion still there?" she demanded, her focus shifting between me and Nash as she held her sister's thin arm with a granite grip. "If we destroy her contract, will that kill the deal?"

"No!" Regan tried to twist away, and Dekker followed Addison's gaze to me and Nash, standing at the edge of the room like freshmen at the prom.

"Who are they?" he asked calmly, clearly speaking to his female colleague, though he looked at us.

The reaper sneered but looked like she really wanted to hiss. *"Bean sidhes,"* she spat.

"Friends," Addison said. "I…invited them."

Dekker dismissed us at a glance and turned back to Addy, flipping open his folder so we could all see that it was empty. Because, as Tod had discovered, demon paperwork was kept in the Netherworld. "It doesn't work like that, Addison." Dekker shot her a smug, patient smile. "Hellion contracts are indestructible by human means. Like fireproof, Kevlar paperwork. And if Regan invokes her out-clause before she has a pedestal to fall from, her willpower and decorum will corrode until she wouldn't recognize a good decision if it ran her over on the street. You'll likely be an aunt in a couple of years, and I'm sure the brat's father will be a convict, or a dealer, or something equally prestigious.

"Regan's flaws will be exploited and magnified, and

because her sister's famous, her every stumble will be front-page news." He paused, and his eager brown eyes seemed to spark with a little extra oomph. "Oh, and any tendencies toward addiction—something she might have inherited, for example?" His raised eyebrows said Dekker was more than familiar with Ms. Page's fondness for prescription drugs. "Well, let's just say they'll be awfully hard for a new, disgraced teen mother to resist…."

Regan stared at Dekker in growing horror, and rage flushed Addy's cheeks. "It doesn't matter," she insisted, while her sister's head whipped back and forth in denial. "She's not taking the out-clause."

"Why not?" Regan demanded, but Addy turned to me without answering her.

"Is the demon still there? I want to talk to him."

"He's gone," I said, remembering the largest of the three dark figures I'd seen in the Netherworld. The one who'd walked away as I let my wail fade.

"Take us," Addy demanded softly. "We'll find him."

"No." Nash shook his head firmly. "You can't go there, and neither can Kaylee. It's not safe."

"Neither is this!" Addison shoved her sister forward, and Nash flinched as his gaze found Regan's newly empty eyes.

"What's happening?" Regan shouted, tears filling

her eyes. "Who're they?" She waved one arm at me and Nash, then her bewildered gaze slid back to Dekker. "Why is he threatening to wreck my life?"

Dekker crossed his arms over his chest, the empty folder flat against his side. "I'm not threatening you. I'm simply stating facts. You've signed a contract, and you'll be expected to stand by your word."

"She had no idea what she was signing," Addy said. "You didn't tell her the truth."

"I never lied," Dekker insisted calmly.

"What are you guys talking about?" Regan demanded, more bewildered than truly scared.

"We're talking about *this!*" Addison whirled her sister around until she faced a mirror hanging on the wall above a beige couch. "Look!"

Regan looked, and her eyes went anime-wide. But though her cheeks flushed bright red, no color returned to her eyes. That beautiful blue was gone, along with her soul.

"What…?" Regan started to step closer to the mirror for a better look, then changed her mind and stepped back instead, shaking her head slowly in denial. Then she whirled on John Dekker and his reaper with a rage and confusion almost equal to her sister's. "What's wrong with my eyes? How can I see if I don't have eyes? You didn't say anything about this."

"It was in the fine print." The reaper crossed her arms over a gaunt, black-clad chest, contempt glittering in her normal gray eyes. "You are old enough to read, aren't you?"

Dekker laid one hand on her forearm, and the reaper seemed to fold into herself, as if he'd just jabbed her off button. "There's nothing wrong with your eyes." His voice was calm and smooth, but it had nothing on Nash. "It's a side effect of the process. And we have an easy fix for this, don't we, Addison?"

Dekker glanced at the older Page sister, but she only glared at him, jaw clenched in vicious anger as he handed two small white boxes to her sister. "These are your prescription, I believe, and a virtual match to your own eye color. I'll have new boxes hand-delivered every six months. These should last until then, but please be careful with them." He winked his own nondescript brown eyes. "They aren't exactly cheap."

Regan's empty eyes filled with tears again, and I couldn't remember ever being scared of a crying eighth-grader before. But I was scared then. The incongruity of her very human tears with those distinctly *in*human eyes gave me chills in places I didn't even know I could get cold. "Will they stay like this?" She turned hesitantly toward the mirror again, then away before she could possibly have really seen herself. "Why do they look so…empty?"

"Because they're empty," Tod said, and we all spun around at the sound of his voice. Tod stood near the kitchen doorway, next to a small redheaded boy who barely came up to the reaper's shoulders. "The eyes are the windows to the soul, and without your soul, there's nothing for them to reflect."

Dekker's pet reaper went stiff on the edge of the room. Was Tod really that scary?

"Do you have another brother?" I whispered, standing on my toes to reach Nash's ear. "And did your dad have red hair?"

"That's Levi," he whispered back, and the little boy nodded politely at me, shrugging with his hands in the pockets of a baggy pair of khakis.

"Levi-the-reaper?" I asked, a little embarrassed when my voice went high with surprise. After all the truly weird stuff I'd seen since discovering I was a *bean sidhe*, a freckle-faced little-boy reaper shouldn't have fazed me in the least. But it did. "Tod's boss, Levi-the-reaper?"

"The one and only." Levi shot me a disarmingly sweet smile. One his eyes didn't match. Then he turned a ferocious glare on the rogue reaper. "Bana."

She froze with that one syllable—her own name, spoken in a child's high, soft voice—and her fingers twitched nervously at her sides. She looked like she wanted to run, but couldn't.

"I wasn't sure who to expect, but I must admit your name never occurred to me." Levi strolled forward like a kid in the park, and I had the absurd thought that he should have been carrying a baseball bat on his shoulder, or a skateboard under one arm. He stopped several feet from Bana and her boss, and gave John Dekker only a fleeting glance, as if he didn't recognize one of the most famous faces in the world.

Which struck me as especially ironic, considering the reaper's apparent age.

"Who is this?" Dekker asked, but before Bana could answer—and I seriously doubt she would have—the boy pulled his freckled right hand from his pocket.

"Levi Van Zant. Senior reaper in this district. I've come to relieve Bana of her duties. And her soul."

Bana's arms went stiff in anticipation, and I realized she was trying to blink out of Addy's house, and out of Levi's reach. My breath caught in my throat. We were going to lose her. But did it even matter? We were too late to stop her from ferrying Regan to the Netherworld.

But despite her obvious effort to disappear, she remained fully corporeal.

And before I could release my breath—before Bana

could even suck one in—Levi's small hand shot out and wrapped around her wrist. His fingers barely met on the back of her arm, but any doubt I had about the strength of his grip was put to rest with one look at her face, twisted in agony, as if his very touch burned.

"Bana, look at me."

She tried to refuse. Her free hand clawed uselessly at the wall behind her, scratching the Sheetrock, resistance etched into the terrified, angry lines of her jaw and forehead. But she couldn't resist. Nor could she blink out. Somehow, Levi was blocking her abilities. Guaranteeing her cooperation.

Would Tod ever have that power?

"Look at me, Bana."

Her eyes flew open, and a cry leaked from her mouth. She looked straight into Levi's green eyes, which seemed to…shine. To glow with a bright, cold light.

We watched, every one of us fascinated. Including Dekker, but especially Regan Page, who was getting her first terrifying glimpse of the world she'd just entered. The world she'd sold herself to.

Bana's shoulders slumped and her eyelids fluttered, as if they'd close. Levi's grip on her arm tightened visibly. Dekker stepped back and the reaper went suddenly stiff.

Her eyes opened again, but began to dull immediately. To simply…go dark.

And that's when the panic hit. My heart pounded, bruising the inside of my chest. Sweat formed between Nash's hand and mine. The cry rose in my throat, clawing me from the inside out, demanding an exit. An audience. Bana's soul song wanted to be heard.

I clenched my jaw against the wail, my mind whirring with questions.

A soul song for a reaper? It made sense—she did have a soul—yet somehow I'd never expected to actually wail for a reaper. Did that mean that Nash and I could save her if we wanted to? But why would we want to? And if we did, would someone else be taken in her place? Did doomed reaper souls require an exchange?

Surely not. Tod had said reaper souls were much rarer than human souls, so if we were to save Bana, would another reaper have to die? Because one human soul wouldn't be enough, would it?

The kernel of an idea I'd had earlier exploded in my head so violently it felt like my skull would split wide open. Because it wasn't just an idea. It was an *idea*. The kind of idea that could change lives.

Or save souls.

My hand clutched Nash's, and he tore his gaze from Bana to look at me in surprise, at almost the exact moment the scream leaked from my sealed lips. Just a sliver of sound at first, sharp and painful, but controlled. For the moment.

"Bana?" he whispered, hazel eyes wide, forehead crinkled.

I nodded and let another slice of sound slide from me.

Tod noticed then, and shot a questioning glance at Nash, who could only shrug. "You can make it stop, Kaylee," he said finally, his lips brushing my ear, his peaceful Influence brushing my heart. "I've seen you do it. Bring it back. Hold it in."

But I twisted away from him, shaking my head adamantly. I didn't want to hold it in. I wanted to let it go. Let my shriek pierce every skull in the room and rattle the windows. And let it capture Bana's filthy soul.

The rogue reaper was about to pay for her part in Dekker's soul-trafficking ring, and I was going to personally wring the recompense from her.

Addy and Regan watched me now, rather than Bana and Levi, and their stares made me nervous. Broke my concentration.

I closed my eyes briefly, then opened them along with my mouth. Sharp spikes of sound burst from me, washing over the room like a wave of glass shards. Addy, Regan, and Dekker flinched as one, as their brains were pierced by the evidence of my intent. Their hands flew to their ears. Their eyes squeezed shut. Their noses wrinkled in displeasure bordering on pain.

Levi shuddered, but his concentration never faltered. Bana was in too much pain from the brutal removal of her soul to even notice what I was doing. But Nash and Tod each wore odd smiles, their faces almost slack in pleasure. They heard my wail as a beautiful, eerie song, a melody without equivalent in the human world. A gift from the female *bean sidhe*, which only the males of our species could experience.

Even the undead males, apparently.

The panic ebbed inside me, riding the sliver of sound out of my core and into the room. With that pressure released, I was able to focus on my part in the plan I was forming. And to somehow communicate Tod's part to him.

An instant later, the last ember of light died in Bana's eyes, and her soul rose from her body. It looked exactly like a human soul—pale and formless. I'm not sure what I was expecting, but that wasn't it. Shouldn't a reaper's soul be different, somehow? And if it wasn't, would my plan even work?

Only one way to find out…

I sang for her soul. Called to it, suspending it in the air like a thick fog as Levi let go of the dead reaper's arm. He stepped back, and she collapsed on Addy's plush living-room carpet, a tangle of bent arms and awkwardly twisted legs.

Dekker jumped away from his dead employee so fast he tripped over his own feet and would have gone down if not for the chair he grabbed for balance. If I hadn't been screaming loud enough to rouse the dead, I'd have laughed. I wouldn't have thought someone who dealt so closely with reapers and hellions would be spooked by a little death.

But despite my fleeting amusement, my plan was not funny. It was born of desperation and inspiration, and it would never work if Tod didn't get on board. Fast.

Unable to take my eyes from Bana's soul, I felt around on my left, reaching blindly for Tod's arm. I found it, and pulled him forward just as Nash bent to whisper into my ear. That was the only way I could hear him over my own wail, and I probably wouldn't have heard a human voice. "What are you doing? She's dead. Let her go. I'm *not* bringing her back."

I shook my head vehemently, frustrated by my inability to communicate. When Tod's head came into my field of vision, I shoved him toward Bana, pointing at her hovering soul with my free hand then at Tod. Specifically, at his mouth. I needed him to suck up her soul, like Libby had sucked up the Demon's Breath.

To hold it, just for a little while.

And finally, he seemed to get it. "You want me to take her soul?" he asked, and I nodded, relief washing through me so quickly the edges of my vision went black.

I grabbed Nash for balance and concentrated on maintaining my song.

"Why?" Tod asked, shrugging when Levi shot him a questioning glance.

But I couldn't explain until he took the soul so I could stop screeching. I made more frantic gestures with my arms, and he finally nodded in concession. Then he opened his mouth and sucked in Bana's soul. In seconds, it was gone.

I closed my mouth and the room went silent, but for the awful ringing in my ears, which I knew from experience wouldn't fade completely for a couple of hours.

Tod wiped nonexistent soul crumbs from his mouth, and I shuddered.

"That was...surreal," I said, my voice as scratchy as an old record player. I stumbled, weak from exertion, and Nash caught me. He half carried me to the couch along the far wall, which was when I realized John Dekker was gone. He'd slipped from the room while everyone else watched me scream, and the front door still stood open.

Outside, tires squealed on the street and headlights faded from the front window. The limo we'd seen out front was gone. As was Regan's soul.

I whirled on the Page sisters, my eyes wide. "Did you catch the hellion's name?"

Addy shook her head slowly, angrily. "They never said it." Her features darkened with tortured disappointment and she glanced at her sister. "Do you know his name?"

Regan shook her head silently, offering no excuses.

"Great. So, what was all that?" Addison asked me, wrapping one arm around her sister's shoulders. Regan only stared, too shocked to form a coherent question.

I knew exactly how she felt.

"Could they see any of that?" I asked, rubbing my throat.

Nash shook his head. "Tod, explain what you can. Kaylee's losing her voice. I'm gonna get her something to drink." With that, he kicked the front door closed and headed into Addy's kitchen, face flushed in barely controlled anger.

Addy didn't seem to notice.

"Bana was a grim reaper," Tod began, guiding both stunned sisters to the empty couch opposite the one

I sat on. "Like me and Levi." He nodded toward the boy still standing in the corner, small hands once again hidden in his pockets, evidently content to watch and listen for the moment. "Only she was…bad. So Levi fired her."

"You mean he killed her," Addison said, obviously struggling not to stare at the corpse on her carpet.

"Well, technically she was already dead." Tod shrugged. "So he really just finished the job. And Kaylee was singing her soul song."

"That wasn't singing." Regan's nose wrinkled like she smelled something awful. "That was a vocal *slaughter.*"

If my throat didn't feel like I'd just swallowed barbed wire, I would have laughed. I totally agreed.

"It wasn't a song like you think of music." Nash emerged from the kitchen with a glass of ice water. "It was a call to Bana's soul. Kaylee suspended it long enough for Tod to…take it."

"Speaking of which…" Tod sat on the other couch, as close as he could get to Addison, their legs touching from thigh to knee while Levi watched with an odd expression I couldn't interpret. "Why did I take her soul? Does this have anything to do with all your reaper questions in the car?"

"In fact, it does," I said, after one long sip of the

water. My throat still hurt, but my voice had decent volume, considering what I'd just put it through. "We're going to barter with Bana's soul."

Nash's brows arched like he was impressed, and the sudden light in Tod's eyes said he understood at least part of what I was getting at. "You said a reaper's soul is rarer than a human's." I shifted my focus from Tod to his boss. "Am I correct in assuming that makes it more valuable?"

Levi nodded, and now his smile showed a line of small white teeth. They were all there, fortunately. If any had been missing, he would have been too creepy to look at.

"As valuable as, say, two human souls?" I glanced at the Page sisters, then back at Levi, whose brows arched in surprise.

"She's smart, this one," he said. "Of course, I can't officially condone what you're thinking, so I'll take my leave now...."

"But I'm on the right path?" I asked as he knelt next to the dead reaper.

"I'm afraid I don't know what you're talking about." Levi winked at me, still grinning. Then he picked up Bana in both arms as if she weighed nothing, though she had more than a foot on him, and they both disappeared.

"What is going on?" Regan finally demanded, impotent fists clenched at her sides.

I smiled gently, trying to set her at ease, though those eerie, empty eyes creeped me out. "We're going to trade Bana's soul to the hellion. For both of yours."

12

"Shh," I whispered to Nash as I closed the front door softly, wondering what the chances were that my father had fallen asleep early and hadn't noticed I was late. The living room was dark, and in the kitchen, only the over-the-sink light was on, so it was looking pretty good so far....

"Kaylee, get in here. Now."

Or not.

Nash squeezed my hand and followed me into the living room, where my father's silhouette leaned forward in the lumpy armchair, outlined by what little light penetrated the curtains from the street lamp outside. I stood in the middle of the floor, staring at the dark spot where his eyes would be, Nash's chest pressed against my back. "Why are you sitting in the dark?"

A shadow-arm reached up and to the left. The floor lamp clicked and light flooded the room. My dad still wore the flannel shirt he'd worked in, and his eyes were red from exhaustion. "Why are you an hour and a half late?"

Technically, it was only an hour and twenty-four minutes, but he looked even less eager to be corrected than I was to discuss my whereabouts.

"It's not even midnight." I tugged Nash forward and he took that as his signal to intervene, though that wasn't what I'd intended.

"Sorry, Mr. Cavanaugh. We didn't realize it was so la—"

"Go home, Nash." A muscle jumped along the line of my father's jaw. "Your mom's waiting for you, too."

Nash's eyebrows rose, and he frowned. "I'll talk to you tomorrow, Kaylee," he said, already turning toward the front door with my hand still clasped in his, our arms stretched between us.

"That remains to be seen," my dad snapped.

I grinned, hoping to lighten the mood. "You gonna ground me from school?"

He was unamused. "Good night, Nash."

"I have to drive him." I probably should have taken

him home first, but I was hoping my dad would be asleep and we could discuss our next move, in light of that evening's failure. I dug my keys from my pocket and turned to follow Nash, but he shook his head with one look at my dad.

"I'll walk. It's only a few blocks." As the door closed behind him, I suddenly wished we didn't live so close together.

"Where were you?" my dad asked as I sank onto the couch on his left. "And before you start, I know you didn't work tonight, and you clearly weren't with Emma."

Great. "It's not whatever you're thinking." I could virtually guarantee that. But I couldn't tell him where I'd really been, because he'd like that even less than the thought that I was out drinking, smoking, or sleeping with Nash.

"Then where were you?" He crossed both arms over his chest, and I thought I saw his irises swirl just a little, though that might have been the flicker of a passing headlight on his eyes.

"Out driving." *Mostly.*

When he leaned forward to peer into my eyes, I realized his irises really were swirling. Weird. He usually had better control over his emotions…

"Is Nash going to be a problem?" My dad's voice was deep and rough. Worried.

I fiddled with a frayed spot of denim over my knee. "Why would he be?"

He closed his eyes briefly, and when they opened, his face held a new resolve and the colors in his irises had stopped moving. He'd regained control over…something. Something I didn't understand and he didn't seem ready to explain. "Kaylee, I know you like him, and I know he's…not a bad kid. And we all know he was there for you when I wasn't, and I'm sorrier about that than I could ever explain. But I don't want you to…"

He hesitated and rubbed his forehead, then started over. "It isn't a good idea for you to get too involved with him. You're so young, and… Damn, I wish your mother was here to explain this…."

Sudden understanding flooded me and blood rushed to my cheeks. "Dad, is this about sex?"

That time he blushed, and I almost felt sorry for him. Full-time parenthood was new for him, and we were still feeling our way around in some areas. Like curfews, and apparently that mortifying after-school-special talk.

"It's not just about sex…."

"Okay, please stop." I held up both hands, palms out, and rolled my eyes. "This is just weird—"

"Kaylee…"

"—and it's really none of your business—" I gestured with one arm.

He stood, frowning down at me. "This most certainly is my business—"

"—and I don't need you stepping in to tell me what I can and can't do!" I stood to put us on equal ground.

"That's my job." His mouth quirked up in an ironic smile, but I refused to see the humor.

"Well, you're not very good at it!"

His smile collapsed, and his eyes swirled slowly. Sadly.

I felt guilty immediately. He was trying so hard. "I didn't mean it like that."

"I know." He exhaled heavily. "But you're still grounded. For coming home late—not for hurting my feelings."

Great. I closed my eyes, trying to think quickly. I knew how to deal with my aunt and uncle, but with my dad, I was in mostly unexplored territory. "Okay, but this is really kind of a disastrous time for me to be grounded." I crossed my arms over my chest. "Can't we work something else out? I'll do the dishes all week. And the laundry." Of course, I already did most of the clothes, anyway, because he kind of sucked at sorting.

"Did Bren and Val really go for that?" Anger edged

his voice now. I was nearing some kind of boundary, and I really had no desire to cross it. My dad was actually pretty laid-back for the most part, and I didn't want to trigger whatever auto-lockdown mechanism most parents have hardwired into their brains. Even recently returned itinerant parents.

"No." They'd rarely actually grounded me; Sophie was usually the one in trouble. Though, I couldn't remember them actually grounding her, either, come to think of it…. "But I have something important to do this week."

"What?"

My entire body felt heavy with guilt. "I can't tell you."

"Like you can't tell me where you were tonight?"

"Kind of." I exhaled heavily and met his gaze. "Dad, I need you to trust me. This is really important."

He held out one hand, palm up. "Give me your phone."

My hand snuck into my pocket, curling protectively around my cell. "Seriously?" He couldn't mean that.

"Yes. One week, no phone."

"No!" Spikes of righteous anger shot up my spine, tingling all the way into my fingers. I was trying to help someone! If he'd been around long enough to get to know me, he'd know that, even without the details.

"It's not safe to run around without a phone!" Especially for someone so deep in hellion business she'd have to look up to wave to the devil.

"Well, that won't be a problem, because you're not going anywhere. Give me your keys. You can take the bus to school tomorrow."

"This is ridiculous!" I shouted, reluctantly digging my phone from one pocket, my keys from the other. "And completely unwarranted. It's not like I was out drinking and sleeping around."

My dad rubbed his forehead and sank back into the armchair, looking as weary as I'd ever seen him. "Kaylee, I don't know what you were doing, because you won't tell me!"

"Fine." I slapped my phone into his waiting palm. "But my reasons for not telling you everything now are just as important as your reasons for not telling me anything over the past thirteen years. And it's completely messed up that you expect me to trust you when you're not willing to return the favor."

My jab found its mark and my father flinched again. "I'm tired, Kaylee, and I don't have the energy for this." He set my phone on an end table and rubbed his face with both hands. "Give me your keys and go to bed. Please."

And what was I supposed to say to Addy and

Regan? *Sorry, I can't save your immortal souls, because I'm* grounded?

I dropped my keys on the kitchen counter, then plodded down the hall to my room, sorting through possible ways around this new complication. How were we supposed to find the hellion without a car? Walk all over the Metroplex?

With my bedroom door open, I sank cross-legged onto my bed and listened as my father locked up, then plodded down the hall to his own room. Fifteen minutes later, his snores echoed in the hall and a bolt of irritation lanced me. Our first real fight hadn't interrupted his sleep in the least.

Still irritated, I crossed the hall to use the bathroom and brush my teeth, then changed into a halter top and baggy pajama pants before collapsing onto my bed again. I had chemistry homework to do, and I was too mad to sleep, but I'd left my books in my car and couldn't get to them without my keys.

"You okay?" Tod asked from the wing chair by my headboard, and I almost jumped off the bed in surprise. "Sorry." He grabbed my arm to steady me.

I was tempted to yell at him, but resisted because for once his intrusion might actually come in handy. And because I didn't want to wake my dad up. "How much of that did you hear?" I waved one arm in the direction of the living room to indicate my fight with my dad.

"Just the last bit. Nash asked me to check on you." He waggled both eyebrows and donned a mischievous grin. "Don't worry, I turned around when you changed."

I couldn't help a laugh. Tod might flirt with me to bug Nash, but he obviously really cared about Addy, beyond whatever crush they'd shared in school. "I'm glad to hear you've retained at least a little moral fortitude since your unfortunate demise."

"I reserve it for special occasions. And people I like."

I threw my pillow at him.

"So is this all because you're late?"

"That, and because I wouldn't tell him where I'd been. I'm grounded for a week."

Tod frowned. "But you're still coming after school tomorrow, right?"

I cocked my head at him, eyes narrowed in mock confusion. "What part of 'grounded' don't you understand?"

"The part where it gets in the way of my plans." But I knew from the serious cast of his scowl that it wasn't really his plans he was worried about. It was Addy's soul.

Since we hadn't gotten there in time to stop Regan from selling out or even to identify the hellion who bought her soul, we were back to plan A: hoping someone at the Demon's Breath disposal facility would be willing to help us. But we had to get there first, which would be difficult without a car.

At least now we had something to bargain with, once we found the hellion. Fortunately, Tod could hold Bana's soul much longer than a reaper could hold on to a lungful of Demon's Breath. Not that I was exactly eager to enact that particular part of the plan…

"Look, it's your fault I'm grounded," I whisper-hissed at Tod. "None of this would have happened if you hadn't dragged me into this in the first place. What do you want me to do?"

"Sneak out." He shrugged, as if that should have been a no-brainer. But that was easy for him to say. He was dead. What else could they do to him, take away his birthday? "If you get caught, I'll make it up to you. I swear. Please, Kaylee. We can't do this without you."

"Yes you can!" I switched to a whisper again, in case my father woke up and heard the single most incriminating words I'd ever spoken. "You have Bana's soul. You can make the deal on your own."

His face fell, and he stared at the pillow in his lap for a moment before meeting my gaze again, frustration flaring like flames behind his eyes. "No I can't. I'm still a rookie reaper, Kaylee. I can only carry a limited amount of cargo to the Netherworld at a time, and I've already got Bana's soul to deal with. Even if I can take Addy, too, I need you to bring Regan. And Nash. I have a feeling we're going to need him."

I felt my eyes go wide, and my reflection in the mirror looked as terrified as I felt. "Can I do that?"

"Can't you?" Confusion flitted across his features. "Isn't that what my mom's supposed to be teaching you?"

"I don't know! She hasn't shown me a syllabus. Can she ferry people?"

"Yeah." He nodded firmly. "And you have to get her to teach you how. We can't do this without you, Kaylee."

I sighed, and the bleak weight of responsibility settled almost physically over me. I had no choice. But my dad was going to kill me when he found out, and the collateral damage would likely include both Nash and Tod. And Harmony, when he discovered her unwitting assistance. But hopefully that wouldn't be until after we'd returned Addy's and Regan's souls to their rightful bodies.

"Fine. But you owe me. Starting now."

"Absolutely." Relief half relaxed his features, and

the reaper leaned forward in my chair. "Whatever you want."

"Can you get my phone out of my dad's room without waking him up?"

"No problem." He was gone before I could warn him to be careful.

Several seconds later, as I sat frozen on my bed, irrationally afraid to move in case the squealing springs woke my father, Tod popped back into my room, cradling my slim red phone in one palm.

He shot me a crooked grin, blue eyes sparkling with mischief. "Did you know your dad sleeps in boxers?"

"Ew. Thanks for the visual." I grabbed my phone and scrolled through the menu to check my missed calls. Five from my dad and four from Emma. We must have hit a dead zone on the highway, and I hadn't checked my messages.

I selected the last voice mail Emma had left and held the phone to my ear, one hand on my hip as I glanced at Tod. "I need my books from my car, then I'll need you to put this back wherever my dad left it."

Tod gave me a mock bow. "Anything else? Can I fan you with a big palm leaf? Feed you grapes while you write your homework in my blood?"

"Shh!" I hissed, waving him off as Emma's

voice spoke to me from my phone. "You said you owed me!"

He frowned and popped out of my room in time for me to hear most of the missed message. "...tried to cover for you, but he called the theater first, and they told him you weren't working. You better call him and do some damage control, Kaylee. I'll see you tomorrow...."

The phone beeped in my ear as her message ended. She'd tried to warn me.

Tod popped back into my room holding my chemistry text and a notebook as I pressed a button to call Emma back. She answered on the third ring, and I gestured for him to set my stuff on my desk.

"Kay? It's twelve-thirty in the morning," Emma mumbled. It sounded like she had her face buried in the phone. "What's wrong?"

"Sorry, Em, but it's kind of an emergency. Can Nash and I get a ride to school tomorrow?"

"'Course." She sounded a little more alert, and springs squealed as she sat up in bed. "What happened to your car?"

"My dad took my keys and my phone for a week."

"Ouch. I'll be there at seven-thirty." Which meant seven-forty-five, in Emma-land. We'd be late to school, but that was better than riding the bus with the freshmen.

"Thanks. You're awesome."

"I know," she slurred, already half asleep again. "Bye." The phone clicked in my ear and Emma was gone. I spared a moment to hope she remembered us in the morning. Then I sank onto my bed, suddenly very sleepy, now that the immediate problem was resolved.

"Tell Nash to be here at seven-thirty if he wants a ride." I'd driven him to school most mornings since we started going out. I glanced at the textbook on my desk, briefly considering my homework. But I was too tired to mess with that. I'd do it at lunch. "So what's the plan for tomorrow?"

"We go downtown and find the disposal facility, then start asking questions until we hear what we need to know," Tod said, slouching in my chair again.

"Simple. I like it." I sat on my pillow and slid my legs beneath my covers. "When?"

"After school?"

"Nope. My dad'll call, and if I'm not here to answer, he'll...I don't know. Call the cops or something."

Tod scowled, an odd look on his cherubic features. "You're not looking at the big picture, Kaylee. Addy's soul is at stake. I've traded two hospital shifts in a row and will probably have to do it again tomorrow. The least you can do is drop off your dad's radar for a couple of hours after school."

"Okay, first of all, we're not out of time just yet. Tomorrow's Wednesday, and Addy's not supposed to die until Thursday. And we can't do this until I learn how to turn myself into a Netherworld ferry." Which meant I'd have to convince my father to let me go for my how-to-be-a-*bean-sidhe* lesson after school, in spite of the grounding.

Then I'd have to talk Harmony into teaching me what I needed to know, without telling her why I needed to know it.

"Besides, we need a car. You can blink into Dallas whenever you want, but Nash and I can't. And I'm not taking the bus in the middle of the night."

"Middle of the night?" He leaned forward in my chair, brows dipped low in concern. "Isn't that cutting it kind of close?"

"We don't really have any choice, Tod." I scooted down on the bed until the covers gathered at my waist. "The only time my dad won't check up on me is when he's asleep, which means we can't leave until tomorrow night. That gives you almost a day to explain everything to Addy and Regan, and to find us a car." Because his mom worked the night shift at the hospital and would need hers. "Do *not* steal one. The last thing we need is to get arrested on the way to the Netherworld."

I could already see the headline: Mentally Fragile Teen Arrested in Stolen Car; Says She Was Looking for a Demon.

Sophie wouldn't have to work hard to convince everyone I was nuts after that.

"That's not enough time, Kaylee." Tod looked as grim as I'd ever seen him.

"It'll have to be." I wasn't sure how best to comfort a reaper. "By Thursday morning, Addy will be in full possession of her soul."

It wasn't much of a promise, but since I couldn't guarantee her life, her soul was all I could offer him.

"Now, could you please put my phone back where you found it? And turn the light off on your way out." With that, I lay back and pulled the covers over my shoulder. I needed sleep.

Tomorrow promised to be the weirdest Wednesday in history.

13

"I REALLY SHOULD JUST LEAVE you here. You deserve to ride the bus, for keeping so many secrets." Emma slammed her locker closed as the last bell rang, but her bright brown eyes gave her away. She wasn't really mad. She was fishing for hints about the super-secret *bean sidhe* mission she imagined we were on.

I settled my backpack higher on my shoulder and tugged my snug tee down over the waistband of my jeans. "Trust me, you're not missing anything." If she knew the truth, her curiosity would no doubt give way to terror. Which was why I couldn't tell her.

But Emma would give us another ride, anyway, to make up for making us all nearly half an hour late to first period. I should have known she wouldn't remember a middle-of-the-night, sleep-foggy promise. She'd actually made it all the way to the school parking lot five minutes ahead of the tardy bell before remembering me and Nash. I would have texted her, but my dad left for work with my phone, and I didn't have her number memorized. Nor did Nash have it programmed.

We all three got unexcused tardies, which made a matched set with my unexcused absence from history the day before. Add to that the half-finished chemistry homework I'd spilled nacho-cheese sauce on during lunch, and I was starting to think I couldn't handle both school and *bean sidhe* business. Not to mention work.

"Hey, Emma," a male voice called from down the hall. We looked up to see Doug Fuller strutting with a huddle of football players in matching school jackets, Nash among them. "You got plans tonight?"

The cluster closed around us in a tall wall of broad green-and-white-clad shoulders, blocking most of the hall from view and effectively trapping us, though Emma didn't seem to notice the sudden suffocating lack of personal space. I stepped back and my bag hit the lockers. There was nowhere else to go unless I was willing to break through the offensive line and expose

my confinement issues. Which would be like waving a
red flag in front of a whole herd of bulls.

Nash must have seen the swirl of panic in my eyes,
because he was suddenly at my side. I let my backpack
slide to the floor, and he wrapped both arms around me
from behind. His breath brushed my ear in a private,
whispered greeting, and I relaxed into him as if the
other assletes weren't even there.

They'd accepted me into their company easily
enough—though I'd only hovered on the fringes
before, thanks to Emma's various adventures in dat-
ing—because Nash and I were practically attached at
the hip.

Or at the crotch, as the other guys no doubt assumed.
After all, why else would he hang out with Emma's
curveless, penniless best friend, even if I did have a not-
hideous face?

A very good question…

Nash had no more money than I did. Maybe even
less. But he was wealthy in another currency: athleti-
cism. He'd helped lead the football team to the regional
play-offs—they were the heavy favorites for Friday
night's game—and would do it again when baseball
season arrived in the spring. That prowess, along with
a face and body—not to mention a voice—few girls
could say no to, kept him firmly anchored in the bright,

shining kingdom of Social Acceptance, a world surely stranger and more frightening than anything I could stumble across in the Netherworld.

Emma had a free pass into that world, issued solely upon the basis of her flawless face and generous curves. She flitted among the chosen ones at will, lingering whenever a strong chin or bulging arm caught her eye. But it never lasted long. She bored easily—especially of guys with wandering hands—and would soon come back bearing tales of bumbling inadequacy unenhanced by enthusiasm.

Outside of school, it was easy to forget that Nash belonged to that world, too, and that he had a lot in common with his friends, minus the bumbling inadequacy part. But I'd rather walk the Netherworld alone, with my soul safety-pinned to my sleeve, than spend a few hours alone with any one of his teammates. Somehow, that seemed safer.

"Yeah, I have plans." Emma stood on her toes and pressed herself into Doug's chest so that her breasts flattened against his letter jacket, her nose inches from his chin. His hand slithered around her waist to spread at the base of her spine, fingers inching lower. "I have very interesting plans…."

His friends snickered and Emma stretched higher, letting her lips brush his jaw near his ear as his hand slid lower, gripping the upper curve of her backside. "Too bad they don't include you."

With that, she dropped onto her heels again and smiled up at him, one hand propped on the dramatic flair of her hip.

I laughed. I couldn't help it. Emma's game was a bit like taunting an angry gorilla through a flimsy window screen, but what can I say? She was fun to watch.

"You'll change your mind." Doug grinned and winked, walking backward away from us to keep Emma in his sight. He was a much better sport than I'd given him credit for.

"Not likely." Emma turned to her locker and threaded the padlock through the holes in the latch, then snapped it shut as Nash waved off several summonses from his friends, so he could hang out with me. And his mother. "Come on, pedestrians, where am I dropping you? Your place or his?"

"His," I answered so quickly Emma's brows shot up in amusement.

"Trouble at home?" She shrugged her backpack onto one shoulder as I grabbed mine from the floor, and we followed her down the hall in the opposite direction of the offensive line.

"No more than usual, but I have a lesson this afternoon." I left it vague because she knew what I was talking about.

Nash climbed into the back of Emma's metallic blue Sunfire and I took shotgun. Her car was far from new—it was a hand-me-down from one of her older sisters—yet it made mine look like an antique in comparison. However, the major advantage to Emma's vehicle over mine was that she was actually in possession of her keys.

I buckled as she pulled out of the lot onto a side street, barely glancing in her rearview mirror before changing lanes right in front of the first stoplight. "Give me a hint." Em glanced sideways at me, when she really should have had her eyes on the road. "Just a little one. Is someone else going to die? Is it another cheerleader?"

I laughed at her lighthearted inquisition.

"Maybe you should tell her," Tod's voice said out of nowhere, and I jumped so hard the seat belt cut into my neck.

"Stop doing that!" Nash shouted, and I turned to see Tod on the bench seat next to him, one finger pressed to his lips in an exaggerated "shh" signal, while his other hand pointed at Emma.

"Sorry!" she snapped, assuming Nash was talking to her. She swerved into the right-hand lane without bothering to flick on her turn signal, and the driver of the car behind us honked, gesturing angrily. "It's not like I'm actually wishing for more dead cheerleaders. I'm just saying, if *someone* has to go…"

Tod snorted. "I like her!"

Nash elbowed him in the side, and Emma raised both brows at him in the rearview mirror. She'd seen the gesture, but couldn't see the reaper now holding his ribs, nor did she hear his *oof* of pain. "Sorry." Nash finally met her gaze. "I wasn't talking to you."

Her mouth opened, but I cut off a question I was sure we wouldn't be able to answer. "Em, go." I pointed out the windshield, where the cars in front of us had already driven through the intersection when the light turned green. The man behind us honked again, and Emma stomped on the gas. We lurched forward, and she forgot about Nash's odd behavior. At least for the moment.

"Does this have anything to do with Eden dropping dead onstage?"

I couldn't think of an answer fast enough, and Em's lighthearted smile died when she realized she'd actually hit the bull's-eye.

"Kaylee…" Tod said from the backseat.

"What's wrong?" I twisted so I could see all three of the other occupants.

"I just didn't see the light change." Emma slammed on the brake when the school bus in front of us slowed to a rumbling stop, the pop-out stop sign swinging away from its side.

Of course, I wasn't talking to her. I was talking to the uninvited, invisible reaper in her backseat.

"I can't get Addy and Regan alone long enough to explain the plan to them. They're constantly surrounded by this whole entourage. Assistants, and publicists, and Security, and their mother, who, by the way—" he turned to Nash "—hasn't changed one bit, except for a whole web of new wrinkles. She still has her nose in everything Addy does."

"Is there a point to this?" I looked from one brother to the other.

"A point to what?" Emma glanced in the rearview mirror again to see what she was missing. "What is wrong with you guys today?"

"Sorry, Em." I turned to face her more directly. "It's—"

"*Bean sidhe* business. I know. And I'm getting pretty damn sick of the whole thing." She smacked the steering wheel with the heel of one palm, then swerved into a right-hand turn without even touching the brake.

I grabbed the door grip, but she only stomped on the gas again before the wheel even straightened out. "I lied to your dad last night, and I got stuck in the ticket booth with Glen 'the human sprinkler' Frank for *four hours* yesterday. And I've driven you around today like your own personal chauffeur. The least you could do is explain why you two are acting so weird."

Sighing, I glanced at Nash, then pointedly at Tod, raising my brows in question. *Should we tell her?*

He shrugged, leaving the decision up to me. She was my best friend.

I shifted to face Emma, exhaling slowly. "I don't want you mixed up in all this. It's dangerous."

She rolled her eyes, and when she turned to look at me, she accidently turned the wheel, too, and the front right tire scraped the curb. Emma didn't seem to notice. "I'm not asking to go with you on some kind of scary field trip. I just hate being in the dark all the time."

I knew exactly how she felt, but before I could say anything, Tod shrugged at me, blue eyes shining in mischief. "Sounds like she wants to help. Ask if we can borrow her car. Preferably before she drives it into the side of a building…"

"No!" Nash and I snapped in unison. Then, before Emma could get even angrier, I glared at Tod. "Show her."

"You sure?" He frowned, no doubt thinking of my standing order for him to stay as far from Emma as possible, and never to let her see him. I didn't want death getting a crush on my best friend.

"Yeah, I'm sure."

"Wha—" Emma started. Then she squealed, and her eyes went huge as she stared into the rearview mirror in total shock. I grabbed the wheel when her hands fell away from it, trying to keep us on the right side of the road while her foot got heavier and heavier on the gas.

"*Told* you this was a bad idea," Tod said from the backseat, as Nash growled wordlessly at him in frustration.

"Em!" I yelled. "Hit the brake!" We were racing toward a four-way stop, where a group of tweens waited to cross the road on bicycles.

"Who…? How…?" She blinked, then actually twisted to look into the backseat, and the car lurched forward even faster when she braced herself against the gas pedal instead of the floorboard.

"Emma, stop!" I shouted, and she whirled around and stomped on the brake, bringing us to a screeching halt two feet from the crosswalk.

"Okay, we probably shouldn't have done that while she was actually driving." Nash studied her profile in concern.

"You call that driving?" Tod crossed his arms casually

over his chest as if we hadn't nearly flattened three kids and totaled Emma's car.

The tweens rode their bikes across the street, glaring at us through the windshield. The last one flipped us off, then tossed long, purple-striped hair over his shoulder and rode off, standing on his pedals.

In the driver's seat, Emma sat frozen, staring wide-eyed into the rearview mirror. Her chest rose and fell heavily with each breath, and her hands shook on the wheel.

"Want me to drive?" I offered, laying one hand on her arm.

She shook her head without taking her gaze from Tod. "I want you to tell me what the hell just happened. Who is he, and how did he get in my car?"

"Okay, but we can't sit here forever." Another car had stopped behind us at the four-way, already honking. "Pull into the lot up there and we'll explain." *Part of it, anyway.*

Emma forced her attention from the rearview mirror with obvious effort. "This is part of your *bean sidhe* business? Who *is* that?" She glanced quickly at Tod again, as she drove slowly through the intersection.

Nash braced his arm on the back of my seat, steeling himself for something he obviously didn't want to say. "Emma, this is my brother. Tod." Calm flowed with his words, and I could tell the moment it hit Emma, because her shoulders relaxed, and her grip on the wheel loosened just a bit.

"You have a… Wait." She turned the car smoothly into a small lot in front of a park full of preschoolers and their parents, then pulled into the first empty spot, facing the road. Emma cut the engine and twisted onto her knees to peer over the back of her seat. "You have a brother?" she said to Nash, after a quick glance at me for confirmation. No one from Eastlake High knew about Nash's dead brother, because he and Harmony had moved—and changed schools—after the funeral two years earlier. "And he can…what? Teleport into strange cars? Is that a *bean sidhe* ability?"

"No…" I started, trying to decide how much to tell her. But then the reaper took that decision right out of my hands, in classic Tod-style.

"Okay, we're kind of on a tight schedule here, so let's get this over with…."

"Tod—" Nash snapped, but his brother held up one hand and rushed on before either of us could stop him.

"I'm a *bean sidhe*, just like Nash and Kaylee. Except that I'm dead. Teleportation—never really heard it called that—isn't a *bean sidhe* ability. It's a reaper ability. I'm a grim reaper. I can appear wherever I want, whenever I want, and I can choose who sees and hears me." He hesitated, and I wondered if my face could possibly be as red as Nash's. Or my eyes as wide as Emma's.

"You're Nash's brother. And a *grim reaper?*" She blinked again, and I readied myself for hysterics, or fear, or laughter. But knowing Emma, I should have known better. "So you, what? Kill people? Did you kill me that day in the gym?" She clenched the headrest, her expression an odd mix of anger, awe, and confusion. But there was no disbelief. She'd seen and heard enough of the bizarre following her own temporary death that Tod's admission obviously didn't come as that much of a surprise.

Or maybe Nash's Influence was still affecting her a little.

"No," Tod shook his head firmly, but the corners of his mouth turned up in amusement. "I had nothing to do with that. I do kill people, then I reap their souls and take them to be recycled. But only people who are on my list."

"So, you're not...dangerous?"

His pouty grin deepened into something almost predatory, like the Tod I'd first met two months earlier. "Oh, I'm dangerous...."

"Tod…" I warned, as Nash punched his brother in the arm, hard enough to actually hurt.

"Just not to you," the reaper finished, shrugging at Emma. "I see you all the time, but you've never seen me, because Kaylee said if I got too close to you, I'd suffer eternity without my balls."

"Jeez, Tod!" I shouted, my anger threatening to boil over and scald us all.

The reaper leaned closer to Emma and spoke in a stage whisper. "She's not as scary as she thinks she is, but I respect her intent."

Em looked like she didn't know whether to laugh or cry, and I rolled my eyes at Tod. "Do you have to be so difficult?"

He shrugged and leaned back in his seat. "You wanted me to show her, so I showed her. Now ask her if we can borrow her car so I can get back to my part in the plan."

"Borrowing a car *was* your part of the plan, and we are not taking Emma's." Even if she was willing to lend it to us, I wasn't willing to ask. I wanted as little contact between her and the Netherworld as possible.

And I was already regretting asking Tod to show himself.

"Wait, why do you need my car?" Emma glanced from Tod to Nash, then to me.

"Kaylee's dad took her keys," the reaper said.

"We don't need your car." I glared at Tod. "Though, we really appreciate you taking us to Nash's house. Assuming you're not completely freaked out by all this."

"Oh, I'm totally freaked." Emma smiled slowly, and I wondered how deep her shock went. "But I asked, right? Besides, this isn't much weirder than you and Nash bringing people back to life. Not really." As if she were trying to convince herself. "And it's much better than listening to you talk to people who aren't there. Or yell at me." She raised one brow at me. "You were yelling at him, not me, right?"

"Yes." I returned her hesitant smile easily. "We yell at Tod a lot."

"I can see why. So…" She glanced at all three of us again. "You need to borrow my car?"

"Yes," Tod said, just as Nash and I said, "No."

"Look." Tod turned a dark look my way. "Everyone I know is dead, and has no use for a car. Except Mom, and she needs hers to get to work tonight. So either you let me take one, let me get your keys back from your dad, or we borrow Emma's car. Those are the options."

"What about Addy?" I demanded, before Emma could break in and volunteer her car. And that's exactly what she would have done. I recognized the gleam of curiosity in her eyes, and I knew that if we used her car, she'd insist on coming with us. And that could not happen. "You can't tell me Addy doesn't have a car."

"She doesn't." Tod scowled, and I got the distinct impression he was a little irritated with his pop princess. "She never got her license, because there's always someone else around to take her wherever she wants to go. Which poses a whole new problem. If we can't get some time alone with her, whether or not we can find a car won't matter."

"Who's Addy?" Emma asked.

"No one." I glared at Tod to keep him from contradicting me. "Just some girl Tod has a crush on."

"It's not a crush," he spat, as if the word burned his tongue. "I'm trying to save her life."

"Not really her *life*," I corrected, when Emma's brow wrinkled in worry. She knew that each life had a price, and I couldn't let her think we were willing to kill some likely innocent bystander to save Tod's girlfriend. "We're trying to save her soul."

"What's wrong with her soul?" Emma asked Tod, having obviously come to the conclusion that he was her best source of information.

The reaper shrugged. "Nothing. She's just not actually in possession of it. At the moment."

"Whoooa…" Emma sank back into her seat slowly, her expression bleak, and I realized that somehow she understood the gravity of what she'd just heard, though she wasn't privy to the whole story. And if I had my way, she wouldn't be. "I get off at eight. My car's yours after that."

"Emma, no." I shook my head, one hand gripping the side of my headrest, but she only shook hers back at me. "Thanks, but…"

"You need the car. Take the car. Don't let some poor girl lose her soul because you were too stubborn to drive a loaner."

I sighed and closed my eyes briefly before giving in with a short nod, despite my better judgment. "Thanks, Em."

"You're welcome." Her smile grew, and her eyes glinted with mischief eerily similar to what I usually saw in Tod's. "And you're buying your own gas. Unless you let me tag along…"

"No." I smiled, to soften the blow. "It's too dangerous. And if you argue, I won't take your car."

"Yeah, I figured. Okay, let's go. I have to be at the Cinemark by four." Emma straightened in her seat and started the car again. "Though, how I'm supposed to serve popcorn for four hours after this, I have no idea…."

14

"Hey, come on in." Harmony Hudson held the front door propped open for us before we'd even made it out of the car. "What's wrong with Emma?"

Nash glanced back at her as he crossed the dead grass, and I followed his gaze to find Emma looking a little dazed as she locked her car, as if what she'd learned had finally truly sunk in. The reaper had disappeared entirely.

"She just met Tod." I stepped into Nash's dark, warm living room and dropped my bag on the floor by the couch.

"Aah…" Harmony smiled knowingly as Emma stepped onto the porch. "You're going to need some processed sugar. Come on in and have a cookie."

Emma didn't even try to resist. She'd had enough of Harmony's treats to know better than to turn down the offer, even though she was already running late for work, thanks to our short detour.

Harmony closed the front door and followed us into the kitchen, where we gathered around the island and a plate of still-warm chocolate cookies, glittering under the fluorescent lights with a sprinkling of granulated sugar.

"I swear, Harmony, if you don't stop baking, I won't be able to fit in my own car. Assuming I ever get it back." I let my backpack slide to the floor while I bit into the cookie, surprised to discover a sweetened-peanut-butter center. "I'm sorry my dad bugged you last night," I said around another mouthful. "He totally overreacted."

"You know, it wouldn't hurt you to check in with him every now and then, to keep him from worrying." Nash's mom reached across the island to smack her son's shoulder. "You, too. You have a cell phone for a reason."

Nash shrugged and avoided answering by shoving an entire cookie into his mouth. But I felt obligated to answer.

"He's my dad. He's going to worry no matter what I do." And part of me was grateful that he was concerned over something legitimate, rather than something stupid, like the lead content of my shampoo bottle. But the other part of me couldn't quite escape the irony. For the past thirteen years, he hadn't even known when my curfew was, and now he'd gone all father-of-the-year.

Before Addy'd called, we were on track to get home before anyone expected us. If I'd known what was going to happen, I'd have called my dad, even if only to make up a reason I'd be late. But after Addy's call, things had moved so fast I'd honestly forgotten I had a cell, much less a curfew.

"Mmm," Emma groaned around her first bite, and I swear her eyes nearly rolled back into her head. "Can I take one for the road?"

Harmony beamed and immediately began rooting through one of the island drawers. "I'll pack several for you."

Emma left five minutes later, armed with a paper bag of peanut-butter-surprise cookies and a private promise to meet us in Nash's driveway at midnight. His mom would already be at work, and surely my dad would be asleep by then. Assuming I didn't wake him sneaking out of the house.

With Emma gone, Harmony sent Nash to his room with a plateful of cookies and a strong suggestion that he take advantage of the privacy to do some homework.

When his Xbox whirred to life a minute later, we shared an eye roll. Nash would leave his homework until the last possible moment, and likely only half finish it. And he'd still manage straight Bs. If he'd ever actually applied himself, he could probably have been valedictorian.

Harmony poured soda over ice in two glasses, then gestured with a nod of her head for me to grab a couple of cookies on our way into the living room. "Your dad knows you're here, right?" She sipped from her glass as she walked backward through the swinging door, to hold it open for me.

"Yeah. These lessons were his idea. He says arming myself with information is the best way to avoid trouble. Or something like that." A fact I'd reminded him of when he threatened to make me come straight home from school.

With any luck, he wouldn't guess that the knowledge I was about to arm myself with could get me into more trouble than he could possibly imagine.

Hopefully it would be enough to get us all out of trouble, too.

I had a vague plan for how to get Harmony to teach me what we needed to know, and to make her think it was her idea. Reverse psychology. It only works on preschoolers and adults.

"We could just skip today's lesson and gorge on junk food instead." I sank onto the couch and set the napkin-wrapped bundle of cookies on the coffee table. "We don't have to tell my dad."

The shades of blue in Harmony's irises churned languidly, and her frown looked impossibly cute for an eighty-two-year-old woman. But then again, she was holding up remarkably well for an octogenarian. "Kaylee, you need to learn about your *bean sidhe* heritage and your abilities. I'd hate for you to stumble into something by accident later, like you did with Belphegore."

"Oh, I won't. Not now that I know what I am. And it's not like I'm ever going to use any of this, right?" I shrugged, but inside I flinched from her hurt look. "I mean, I already know how to hold back my wail, and that's all I really need, right?" I hated feigning disinterest in what she had to show me, when I was really very curious. And I hated it even worse that I sounded ungrateful for her help. But Addy's and Regan's souls depended on making Harmony want to teach me something my father wouldn't approve of. Something she'd normally never show me.

"You never know, Kaylee." She drank from her glass again, probably to hide her disappointment, which had virtually erased the deep dimples from her cheeks.

"Emergencies happen, and you might need to know how to go to the Netherworld someday, instead of just peeking into it."

I frowned, showcasing my hesitance as I chewed my last bite of cookie. "Isn't that dangerous?"

She shrugged and pushed up the sleeves of her snug lilac sweater. "Unsupervised, yes. But the risk would be pretty minimal if we cross over from here."

"Because human houses don't exist in the Netherworld?" I was thinking of what she'd told me on Sunday.

"That's true, but Netherworlders do have homes of their own, and if you cross over without knowing where you'll come out, you could wind up somewhere you don't want to be."

I was betting that was a pretty big understatement.

"Can't we just peek in and see what's here on the Netherworld plane?"

"Kind of." Harmony sat straighter; she was perking up now that I was openly curious. "When you peek into the Netherworld from here, or vice versa, you're seeing the two realities layered, one over the other. That can be really confusing if you aren't used to mentally sorting out what you're seeing. You could easily overlook something important. Or dangerous."

"So, how do you know it's safe to cross over from

your house?" I asked, then let my brows rise in eager-ness. "You've done it, haven't you? Where would we wind up?"

Harmony set her glass on the end table, then met my gaze frankly. "Yes, I've done it. I had to cross over when we first moved here, to make sure it was safe in case of an emergency. I still do it periodically, to make sure nothing's changed."

"What could change?"

She shrugged. "The landscape there evolves, just like ours does, based on the needs of the populace."

"So, is it safe?"

She smiled, obviously enjoying my interest. "Yes, it's safe. Comparatively speaking, anyway. This spot in the Netherworld—" she spread her arms to take in her entire house "—is…unoccupied. But, Kaylee, things are different there. It's like a warped reflection of our world. Everything is skewed, like the world kind of *shifted* after everything was built."

I knew exactly what she meant, though I'd never actually been to the Netherworld, because I'd seen the things that lived there. They were skewed, too. Dispro-portionate, like images stretched or squished in carnival mirrors. I could only imagine what their surroundings must look like.

And I only *wanted* to imagine. But my imagination

wouldn't get the Page sisters back their souls. Or get me out of my house if my father didn't go to bed at a decent hour...

"Have you ever crossed over from my house?" My heart thumped painfully as I said the words. She'd see through my question. She'd know what I was up to. She'd tell my dad, and it would all be over. Addy would die soulless, and Regan would follow her sister, whenever her time came.

But Harmony only cocked her head to one side, frowning at me as the unpleasant possibilities occurred to her. "Only once. Why?"

I thought quickly, and went with a half truth. "It creeps me out to think that someone else—some weird Netherworld family—could be living in an alternate version of my house. What if I have one of those emergencies and have to cross over? I'd rather know what I was getting into before I actually get there. To make sure it's safe." I quoted her own words back to her, and Harmony's bright blue eyes darkened for a moment, before clearing like the sky after a summer storm.

I admired her control. Her perseverance. Harmony had picked herself up and pieced her life together twice, after the deaths of both her husband and her oldest son, and she still found enough of herself to share with people who needed her. To protect both me and Nash, and by extension, Emma, Addy, and Regan.

"You don't have to worry about that." She handed me the cookie she had yet to taste, as if a little sugar really could make everything all better. "The Netherworld is much more sparsely populated than our world," she continued as I bit into the cookie. "So it's not like every house here represents a house there. If you crossed over from home, you'd find overgrown fields, with buildings in the distance, in the direction of our downtown district. Very similar to what you'd see if you crossed over from here."

Good. I kept chewing to disguise my exhalation of relief.

"But, Kaylee, that doesn't mean you should try it." She was solemn now, blue eyes glittering with urgent warning. "The Netherworld is dangerous, especially for *bean sidhes*, and you should never go there unless you literally have no other choice."

I could only nod. "But if I needed to? If I had that emergency?" I paused and met her eyes, letting mine shine with equal parts eagerness and careful dread. As if I wanted the knowledge but hoped never to have to use it. Which was totally true; my fear was real enough to pass scrutiny. "You said it works just like peeking, right?"

"Yeah." She held her glass in both hands and leaned back against the arm of the couch, looking easily a quarter of her actual age with one foot tucked beneath her slim leg. "The difference is in the intent. If you call your wail on purpose, like you learned to do on Monday, but with the intent of going to the Netherworld, rather than just peeking in, you'll cross over." She set her glass down again and sat straighter, as if to underline the importance of whatever she was about to say. "It's frighteningly simple, Kaylee. The most important thing to learn is how *not* to go, when you just want to peek, because once you've crossed over that first time, your body remembers how. And sometimes it seems like *it* wants to be there, even if you don't."

Okay, that's *scary.* I shivered with a sudden surge of fear that left chills the length of my arms.

"Which is why we're not going to try it." Harmony leaned back again, and her usual pleasant smile was in place. "I think theoretical knowledge is enough for now."

I found myself nodding, even though I really needed the actual experience. "Once you're there, do you get back the same way? By wailing with the intent to go home?"

Harmony nodded. "But, Kaylee, this knowledge is for emergencies only. I can't emphasize that enough."

I nodded, but she continued. "Do not go sightseeing in the Netherworld. You practically shine with youth and vitality, and that will attract...people. Netherworlders."

Aaaand, it gets even creepier....

"Don't worry." I exhaled and smiled to set her at ease. "I don't go around looking for danger." Yet somehow, it always seems to find me....

"I know."

She drank the rest of her soda and we sat in silence for nearly a minute, listening to the canned fight sounds from Nash's room. Then, though I was more on edge than I wanted to admit by what I'd already learned, I played my last card, desperate for that remaining piece of information.

"Since you checked to make sure it was safe to cross over from here, my dad probably did the same thing, right? Crossed over from our house to make sure it's safe?"

Harmony grinned like I'd just asked her to explain the difference between boys and girls. "Not exactly," she said, still smiling. "Your dad can't cross over on his own." Which I'd already known, thanks to Tod. "So I took him. Humans and male *bean sidhes* can't cross over without a female *bean sidhe's* wail."

"Oh," I let my eyes widen in surprise and concern.

"What if we have an emergency and we both need to cross over? How can I do that? Take him with me?"

I didn't think she'd answer. I truly didn't. And she probably wouldn't have, if not for the obvious guilt she felt over having scared the crap out of me with the knowledge that I might someday have to abandon my father in a burning building because he can't cross over.

"You just have to be holding on to him when you cross over, and he'll come with you. That's the same way it works with whatever you're holding or wearing. Which is what keeps you from showing up naked in the Netherworld." Harmony grinned at her own joke, and I forced a laugh to let her know I wasn't totally freaked out.

"You two about done?" Nash asked, and I looked up to find him watching us from their short, dark hallway. He glanced pointedly at his watch, then at me. "It's nearly four-thirty. What time are you supposed to be home?"

"My dad'll probably call to check on me soon. You know, to make sure I'm not having any fun or acting like a teenager." I stood and picked up my backpack, and Harmony stood, too. She got the message.

"Go easy on your father. He's pretty new at this."

"I know." But that was his fault. He'd had the past thirteen years to reestablish his role in my life after my mother died, and so far, late was proving to be only marginally better than never. "Walk me home?" I asked Nash, already headed for the door.

"Love to."

"Thanks for the cookies, Harmony. And the lesson," I added, still trying to make up for acting like I didn't care about her efforts to help me.

"No problem." She headed toward the kitchen with both empty glasses. "And, Nash, please don't linger. I doubt hanging out with you is on Kaylee's list of approved activities at the moment."

That was an understatement, considering that whatever my dad thought I'd been doing, he knew I'd been doing it with Nash.

Nash rolled his eyes at his mom and held the screen door open as I stuffed both arms into my jacket sleeves, then took the backpack he held for me. "Bye, Mom…"

We didn't hear her reply, because the door closed behind us, and we were already walking hand in hand, in spite of the cold numbing my fingers. We walked in comfortable silence, and I opened my own front door with a key ring conspicuously missing my car key. Nash came inside, in spite of his mother's warning.

"Want a snack?" I shrugged out of my jacket and backpack and let them fall onto the couch, and when

I looked up, Nash was there, so close I caught my breath.

"I want you." His eyes smoldered, and his lips came apart a tiny bit. Just enough to make me want to fill that gap with my own. To taste his lower lip, and leave a trail of kisses over the stubble on his jaw and down his neck.

"Mmm," I murmured as his lips found the hollow below my ear, and vaguely I realized that was the same sound Emma had made when she bit into her first cookie.

Nash was just as delicious, in a completely unsatisfying way. Unsatisfying, because no matter how much time we spent together, no matter how closely I pressed myself against him, I always wanted more.

But what if more was too much for me, and just enough for him? That fear lingered, that secret certainty that if I slept with Nash—if I gave us both what we wanted—he would move on in pursuit of the next challenge. It had happened before, over and over again. The list of his past conquests was long and distinguished, at least by Eastlake standards.

I couldn't put my paranoia to bed. In fact, it grew with every groan he let slip, because they told me how badly he wanted me. But what if wanting me was like waiting for popcorn to pop, or coffee to brew? They both smelled so good, but the taste could never live up to such delectable scents. And neither made a very satisfying meal.

What if I was the sexual equivalent of popcorn? Suitable for light snacking only?

Nash's lips met mine, and I pushed those fears away. I opened for him, sucking his tongue into my mouth, tasting it. He leaned into me, and we would have fallen onto the cushions if he hadn't braced his hand against the back of the couch. He shoved my backpack and jacket to the floor, then lowered me gently, slowly. With infuriating patience.

Even drowning in my own doubts, I had no patience.

He settled over me, hips pressing into me, chest heavy on mine, holding himself up on one elbow. His knee slid between mine and I gasped, sucking air from him. Heat rose from the pit of my stomach, tingling all the way up. He tasted so good. Felt so good. And I understood him in a way no human girl ever could.

Surely he knew that…

Nash's lips trailed down my neck, setting off a series of tingly explosions, adrenaline pumping through my heart. My hand clenched the tail of his shirt, then I pushed it up, trailing my fingers over his stomach.

And in that moment, I became a fan of football, for the simple fact that it had literally shaped him. I couldn't resist running my hands around to his back as it twisted and bunched beneath my fingers. He was strength personified, and simply touching him made me stronger. Harder. More capable of everything ahead of us.

If I had Nash, I could do it. I could do anything.

The phone rang, and Nash groaned into my ear, his breath a puff of warm frustration fueling my own. "Your dad?"

"Probably."

He collapsed on me, pinning me to the couch momentarily as the phone rang again, and I didn't want to move. Didn't want him to get up. He had to, of course, but he did it slooowly, sliding off me one delicious inch at a time until he sat on the floor beside the couch, one hand flat over my stomach.

I arched one arm over my head and grabbed the phone, moving as little of my body as possible. "Hello?"

"I take it you're at home?" my father said as metal clanged in the background.

"I answered the phone, didn't I?" I closed my eyes in regret; my answer had come out harsher than I'd intended, my voice sharpened by irritation at having been interrupted.

My dad sighed, and I heard hurt in his exhalation. "Is Nash there?"

"He walked me home."

He sighed again and raised his voice. "Nash, go home."

Nash scowled. "I was...just going."

"Say hi to your mom," my father said. Then there was only silence and the clang of more metal over the line, and I realized he was waiting for Nash to leave. Right then.

"Um, I will." Nash stood and leaned down to kiss my cheek, the most he would do with my father there, even if only in spirit. And in voice. "See you later, Kaylee," he said, then closed the door on his way out.

"Happy?" I snapped into the phone. I wasn't sorry that time.

"No, Kaylee. I'm not happy. I'll be home by seven-thirty with dinner. What do you want from the Chinese place?"

I bit my lip to keep from saying something I'd regret later. Likely much later. "Shrimp fried rice. Want me to call it in?"

"That would be great. Thanks." He hung up, and I stared at the empty living room, wishing I knew of some way I could get along with my father *and* save Addy's soul. But so far, the two seemed to be mutually exclusive. Fortunately, it would all be over in a matter of hours, and my life would go back to normal.

Assuming I survived the night.

15

My dad walked in the front door at seven twenty-four, carrying a white paper bag and smelling of metal and sweat. He looked awful. Exhausted. I felt bad for him. And really guilty.

After my mother died and I'd been handed over to my aunt and uncle, my father had gone to Ireland to run the pub his parents owned. He'd made a decent living, but most of his extra money went to pay for my incidentals and to fund my college account. So when he came back to the States, he'd brought nothing but a suitcase and enough cash to put down a deposit on a rental house and buy a second used car—I still had the one he'd bought me for my sixteenth birthday.

Now he worked in a factory all day, taking overtime where he could get it, because he thought he should at least try to make as much money as his brother did.

I didn't care about the money. A little money only made people want more of it. And I liked our used furniture, because if I spilled on it, no one got mad, which meant I could snack in the living room, in front of the television. But my father insisted we eat dinner together every night. Our crappy kitchen card table was the magic wand he kept waving to turn us into a real family. But on some nights, all that magic seemed to do was irritate and frustrate us both.

And still he tried….

"I got some fried wontons." He set the greasy bag on the card table and draped his jacket over the back of a folding metal chair.

"Thanks." He knew they were my favorite. He knew all my favorite takeout, because he rarely had time to cook, and I didn't care if I never ate another bite of homemade health food after living with Aunt Val for thirteen years.

We ate in near silence, except for the occasional intrusion upon my thoughts when he asked if I'd done my homework—yes—and how Nash and Harmony were doing—fine. He never asked about Tod, which was just as well, because if he had, he'd know from my answer that I'd been hanging out with the reaper, too. And that would just make him even angrier, and more worried.

"How long is it going to be like this?" my dad asked as I pushed back my chair and tossed my paper plate into the plastic trash bin. "How long are you going to be mad?"

"I'm not mad." I trudged into the living room and shoved my trig and history books into my backpack, the corresponding homework assignments folded in half inside them. "I just…" …*have things I can't tell you. Things you could probably help me with. But you won't. So talking does us no good.* "I have stuff on my mind. It has nothing to do with you."

I wanted to explain that things would get better. He would stop trying so hard—start realizing I was sixteen, not six—and eventually he'd understand that Nash was keeping me out of trouble, not getting me into it. When that happened, we could both relax. Maybe he could even tell me about my mother without tearing up and making some excuse to stop talking.

But not yet. None of that could happen while I was still helping Addy and Regan behind his back. Because he knew something was wrong, and he couldn't move beyond that until it was resolved, and I couldn't look him in the eye until I was done lying.

Soon, though. It would be soon.

My dad fell asleep in his recliner shortly after eleven, and he sat there snoring for several minutes before I thought to turn off the television. I could only stare at him from the couch, boiling with frustration.

He was supposed to fall asleep in his bed, not in the living room!

I could wake him up and tell him to go to bed. That would still leave more than half an hour for him to go back to sleep before I had to leave for Nash's. But the last time I'd done that, he'd decided he wasn't ready for bed yet, and he'd stayed up to watch some stupid action movie until after midnight.

I could leave him where he was and hope he didn't check on me when he went to bed. But then I'd run the risk of waking him when I opened the front door. Because the window in my room was painted shut, and the screen on the back door squealed like a pissed-off harpy.

That only left my backup plan, which I'd really hoped to avoid.

My dad's bedroom door stood open, and I saw my cell phone on his nightstand, all alone and sad-looking. He'd never know if I took it, and I'd have a safety net in case something went horribly wrong while I was out.

I took my phone—I was too big of a wimp to walk

into something so dangerous without a safety net—then stared at myself in the mirror over my dresser, wondering if I had the courage to do what needed to be done. I tucked a strand of straight brown hair behind my ear and wondered if my irises were swirling. I couldn't see them myself, but if Nash were there, would he see the shades of blue twisting with the fear that pulsed through my veins, leaving icicles in its wake, threatening to shatter with my next movement. Could I walk into the Netherworld like I belonged there? Could I demand an audience with a hellion and offer him a trade?

Even if I could, would I survive such an audience? And if I did, what was I opening myself up to? It seemed like an extraordinarily bad idea to bring myself to a demon's attention. Pretty much the opposite of my dad's lay-low-to-survive philosophy.

At least I wouldn't be alone. I'd have Nash and Tod. Assuming I survived sneaking out of my own house.

What should I take?

Something that would actually function in the Netherworld. Traveling light seemed wise, but did I really want to step into another reality carrying nothing but a useless phone and some pocket lint? I slid my pitifully incomplete key ring into my pocket. Cash would do me no good in the Netherworld—Nash said they spent other, unthinkable currency—but it might come in handy before we crossed over.

A small stone box on my dresser held everything of tangible value I owned: my mother's engagement ring and the forty-eight dollars left over from my last pay-check. I stuffed the bills into my front pocket. Usually a small lump of cash felt reassuring; it represented emergency gas money, or bus fare home, should I need it. But this time I still felt woefully unprepared to face the world with so little going for me.

What I really needed was a weapon. Unfortunately, the most dangerous thing in the entire house was my dad's butcher knife, and something told me that wouldn't be much use against anything I ran into in the Netherworld.

I pulled my hair into a ponytail and shrugged into my jacket, then pronounced myself ready to go. At least, as ready as I was going to be.

My heart beat fiercely, and suddenly my throat felt too thick to breathe through. My father would wake up if I tried to unbolt and unchain the front door, but there was no telling what *else* I'd wake up if I crossed into the Netherworld. Harmony said there'd just be an empty field, but what if she was wrong? What if things had changed since she'd last crossed over?

I shook off fear, forcing my spine straight and my

head up. The best way to enter the lion's den is one step at a time.

With that, I dove into my remembrance of death. It was like tumbling headfirst into a pool of grief and horror, and at first, it seemed I would sink. I would drown in sorrow. Then I forced my heartache into focus, scrambling desperately for a handle on my own emotion. *Sophie. Emma.* And finally my mother—what little I could remember of her. The memories of their soul songs bubbled up inside me. Darkness enveloped me, and sound leaked from my throat.

I pressed my lips together to keep it from bursting forth in a silence-shattering wail of grief and misery. If my father heard me keening—or singing, from his perspective—it was all over. So I swallowed the sound, like Harmony had taught me. Forced it down and into my heart, where the echo resonated within me, hammering at my fragile self-control, clawing at my insides.

It was easier this time, just like she'd promised. Or rather, like she'd warned. I could see the Netherworld haze blooming before me, a gray filter laid over my room, covering my bed, my dresser, and my desk in various shades of gloom. Now I only had to add intent to my wail.

Whatever that meant…

I intend to cross over, I thought, closing my eyes. When

I opened them, my room was still gray, and still just as *there* as it had been a moment before.

It would be so much easier if there were a secret password, or handshake. *Netherworld, open sesame!*

Yeah, that didn't work, either.

I closed my eyes again, careful to keep the wail deep in my throat—all but one slim curl of sound that wound its way up and into the room, like a thin ribbon of Netherworld energy being pulled through me and into the human plane. If I could just follow it, like a bread-crumb trail, I was sure it would lead me where I needed to go.

Where I was already going...

The background hum of the refrigerator faded and cool air brushed my face. I opened my eyes and gasped so suddenly I choked on my own keening. I coughed, and the thin stream of sound ended in a wet gurgle.

My room was gone. As was the whole house. The walls, the doors, the furniture. All gone. My father, too.

I stood in the middle of a large field of some kind of grass I didn't recognize. It grew tall enough that the thin seed clusters on top brushed my elbows, and I knew without taking a single step that it would be a pain to walk through.

I ran my fingers over the grains, surprised by the

rough, whispering sound they made against my skin. The stalks were stiff and brittle, and oddly cold to the touch, as if they were nourished by a chill wind rather than by the sun. And they weren't green or even fall-brown like the November-hued grass was in my world. The entire field was an earthy olive color, with shades of deep umber near the base of the stalks.

Curious, I bent one seed cluster and nearly jumped out of my own skin when it broke with an audible *snap* and shattered between my fingers. It didn't crumble. It splintered into hundreds of tiny, cold plant shards. The slivers tinkled like tiny bells as they fell, brushing the other stalks on the way down.

One sharp grass shard got caught with its point through the weave of my jeans. When I tried to brush it off, I accidently pushed the splinter deeper, flinching when the tiny point jabbed my skin. I used my fingernails like tweezers to pull it out carefully, and was surprised to see a little dot of blood staining my jeans.

Stupid sharp grass had cut me! *This gives all new meaning to the phrase "blades of grass…."*

I looked up slowly, then turned to see as much as I could of the grass surrounding me without breaking any more stalks. I was in the middle of the field, at least a hundred feet from the nearest edge, which was in front of me. I couldn't walk through the grass without getting shredded in the process.

Crap! When Harmony said the Netherworld was dangerous, I'd thought she'd meant the residents!

I glanced around at my foreign surroundings, hoping for inspiration from the scenery. What I could see of the Netherworld was beautiful, in a dark, eerie way. The night sky was a deep, bruised purple streaked with ailing shades of blue and green, as if the earth had beaten its canopy into submission.

The slim crescent of a moon was dark red, like the harvest moon after a slaughter, and its sharp points seemed to pierce the sky, rather than to grace it. It was beautiful-scary, but absolutely no help in getting me out of the field. I could *not* make it across one hundred feet of fragile glass spires without getting all sliced up.

But maybe I wouldn't need to….

I only had to stay in the Netherworld long enough to get out of my house, to keep from waking my dad.

Would it have killed Harmony to mention that the plant life in the Netherworld was painful?

Okay, Kaylee, focus…. How far was it from my room to the side yard outside my window?

Before I'd crossed over, I was standing in front of my mirror. I closed my eyes and visualized turning, then crossing my narrow room toward the far wall.

Ten steps, give or take. If I could make it eight feet to my right, I'd wind up just outside my bedroom window. Assuming I didn't misjudge and cross over inside the brick wall…

Better go nine feet, to be safe.

I took a deep breath and lifted my arms to keep them from brushing the grass stalks and getting chewed up. Then I slid my right foot to the side, one step.

Four glasslike stalks shattered as my foot went through them. They collapsed to rain sharp chunks of Netherworld vegetation on my leg, and those chunks shattered even further. But the damage to my body was minimal, because I didn't try to brush the shards off.

On my left, something growled softly, and a slithering sound approached from near the ground. Ten feet away, several stalks shook without breaking.

My pulse raced, and I began to sweat in spite of the cold. A stray strand from my ponytail fell over my eyes, and I brushed it back, on alert for more movement or noise from the ground around me. But there was none, at least for the moment.

I moved quickly after that, shuffling sideways through the grass, pausing after each step to let the vegetation settle and to make sure I hadn't been cut very badly. More dry rustling met my ears, and was followed by a quick, nausea-inducing burst of panic. But I saw no more movement.

Plants crunched beneath my shoes, and I soon learned to angle my right foot so that the stalks fell away from me, rather than on me. The slithering noises continued, like a dark echo from some panicked part of my brain, and I moved in the opposite direction, praying that whatever was making those sounds wouldn't pounce. Or bite. Or whatever.

Ten steps later, I was sure I'd gone far enough. I closed my eyes and stuck my fingers in my ears to block out sights and sounds of the Netherworld, unconcerned with how stupid I must look.

I wanted to look stupid in my own yard.

The wail came even easier this time, and rather than worrying about that, I reveled in it, grateful that I didn't have to fight for concentration with that slither-creature sliding toward me. Intent wasn't hard to come by that time, either. I seriously wanted to go home. Just in time to sneak out.

I kept my eyes open, and was amazed to see the Netherworld simply fade around me, going first gray, then insubstantial. The sharp stalks blurred, then finally disappeared, and I found myself standing in short, dead grass, a mere six inches or so from the brick wall of the house and my bedroom window.

Oops, cut that one kind of close. Though, I'd gone two extra steps, just to be sure. Were distances skewed in the Netherworld?

My brain danced around the possible implications of that thought, but then I shook it off. I had to get to Nash's.

I spared a moment to pluck the obvious shards of Netherworld grass from my jeans, vaguely frightened that they hadn't simply faded from existence with the rest of the Nether. Then I zipped up my jacket and took off toward Nash's house at a jog, hoping the remaining slivers would shake free with the movement.

Any other night, I would have been nervous to be out alone, but after several minutes in the Netherworld, edging my way through a field of deadly grass to get away from something slithering through the stalks after me, nighttime in the human-world seemed downright welcoming.

I was breathing hard by the time I got to Nash's house, where he, Tod, and Emma were piling into her car. "Leaving without me?" I panted, leaning with my hands on my knees to catch my breath.

"Kaylee, jeez, you scared me!" Emma cried, loud enough that if any of the neighbors had been awake, they'd have heard her.

"We weren't leaving without you." Nash greeted me with a tame kiss on the tip of my nose, a greeting that spoke of relief, rather than heat. "We were coming to find you."

I wrapped my arm around his waist, pressing into him to share his warmth. "I'm only a couple of minutes…" My voice trailed off as I glanced at my watch. It was twelve thirty-five. I'd left my room around eleven fifty-five, and it had taken me no more than ten minutes to jog from my house to Nash's. And I'd spent less than five minutes in the Netherworld. I was sure of it.

Which meant I was missing twenty-five minutes….

Fear washed over me like a cold ocean wave, and both Hudson boys saw it on my face.

"How did you get out of your house, Kaylee?" Tod asked, his voice deep with suspicion, and when all heads turned his way, I knew Emma could both see and hear him.

I squeezed Nash and stared at my feet. "My dad fell asleep in the living room. I didn't have any other choice."

"So you crossed over?" Nash's voice was lower and more dangerous than I'd ever heard it, and his words held no hint of calm. He held me at arms' length, both hands on my shoulders. "Don't ever do that again. Do you understand?"

I shrugged out of his grip, my temper flaring to a hot, sharp edge. "It'll be pretty hard to get Addy's soul back without crossing over," I snapped.

"Crossing over?" Emma's brows sank in confusion. "To where?"

"I mean alone," Nash clarified, ignoring her question. "You can't go there alone, Kaylee. You have no idea what…stuff is out there."

"What stuff is where?" Emma demanded, propping both hands on her hips.

"Well, I know a little better now." Turning from Nash, I slid into the passenger seat, then I caught Emma's eye and tossed my head toward the driver's side, urging her silently to get in.

The guys followed our lead reluctantly.

"What happened?" Nash demanded softly, as he clicked his seat belt home in the backseat. "Did you see something?"

I twisted around and smiled to relax him. I didn't like the bossy side of him, but knew it stemmed from concern for me. "Just a field full of weird grass with something slithering through it."

"Lizards," Tod said, and I knew based on Emma's reaction—or lack thereof—that he hadn't let her hear him that time. Which meant we weren't talking about ordinary lizards.

I glanced at Nash with my brows raised in question, but he only shook his head. We'd talk about it later, after we'd dropped Emma at her house. Or rather, after she'd dropped herself off.

Em was still irritated by our refusal to explain what was going on, but she hugged me when she got out of the car and told me to be careful doing...whatever we were doing.

I hugged her back and thanked her sincerely. Then I hugged her again, hoping it wouldn't be the last time I'd see her. I really didn't want to die in the Netherworld. Or anywhere else, for that matter. Not yet, anyway.

I slid into the driver's seat and Nash climbed over the center console to sit next to me. Then I twisted to look out the rear windshield as I backed slowly out of Emma's driveway, while she let herself into her house. "So, time moves slower in the Netherworld? That would have been nice to know."

"If we'd known you were going, we would have told you," Tod said matter-of-factly. "Along with the fact that most species of Netherworld lizards are poisonous to humans."

"And to *bean sidhes*," Nash clarified, in case I didn't get it.

"Yeah, thanks. And the plant life isn't exactly amber waves of grain."

Tod grinned, and I knew that he, at least, had forgiven me. "It won't be like that closer to the city. The Netherworld is like a reflection of our world, anchored at certain, highly populated spots. Like public buildings. But the farther you go from those meccas, the less the Netherworld resembles our own. Including plant and animal life. And space and time."

So I really *had* gone farther in the Netherworld than I had on the human plane.

"Space and time?" I took the next corner too fast, distracted by the new information.

"Yeah." Tod shifted onto the center of the back bench seat so I could see him better in the mirror. "The human world is the constant, and time in the Netherworld will never go faster than it does here. And you'll never move farther here than you would have there. But time will move slower in the parts of the Netherworld that are least firmly anchored to the human plane, and it's very easy to think you've traveled far enough, yet when you cross back over, you haven't gone as far here as you thought you had."

Which was exactly what had happened to me.

"So, how are we supposed to get around in the Netherworld, if we never know where or when we'll be when we cross back over?" I shot a worried glance at Nash.

"Very carefully," he said, his voice grim and dark again. But this time he let a thread of calm snake through it to wrap around me, and I settled into that calm, inhaling it just for the taste of Nash. "Because most mistakes made in the Netherworld can't be fixed."

16

WE TOOK I-30 to Highway 12, in Irving, where the Dallas Cowboys were finishing their last season in the old stadium. I drove and Nash navigated. Fortunately, he'd been to Texas Stadium a bunch of times, and except for one missed exit—I hate it when highway signs aren't marked well in advance—we had no problems getting there. Though, I was a little creeped out by the late-night, nearly deserted feel of the area.

We parked in a lot south of the stadium, and the sound of my car door closing echoed across the expanse of bare concrete. The air outside was warmer and more humid than in the car, but goose bumps popped up all over my arms, as if my skin knew better than my head that I ought to be afraid.

The dark chill of anticipation could probably be attributed to my imagination. Or to the fear that I would cross over from the human plane into another field of glass spears, or something even worse.

"You ready?" Tod asked from the other side of Emma's car, one hand on the roof between us. Nash stood next to him, watching me carefully, as if I might melt into a puddle of fear and raw nerves any minute. Or maybe burst into tears.

Did he really think I was that fragile?

No, I was not ready. But neither was I going to delay our mission. Addy's time was running out.

"This is a public place with a very large concentration of human life force most of the time, so this section of the Netherworld should be pretty well anchored to ours," Tod began, stuffing his hands into his jacket pockets. "Which means that, for the most part, you can trust that time and space are running along pretty normal lines."

"But there hasn't been a game here in a couple of weeks, right?" I glanced from one brother to the other. "Shouldn't that lack of human activity cause the anchor to slip a little?"

Nash rounded the hood of the car to take my hand, and his brother shrugged. "It might slip a bit during the off-season, but there's been so much human energy built up here over the years that two weeks isn't enough to make much of a difference." The reaper ran one hand through his blond curls and joined us at the front of the car. "There might be a slight time and space discrepancy because it's the middle of the night and no one's around right now, but it'll be very small. Definitely much less than what you felt at home."

"What about the grass? Are we going to be shredded by vegetation when we cross over?"

Nash rubbed my upper arms through my jacket as I shivered. "I doubt it. There's too much activity here for razor wheat to get a foothold on the land. It takes a while for that shit to establish strong roots, which it can't do with Netherworlders stomping through it all the time. Right?" He glanced at Tod for confirmation, and the reaper nodded. Then Nash lifted my chin until my gaze met his. "And by the way, if you ever have to do that again—which I would not recommend—wear waders. Waist high, at least. Mom says that's the only way to get out of razor wheat without getting sliced to bits."

I nodded and bit my lip to keep from telling him about the whole sideways-step procedure, because that would make it sound like I'd mastered the razor wheat and intended to maintain my skill. Which I did not.

Unless I had to.

Still, waders sounded like a good idea….

"So, if the Netherworld parallel to my house is a field of razor wheat, that means no one's been there in a while, right?"

"It means there hasn't been enough activity there to keep it from growing or to stomp it down," Nash said as Tod headed across the lot toward the stadium, with us trailing him. "That's probably why your dad picked that section of the neighborhood."

His guess felt right. I could easily see my father trying to protect me by isolating us from centers of Netherworld activity.

A pang of guilt rang through me at that thought, for the way I'd yelled at him. Yes, he was being a real pain, but only because I wouldn't tell him what I was doing. It wasn't his fault. When this whole mess was over and I was done lying, I'd make him a pan of brownies.

Chocolate says "I'm sorry" so much better than words.

"The fact that there probably won't be razor wheat doesn't mean the plant life will be safe." Nash sounded grim and almost angry as he stepped over a concrete wheel stop. He didn't want to cross over, and honestly, neither did I. "Don't touch anything, just in case."

"So, all the plants are dangerous?"

Tod cleared his throat and pivoted to walk backward,

facing us as he spoke, walking right through steel barricades and light posts. "The sun in the Netherworld doesn't shine as purely as it does here. It's kind of... filtered. Anemic. So the plants have adapted. They supplement their diet with blood, from wherever they can find it. Mostly rodents, and lizards, and other scuttlers. But they'll try for your blood, too, if you flaunt it."

Lovely... A dark chill washed over me, and I rubbed my arms for warmth. I hated the Netherworld already, and I'd spent only minutes there. "It sounds like *Little Shop of Horrors.*"

Tod gave a harsh huff and turned smoothly to face forward. "That was only one plant."

I stepped onto the raised sidewalk in front of the stadium, walking confidently to hide the fear pumping through my veins, chilling me from the inside out. "So, don't touch anything and stay away from the plant life."

"Right." Tod nodded, apparently satisfied. "Let's go. It's not getting any earlier, on either plane."

Keening was even easier that time than the time before, and to my surprise—and concern—I was able to do it without consciously remembering anyone's death. Instead I forced myself to endure the nightmare unfolding in my mind, like a bloom dripping blood.

Nash's death.

It wasn't a premonition. I knew that at the first touch of the terror-soaked, thorny vine creeping up the base of my skull. I wasn't predicting Nash's death. I was imagining it in horrifying, soul-wrenching detail. My biggest anti-wish. It played out behind my closed eyes, drawing from me a wail so strong the first thin tendrils of sound scorched my throat like I'd choked on living flames.

I wanted to spit those flames back up. Needed to purge them from my body for my own sanity. But I made myself swallow them, all but a ribbon of sound vibrating from my vocal chords, bypassing my sealed lips. My insides smoldered, ethereal smoke making the back of my throat itch.

I opened my eyes, and the world had gone gray.

The stadium was still there, rising in front of me like a domed, steel-and-concrete mushroom. But now an otherworldly fog shrouded the exposed beams and the underside of the massive stands.

Nash stared at me, his eyes churning colorlessly in fear for me. Fear for us all.

Tod watched us both carefully, and I read doubt in every line on his face. He wasn't sure I could cross over. Or at least that I could take Nash with me.

The reaper's skepticism fueled my determination, pushing me past the pain in my throat and the awful bloated feeling in my core, as if my insides would soon rupture from holding back my own wail. I thought of the Netherworld, and my intense need to be there. To find the hellion who'd sucked the Page sisters' souls. To get those souls back.

At first nothing happened. Then, just when frustration threatened to rip the full cry from throat, I realized the problem. I was still thinking about the razor wheat, and my desire never to step into it again. And those thoughts interfered with my intent to actually cross over.

Growling a bit, in sharp, dissonant harmony with my keening, I forced thoughts of the glasslike stalks from my mind and concentrated on Nash's assurance that it couldn't grow in such a populated area.

Suddenly the stadium began to fade into that featureless haze, and for one long moment I saw nothing but gray. Felt nothing but gray. I'd had my eyes closed the first time I'd crossed over, so I'd missed this claustrophobic emptiness, as if the world had swallowed me whole and wrapped me in fog.

My hands flailed in front of me, reaching desperately, blindly for Nash, before it was too late to take him with me. I did not want to have to cross over again.

His hands closed over mine with a familiar, soothing warmth. My finger brushed the pencil callous on the middle finger of his right hand, and the long, raised scar on his left palm, where he'd sliced it open working on his bike when he was twelve. I squeezed his hands, and an instant later the world whooshed back into focus around me.

Only it wasn't our world. It was the Netherworld. Again.

My previous crossover had prepared me for this trip no more than a trip to the farm would prepare an alien visitor for an evening in New York City.

My biggest surprise was that the Netherworld had sidewalks—a sign of civilization and advanced order I had not expected. I'd known the stadium would exist on both levels. As a center of high-volume human activity, it was one of the anchors pinning the human plane to the Netherworld like a dress pattern over a bolt of cloth. Where the pin pierced both, the layers remained flat and even, and time and space were relatively constant. But between the pins, the bottom layer—the Netherworld—could bunch, and shift, and wrinkle. And that's where things were likely to get the weirdest.

Not that they were exactly normal even at one of the anchors....

"How did the Netherworld get sidewalks?" I whispered, letting go of Nash's hands to wipe nervous sweat on the front of my jeans. My pulse pounded in my ears so fast I was actually a little dizzy. "And parking lots? Is there some kind of creepy concrete company around here?" I didn't even want to know what the Netherworld mafia might bury in building foundations....

"No." Tod sounded amused again, in his own bleak way. "All of this is drawn through from our world, along with enormous amounts of human energy. The stronger the anchor, the more closely the Netherworld mirrors our world."

"So, the Netherworld equivalents of places like L.A. and New York must look—"

"Just about the same," Nash finished for me, smiling in spite of the circumstances. "Except for the people walking down the sidewalks."

I propped both hands on my hips, below the hem of my jacket, and took a long look around. "The stadium doesn't look much different—" though, the few vehicles sprinkled around the lot and the area surrounding the huge complex on the human plane were gone "—so where's the disposal facility?"

"Um…" Tod gestured toward the stadium. "I think that's it." He shrugged. "It's not like they actually play football here, right?"

I studied the stadium more carefully, looking for some sign of activity. Surely if this place was a repository for dangerous substances, there would be Security, or warning signs, or something. "Where is everyone? What about those fiends? Shouldn't they be around here somewhere?" Not that I was eager to find them. Unless, of course, finding them helped us avoid them.

"I don't—" Tod started.

But then Nash grabbed my arm, whispering fiercely. "Did you see that?"

I followed his gaze to the main entrance and the thick bank of shadows cast over it by the strange red crescent moon. On its own, such a feeble moon shouldn't have been able to produce much light, but again I noticed that the Netherworld night sky was not as dark as the one I'd grown up beneath, and the odd purple expanse cast a weak glow of its own.

Still, the shadows were virtually impenetrable, and at first I could see nothing in their depths.

Then something moved. The long, dark expanse seemed to writhe. To *wriggle,* as if the shadows cloaked some huge nest full of bodies crawling all over one another, vying for what little light reflected from the oddly colored sky.

"What is that?" I'd wandered several steps closer before I even realized I'd moved. Nash came with me, but Tod put a hand on my shoulder to hold me back.

"I think those are the fiends."

Great. "Okay, maybe there's a back door." 'Cause we

were not fighting our way through a mass of wriggling fiends. Whatever those were. "Let's walk around," I suggested. And since neither of the guys had a better idea, we walked.

I couldn't get over how normal things looked—so long as I stared at the ground. The parking lot was virtually identical to the one in front of our own Texas Stadium, potholes and all. There were faded, chipped lines of yellow and white paint on the asphalt, and even several dark streaks of burned rubber, which had crossed over with the entire lot.

The closer we got to the building, however, the more the small differences began to jump out at me. The first was the flags. On the human plane, the stadium was ringed with a series of blue-and-white flags showing a football player in his helmet, and the Texas Lone Star. But in the Netherworld, those flags were stained, streaked banners of gray, torn by some otherworldly wind. Several had been reduced to ribbons of colorless cloth, virtually shredded by time and neglect.

The murals, too, were gray and largely featureless, showing just a hint of a humanlike outline. Several of them seemed to have extra limbs. And I could swear one had two heads.

"This is weeeeird," I sang beneath my breath, curling my fingers around Nash's when his warm hand found mine. "Let's just find a way in and ask the first person we see. Maybe Libby will be here…."

"She won't help." Tod veered slightly to the right, away from the main entrance, where those writhing figures were slowly coming into focus. "She's already told us everything she can, and I doubt any other reaper will do more. We'll have to ask someone else."

"What *are* those?" I asked, again squinting into the shadows beneath the awning. I could discern individual bodies now, and was surprised to realize that they were not serpentine in the least, in spite of the mental image their writhing had called up in my head.

They had heads—one apiece, fortunately—and the proper number of arms and legs. But that's where the similarity to my species ended. These creatures were small—though I couldn't judge how small from such a distance—and naked. Their skin was darker than mine and lighter than Libby's, but I couldn't tell how much of their coloring was due to the thick shadows they crawled through.

Oh, and they had tails. Long, thin hairless tails that coiled and uncoiled around legs and other appendages with such fluidity that they couldn't possibly have contained rigid bones.

And their tails weren't the only hairless parts. These little creatures were completely bald, and some part of me wondered if they wallowed all over one another just to stay warm. Some sort of group defense against the cold?

"Those are the fiends," Tod said softly, and for the first time, I realized he was acting weird. Speaking softly. Walking with us, rather than blinking to the other side of the stadium to scan for other entrances. Did his reaper abilities not function in the Netherworld?

"They can't be fiends," I said, deciding to hold my question for later. "They're too small." They didn't even come up to my waist, and the way Libby described fiends, I was expecting huge, burly monsters, pounding on the doors of the facility, literally fiending for another hit of Demon's Breath.

"Size isn't everything," Tod said, and my jaws clenched in irritation over his wiseman tone. "Those are the fiends. Look how they're crawling all over one another to get to the door. Not that that'll help. It's probably bolted from the inside."

Oh. They weren't trying to stay warm. They were trying to break in. I kicked a loose chip of concrete, thinking. "If it's bolted from the inside, how do the reapers get in?"

"They probably cross over from inside the stadium." An easy feat for a reaper, who could blink himself right onto the football field on the human plane, even after hours.

"So how are we going to get in?"

"Don't know yet." Tod frowned, still watching the fiends.

"Can't you just blink yourself inside from here?"

He shook his head slowly and feigned interest in a crack in the sidewalk.

Nash huffed, sounding almost smug. "Most reaper skills don't work here," he said, confirming my earlier hunch.

Tod sighed and met my gaze, his forehead lined deeply in frustration. "I could have done it from the human plane, but I doubt whoever works in there would be eager to help one rookie reaper who pops in without permission, bearing no Demon's Breath."

"So you're just like us down here?" I couldn't tear my gaze from the small bodies climbing all over one another in a bid for the door. As I watched, one creature's tail encircled another's neck and wrenched him forcefully from the top of the pile, only to drop him several feet from the ground. The displaced fiend bumped and rolled down the mountain of squirming bodies until he hit the concrete, where he scraped the side of his face and came up bleeding.

Wow. It was like watching a panicked crowd fight its

way out of a burning building, only they were trying to get in.

And that's when I noticed that several fiends stood at the edge of the crowd, watching their spastic brethren jostle for position. Other than the occasional manic, full-body twitch, they looked pretty normal. For little naked guys with tails.

"Maybe we should ask one of them," I whispered, pointing out the fiends on the fringe. "They look like they come here pretty often."

"Kaylee, you can't just walk up to a fiend and start a conversation," Nash whispered, pulling me close with one arm around my waist. But this time, the motion felt less like it was intended to comfort me than to protect me. To draw me away from the minimonsters.

"Why not?" I frowned and glanced again at the pile of fiends trying to scale the exposed beams and smooth, glass doors. Okay, yes, they looked pretty fierce. But they were also pint-size. If one attacked, surely we could just…step on him.

"Because they're poisonous," Tod answered, coming to an abrupt stop. "And they bite."

"They eat people?" I took several slow, careful steps backward, squinting harder at the fiends. They weren't big enough to eat more than my hand in a single sitting.

Maybe they share….

Though, judging from the competitive nature of their desperate climb, I highly doubted it.

"No, they don't eat people. Not humans or *bean sidhes*, anyway. There aren't many of us around here. But they bite anything that gets in their way, and their saliva is toxic to creatures native to the human world."

"Lovely." I took another step backward, but it was too late. We'd caught their attention. Or rather, I had.

The fiend in the middle crossed the lot toward me, almost bouncing with each step, and two more came on his heels, twitching noticeably every few seconds.

"Snacks?" the second fiend asked, his voice high-pitched and eager, like a child high on sugar. And when he opened his mouth, I glimpsed double rows of sharply pointed, metallic-looking, needlelike teeth, both top and bottom.

They glinted like blood in the red moonlight.

The fiends grew closer, fingers twitching eagerly. Saliva gathered in the corners of their thin gray lips.

My heart lurched into my throat, and to my own humiliation, I yelped and grabbed Nash's arm. I tried to take another step back, but my foot caught on something, and I would have gone down on my face if not for my grip on Nash's jacket sleeve.

One glance down revealed the problem, and pumped more scalding fear through my bloodstream, fast enough to make my head swim. A thin, bright weed grew from a crack in the concrete, red as Japanese maple leaves in the fall. The damn thing had wound around my right ankle, clinging to my jeans with thorns as sharp as the teeth of a tiny saw.

I jerked on my foot, my gaze glued to the fiends still approaching slowly, but that only pulled the vine tight. The thorns pierced denim and speared my flesh in a dozen tiny points of pain. "Ow!" I cried, then immediately slapped my hand over my mouth. The last thing I needed was to draw more attention our way.

Nash glanced down, and in a flash he'd dropped to one knee, a pocketknife drawn and ready. He couldn't fit it between the vine and my leg without cutting me, so he simply sliced the weed out of the ground, and pulled me back before the surviving, grasping tendrils could grip me again.

The severed weed dripped several drops of dark red on the concrete. Or maybe that was my blood. A sick feeling wound around my stomach, tightening like the vine around my leg.

What am I doing *here?* My ankle burned where the thorns had pricked me, my pulse raced in my ears, so loud I could hardly hear the scrambling of the fiends against the glass anymore.

Was there time to cross back into the human world

before the approaching fiends pounced? Because I was suddenly certain that's what they were planning.

"They smell yummy," the third said, followed by a peal of high, maniacal laughter. "Do they kiss hellions?" His teeth clanged like hollow metal when he closed his mouth, and my pulse lurched again. "Do they breathe Demon's Breath?"

"No," the first one said, as Nash, Tod, and I slowly backed farther from the small monsters now clearly stalking us. I wasn't sure if they could hurt Tod, but he obviously wasn't taking any chances. "They are clean."

"Pity…" the second high-pitched voice sang. Then the two fiends in back turned on their small, bare heels and twitch-bounced back to the group scaling the walls of the stadium.

My pulse slowed just a bit, with the threat decreased by two-thirds. But the first fiend still eyed us. Eyed *me*. He sniffed, tiny, flat nostrils flaring. "Foreign." His left arm twitched violently, as if it were trying to fight free from the rest of his body. Then his right foot jiggled, like he was trying to wake it up. Only, I was sure he hadn't done it on purpose. He was in desperate need of a hit, and his body wouldn't work properly until he got it.

"You don't belong here, humans." He stepped forward as one corner of his mouth began to jump. The fiend eyed me boldly, assessing me, and I realized that though he was clearly in the grip of some sort of withdrawal, he was still thinking and speaking somewhat coherently. At least, more so than his friends. "Stay, and something bigger will surely eat you…."

"We're not—" I started, but Nash squeezed my hand ruthlessly, stopping me from denying our humanity. "We're looking for a hellion," I said instead, and Nash groaned audibly. Evidently that wasn't a good conversation-starter in the Netherworld.

Who knew?

But the fiend surprised me. "As are we all," he said wistfully, and I felt my brows arch almost off of my head. Yet that made sense. They were desperate for a hit of Demon's Breath. Of course they were looking for a demon.

"Um, I mean we're looking for a *particular* hellion." This time, Tod squeezed my other hand, but I ignored him. If the fiend wanted to bite us, he could already have done it several times over. "Do you know a hellion of avarice?"

The fiend's flashing yellow eyes gleamed brighter, and they may have moistened just a bit, as if with a fond memory. "Ah, avarice…" he breathed, squeaky voice piercing right to the center of my brain. "My favorite flavor."

Excitement traced my veins, chasing out those last, healthy jolts of fear. He knew the hellion of avarice. Or at least, he knew *a* hellion of avarice.

I dared one step forward, fighting the urge to squat and look him in the eye, and Nash held tightly to my hand so I couldn't go any farther. "Can you tell us where to find this hellion?"

"I can." The creature nodded his bulbous, bald head, and in the reddish moonlight, I got a good look at the dark veins snaking over the top of it, bulging like a serious weight lifter's. "But there is a price."

I frowned. "I don't have much money. Not quite fifty—"

"Kaylee…" Nash refused to relinquish my hand when I tried to dig in my pocket.

"I have no use for your worthless paper currency," the fiend spat, gray lips turning down around razor-sharp teeth. "I will tell you where to find your hellion—for a portion of his breath. Payable in advance…"

"What?" Anger burned in my cheeks. The fiend's nostrils flared again, as if my ire scented the air, and for all I know, it did.

"Let's go…." Tod tugged on my other arm.

"No!" I turned back to the fiend, trying to get my

voice under control. My anger clearly pleased him, and that wouldn't help my case. "If we knew where to get a dose of his breath, we wouldn't have to ask you where to find him!"

But the fiend only blinked up at me, tiny hands twitching, clearly unconcerned with how I came up with the payment. Did logic have no place in the Netherworld? How was I supposed to...

I stood straight as a sudden possibility occurred to me. "Is an hour soon enough?" My lips curled up into what felt like a sly smile.

The fiend nodded slowly. Eagerly. "I will wait here. One hour. My time," he said, as if in afterthought.

"Deal." My smile widened.

Nash and Tod frowned at me, but instead of explaining, I dismissed the creepy little monster and rushed across the lot with both guys on my heels, my focus on the ground ahead, on the lookout for anything that could poison, grab, or eat me.

Because the guys were right: If I wasn't careful, I had no doubt this monstrous wonderland would swallow Alice whole...

17

"WHERE ARE WE GOING?" Nash asked from the driver's seat as I propped my right foot on the dashboard, glad to be back on my own side of the looking glass, even if only temporarily.

"I don't know yet. Here." I twisted to toss my phone over the backseat to Tod. Unfortunately, he was no longer fully with us—non-corporeal due to stress, maybe?—and the phone dropped through his body to land on the seat, like it had fallen through a hologram. His rear and my phone now occupied the same space at the same time.

Wasn't an event like that supposed to make the world explode, or something?

The reaper glanced down in surprise, then reached through himself to grab my phone from the seat—which had to be one of the weirdest things I'd ever seen. Even weirder than killer plants and little bald fiends with tails and needle-teeth.

Tod's body solidified, and he stared at me blankly. "What's this for?"

"Well, most people use it as a form of communication, but it would probably work as a projectile, in a pinch."

Tod frowned. "Funny. Who am I supposed to call?"

"Addy. Find out where she is. I have an idea." While he dialed, I turned my attention to the thorny coil of vine still wrapped tightly around my ankle. Nash had cut it close to the ground to get me loose, but there was still enough of the weed left to encircle my leg twice, long, thin thorns piercing both the denim and my skin. At two-inch intervals, thin four-leaf clusters dangled, dark green at the centers, bleeding to red on the serrated edges.

"Be careful with that," Nash warned, glancing from the road to my ankle, then back. "I think that's crimson creeper, and if it is, the thorns are poisonous."

Of course they were. Was anything in the Netherworld nontoxic?

"It's a little late for that. The stupid thorns went all

the way through my jeans." I pinched the end of the creeper vine between my thumb and forefinger, completely horrified when thin red liquid dribbled from the severed tip, and gingerly pulled it away from my leg. Fortunately, now that the weird red vine was dead, it uncoiled easily. But each time a thorn pulled free from my skin, a fresh jolt of blazing pain shot through my ankle, as if I were being struck by tiny bolts of lightning. By the time I dropped the plant on the floorboard—the vine had to be eight inches long—a hot ache had settled into my ankle joint, throbbing with each beat of my heart.

I bit my bottom lip as I carefully rolled up the cuff of my jeans. Then I gasped in shock. My ankle was already swollen. Each of the dozen or so tiny holes was raised and puckered, and the wounds were almost as red as the vine itself.

"Shit!" Nash whistled through his teeth. "Definitely crimson creeper. My mom will know what to do for that, but if we tell her, she'll call your dad." Nash's eyes found mine, and I wondered if I looked as conflicted as he did. "Do you think you can wait a couple of hours, or do we need to go now?"

To the hospital, of course. Where Harmony worked as a third-shift RN on the orthopedic ward, where the patients were least likely to die.

I pressed my foot against the dashboard experimentally. The pain was constant, and did not increase with pressure, which meant I could probably walk on it. "I can wait." I closed my eyes briefly and exhaled, mourning the last of my hope that my dad might never discover what we were up to. Now that I was injured, full disclosure was unavoidable—hopefully after we'd reclaimed Addy's and Regan's souls.

When this was all over, I'd probably be spending a lot of time alone in my room.

"Hello, Addy?" Tod said from the backseat, and I loosened the chest strap of my seat belt so I could twist around to watch him, studying his face for any clue about Addison's half of their conversation. "Did I wake you up?"

She laughed bitterly over the line, but I couldn't make out her actual words.

"Yeah, I probably couldn't, either." Tod plucked a frayed thread from the thin layer of denim over his right knee. "Listen, where are you? I think we need to drop by for a minute…." He glanced at me to confirm, and I nodded while Addison said something else I couldn't understand. "Good. Can you arrange for a few minutes of privacy?" Another pause. "We'll be there in ten minutes."

"Twenty," I corrected him. "We have to make a stop first."

Tod relayed the correction to Addison, then said goodbye, hung up, and tossed my phone back to me. "She's at her mom's house. It's the only place she can avoid most of her entourage."

"Good." I slid my phone into my pocket and glanced out the windshield to read the passing highway signs. "Nash, we need an all-night Walmart, or grocery store. Or maybe a drugstore."

He nodded and slid smoothly into the right-hand lane, barely pausing to flick on Emma's blinker. "There's a twenty-four-hour Walgreens a couple of miles from Addy's house. Will that work?"

"With any luck. Do you think I should get something for this, while we're there?" I raised my cuff to show him my ankle, and Tod sucked in a sharp breath from the backseat, then leaned forward, gripping my headrest.

"Damn, Kaylee, is that from the weed?"

"Yeah." I poked gently at one of the swollen puncture marks, then hissed when a fresh jolt of pain shot through my tender flesh and into the core of the joint. A small bead of clear fluid oozed from the hole, and I dabbed at it with a tissue from the box on Emma's center console. "Nash thinks it's crimson creeper."

"He's right. Thank goodness it was a little one. Of course, if it was fully grown, you never would have stepped on it."

"Fully grown? How big do they get?"

Tod raised both brows, surprised by my cluelessness. Though, he shouldn't have been, considering that a couple of months ago I didn't even know my own species. "Fifty feet or better. And a puncture from one that size will kill you in a couple of hours, if it doesn't break your spine first. They're like giant pythons with roots."

"And thorns," I added bitterly.

Tod looked like he wanted to say something else, but whatever he was thinking was lost when Nash spoke up.

"You're gonna need something for that ankle." Nash glanced at it again, until I pulled my cuff down and set my foot on the floor. "But I have no idea whether or not human-world medicine will work on Netherworld toxin." He paused and flicked the right blinker on again, when he spied our exit. "So what else do we need at Walgreens?"

"Balloons." I smiled at Nash's perplexed expression, enjoying understanding more than he did for once.

Tod stuck his head between the front seats, looking just as confused as his brother. "We're taking Addy balloons? Should we stop for a cake and a present, too?"

My smile widened. "The balloons aren't for Addison. They're for the fiend. Addy's just going to…blow one up for us."

For a moment, Tod's eyes narrowed even further. Then his expression smoothed as comprehension settled in, and one half of his mouth quirked up.

"Clever…" Nash nodded at me in obvious respect. "I like it."

"Let's just hope it works."

At Walgreens, Tod found a bag of multicolored latex party balloons while Nash and I hunted down a tube of antibiotic cream. When we met at the cash register, the reaper also snagged three bars of chocolate. I paid—I knew my "paper currency" would come in handy!—then we rushed to Addison's house, beyond grateful for the light, middle-of-the-night traffic, because we had to be back at the stadium in half an hour.

We parked next to a shiny Lexus in Addison's driveway, and she must have heard the engine, because she pulled the front door open as we climbed the steps, then ushered us into the empty living room.

Addy closed the door behind us and stood in the entry with her hands deep in the pockets of a pair of snug, faded jeans. She was still fully dressed. She hadn't even tried to go to sleep. Not that I could blame her.

"Where's your mom?" Tod asked from the middle of the room. No one sat.

"She's passed out in her room." Addy's ironic smile said that for once, she was grateful for her mother's "issues."

"What about Regan?" I rubbed my left shoe against my right ankle, barely resisting the urge to bend over and scratch because that would have exposed my Netherworldly injury and led to questions we didn't have time to answer. And because I was pretty sure scratching would make more clear liquid run from my puncture wounds, rather than easing the fierce, burning itch that had settled in.

"She's sleeping off a couple of Mom's painkillers." Addison glanced at me, then down at her unpainted toenails. "I *had* to give them to her. She was freaking out, and I just wanted her go to sleep and shut up. I tried to warn her, but she didn't listen. She never listens…."

My heart ached for Addy, and her splintered relationship with her sister. They reminded me of me and Sophie, and that thought left a bitter taste in my mouth, as if I'd swallowed one of Addy's mother's pills.

"It's fine." Tod clearly didn't care what happened to

Regan. He had eyes—and concern—only for Addison. "We're a step away from finding the hellion, but first we need you to blow up one of these."

"Maybe two or three of them," I interjected, tossing Tod the bag of party balloons. "I'm not sure what dose the fiend is looking for, or what the concentration is… inside her. So it might take more than one."

Tod ripped open the bag while Addison glanced from one of us to the other like we'd lost our minds.

"It's in your breath," I explained, while Tod pulled a cherry-red balloon from the bag and stretched it to make it easier to inflate. "The Demon's Breath. It rests in your core. And in your lungs, and I think that every time you exhale, you breathe a little bit of it into the air."

I'd gotten the idea from the fiends, who'd wanted to know if we exhaled Demon's Breath. We didn't, of course. But Addy might.

I wasn't sure how it worked. If she lost a little bit of the force keeping her alive with each exhale, or if the Demon's Breath replaced itself as each little bit was lost. But I was virtually certain—based on the fiends' odd dialogue—that Addy carried within herself the very currency we needed.

She took the balloon from Tod and stared at it for a second as if it might grow teeth and bite her. Then

Addy put the latex to her mouth as we watched from a loosely formed semicircle on the beige carpet.

"Wait." I shrugged, my arms still crossed over my chest. "It seemed to me when Eden died that Demon's Breath is heavier than air, so it's probably at the bottom of your lungs. You'll have to empty them to exhale what we really need. So blow out as much as you can on each breath, okay?"

Addison nodded hesitantly, then put the red balloon to her lips again as Tod pulled a yellow one from the bag. She began to blow, and the balloon grew slowly, becoming more translucent with each millimeter it gained in circumference. She blew without inhaling, forcing more air from her lungs than I'd have thought possible, until her face was nearly as flushed as the balloon.

Singers must have very good lungs.

When she could exhale no more, the balloon was half-filled. She pinched it closed between her thumb and forefinger, and I took it from her to tie off the opening. When I let it go, the balloon sank quickly, as if it were tethered to some small weight.

Tod handed her the yellow balloon and she repeated the process without a word or a glance at any of us. When the second balloon had joined the red one on the floor, I couldn't help but smile as I stared at them, the room silent but for Addy's forceful exhaling into a third, purple, one.

The balloons on the floor looked festive, in a cheesy, child's-birthday-party kind of way. They seemed to mock their own dangerous content. But then, maybe that was appropriate, considering the origins of that content: a world where the residents would gladly eat us alive. If the plant life didn't get us first.

When Addy had finished the third balloon, Nash decided we had enough. Not because we were sure we actually *did* have enough, but because we were running out of time. Why hadn't I asked for two hours?

Not that it mattered. Addy's life-clock was ticking toward its last tock even without the fiend's deadline. According to the digital numbers on her DVD player, it was just after one o'clock on Thursday morning. Addy would die sometime in the next twenty-three hours— probably sooner, rather than later—and every moment we wasted brought that unknown time closer.

"We'll come back for you as soon as we can," Tod said as I gathered the filled balloons. "Get Regan up and moving." If she'd already been conscious, we could have just taken both Page sisters with us. "We'll call when we're on the way, but I can't promise much notice."

Because we had no idea where this hellion was going

to be, or how long it would take to get there. And to find him.

"I'll try." Addy frowned, glancing toward the kitchen. "She won't touch coffee, but I think we have some Jolt in the fridge."

"Good. I'll call you when we know more," Tod promised, and left a kiss on her cheek on his way out the door.

Addison watched us from the front porch as we backed down the dark driveway, her arms crossed over the front of a thin, long-sleeved T-shirt, apparently oblivious to the middle-of-the-night November cold. My guess was that it was nothing compared to the chill inside her.

Nash drove again, and I spent the first part of the ride to the stadium applying antibiotic cream to my ankle, and the second part desperately wishing I hadn't. I'd barely wiped the thick white cream from my fingers when the puncture wounds began to bubble and hiss softly, as if I'd poured on hydrogen peroxide instead. The annoying ache/burn I'd been trying to ignore for the past forty minutes roared into a full-blown bonfire in my ankle.

I wiped off all the cream I could with more of Emma's tissues, wishing she had something wet so I could get all of it. The little bit that remained in the holes in my flesh bubbled softly, leaking tiny drops of white-tinged liquid now. By the time we pulled into the stadium parking lot, thin, red, weblike lines had begun to snake out from the double ring of punctures in all directions. The webbing extended less than an inch so far, but I had no doubt it would keep spreading.

Nash glanced at my ankle twice, his frown deepening each time, and I seriously considered his offer to take me to the hospital. To end the pain creeping up my leg and get our confession over with. But that would effectively end our night, leaving Addy to die without her soul. Damning her to an eternity of torture. And I couldn't do that. Not knowing what had happened to the souls my aunt had bargained with. How could I let Addy suffer the same fate?

Besides, there would be time to treat my injury after we'd reclaimed the Page souls, right? Because according to Tod, no matter how bad my ankle got, I wouldn't die until my name showed up on some reaper's list, and if that happened, no amount of Netherworldly cream or pills could save me. I refused to think about the fact that Tod's list couldn't predict the loss of my leg or foot. So I pressed on, in spite of the pain.

We negotiated the parking lot on the human plane— brightly colored balloons tucked under both of my arms and one of Nash's—to avoid stepping on any more crimson creeper, and we didn't stop to cross over until I judged that we were approximately where we'd stood when we'd bargained with the fiend. Then we moved several feet to the left, to avoid that stupid vine. I was pretty sure my estimate of the distance was good enough, because as far as I could tell, we hadn't lost any time crossing over earlier. The anchor at the stadium was very strong.

Tod crossed over first, to make sure all was clear, and that the fiend was waiting for us, because I wasn't going to make the effort if the little monster had ditched us, or if it wasn't safe to be in the Netherworld at that particular place and time. Only once he'd returned with the all clear did I summon my wail—with less effort than ever now—and haul Nash into the Netherworld with me.

The fiend stood very close to where we'd left him, running the tip of his tail through one small, loosely clenched fist over and over. His gaze jumped from place to place. His twitches had grown stronger, and he clearly could not stand still. And suddenly it occurred to me with an indescribable jolt of horror that I'd become a Netherworld drug dealer.

After several deep breaths, I decided I could live with that, so long as the ends justified the means. I hadn't gotten the little monster hooked on Demon's Breath in the first place, and I was only enabling him for one hit. Right?

The fiend's eyes widened at one glimpse of the balloons we carried, and I noticed for the first time that his bright yellow eyes were drastically dilated and shiny.

"Give!" he panted, reaching up with both short, stubby hands for the red balloon, the first to capture his attention. I wondered briefly if he were color-blind, and I was relieved to notice that he had no fingernails. At least I wouldn't have to worry about him clawing me in a rush for his fix.

"Information first," I insisted, holding both balloons over my head by the knots sealing them.

"No!" His arms began to tremble, even as his tail twitched furiously. He was hurting badly, and if he didn't get what he needed soon, someone was going to get hurt. Unfortunately, I didn't have needlelike metallic teeth with which to defend myself.

But my spine was starting to feel quite a bit like steel.

"Tell us where to find the hellion of avarice, or we'll pop the balloons one at a time. Too high up for you to inhale." I nodded at Nash, and he produced his folding knife from one pocket, flipping it open with the press of one button.

"No!" the fiend screeched, jumping for the balloon in vain.

Nash jerked back in surprise, and the point of his knife pierced the balloon he held. The latex exploded, showering him with bits of purple rubber. He coughed and waved a hand in front of his face, casually clearing away the very substance our little informant craved. *Needed*...

The fiend dropped to his knees, picking up one scrap of latex at a time, sniffing them desperately. But after several seconds, he looked up at us in bitter, pained defeat.

I held up the red balloon. "Tell us, or we'll pop this one, too," I threatened softly, hoping not to attract the attention of the fiends still madly trying to scale the stadium walls. Many of them now lay unconscious on the sidewalk, either from denial of their chemical fix, or from being stomped on by their stronger brethren.

The fiend squealed in fury, and his hands squeezed into tiny fists, his tail whipping behind him angrily, stirring dust from the surface of the parking lot. "Fine. Human monsters. No mercy..." he mumbled, and I almost laughed. His entire species seemed ready to bring about its own end for one more hit of a substance they had no business snorting. Or sniffing. Or whatever. Yet *we* had no mercy?

"Talk." I held the red balloon closer to Nash's knife, as he posed with it threateningly.

The small creature drew himself up straight and squared his shoulders, drawing what little dignity he still possessed around himself like a cape. "Hellions loiter where they feed. You want Avari, a hellion of avarice. He will be where greed best festers."

"Which is where?" I inched the red balloon closer to Nash's knife point.

The fiend shrugged, but the motion was not smooth enough to disguise the tremor now shaking his entire body. "Downtown. The greatest bastion of greed I know." The fiend gasped, as if he couldn't suck in a deep-enough breath. At least, not one that wasn't polluted with his poison of choice. "Humans call it Prime Life."

"The insurance company?" Nash cleared his throat gingerly, as if it hurt. Prime Life was the largest insurance firm in the country, and it was headquartered in Dallas.

Hmm, I thought, a moment before the fiend nodded silently. *That kind of makes sense.*

"Bastion of greed…" the fiend repeated. "Probably there now…" He extended both small arms, like a child begging to be picked up. Only this child wanted a party balloon filled with addictive Nether-toxins.

I handed it over, though my stomach churned in response to a less-honorable action than any I'd ever taken. After a second thought, I gave him the yellow balloon, too. We had no use for it, and he clearly needed it. The thought of which made my stomach pitch even harder.

But we'd gotten what we'd come for, and I crossed back into the human world satisfied, if not exactly pleased with myself.

The ends would eventually justify the means, right? So how come I felt like *I'd* just sold *my* soul…?

"YOU OKAY?" Nash asked, when he noticed me limping back to the car.

"Fine." Though, I wasn't at all sure of that. My ankle burned fiercely, and was so swollen it seemed to jiggle with each step. But I was afraid to look at it, so I glanced at my watch instead.

It was 2:15 a.m. on the day Abby was fated to die. Unfortunately, we hadn't thought to ask Libby for a specific time, and Levi had been closely guarding the reapers' list ever since Tod stole a peek at it six weeks ago, so I already felt like we were working in the dark. Regardless, there wouldn't be time to seek medical attention until Addy and Regan had their souls back and evil had met its match. Until then, I would pretend my ankle was made of steel, like some kind of bionic joint, and that I could feel no pain. I was superhuman. I could do anything.

But I'd take some Tylenol, just in case. Lots of Tylenol.

Nash slid behind the wheel of Emma's car again, because I didn't feel like driving. I felt like sleeping, but sleep, like everything else appealing, wasn't an option at the moment.

Nash twisted the key in the ignition and glanced in the rearview mirror at his brother. "We'll pick up Addy and Regan." He turned the wheel to the left as far as it would go, to cut a tight circle in the deserted parking lot. "You go on to Prime Life and see if you can find Avari. Here, take this." Nash arced one arm backward over his shoulder to Tod, his cell phone clenched loosely in his fist.

"That won't work in the Netherworld," I said. And even if it did, I bet he'd rack up one hell of a roaming charge.

Tod scrolled through his brother's contact list. Or maybe his playlist. "Yeah, but once I find Avari, I can cross back over and call you."

Oh, yeah.

Tod pocketed the phone and leaned forward to stick

his head between the seats. "Thanks, guys I really owe you for this."

I'm sure my grin looked more like a grimace. "And for this…" I propped my foot on the dash again and pulled up my jeans cuff to reveal my ankle. At which point my grimace contorted into an expression of disgust and fear, and my words trailed into shocked silence.

My ankle was twice its normal size. The flesh beneath the double ring of punctures was inflamed and covered in those weird, red webbed veins, which now crept beneath my sock and halfway to my knee. Fluid sloshed beneath the skin over my ankle, hanging lower at the back, just above my shoe, where gravity tugged hardest.

Nash's sudden intake of breath hissed throughout the car, and I looked up to see him watching me, rather than the road. "Kaylee, we have to get that looked at."

"Ya think?" I tried to smile, but my sense of humor had deserted me. "Eyes on the road!"

He jumped, then turned the wheel back on course, but kept sneaking glances at my ankle while I tried to decide whether or not to poke it. "That antibiotic cream made it worse," I said. "Will a human doctor even know what to do for this?"

"I doubt it." Nash divided his attention between my ankle and the lightly populated highway. "But Mom will."

I glanced at Tod, eager for a second opinion. "What do you think? Can this wait?"

The reaper swallowed thickly and studied my ankle for a moment. Then he met my gaze, his blue eyes shadowed in the backseat. "I think so."

"You sure?" I asked. Because he didn't sound very sure.

"Yeah." Tod nodded firmly. "You'll be fine. We're not looking to drag this out, anyway."

"Okay. Good." I sank back into my seat, feeling a little better now that we'd decided on a course of action. "As soon as we're done at Prime Life, we'll call your mom and have her meet us at your house," I said to Nash, then twisted to look at Tod. "I'll call Addy and tell her we're on the way. You go find this hellion. Avari. But try not to let him see you. And if he does, don't tell him we're bringing Addy and Regan. Somehow I doubt he'll be eager to give their souls back, even if he thinks he'll be getting two more in exchange."

For once, Tod nodded without arguing. Then he gave me an unexpected kiss on the cheek and disappeared with Nash's phone before I could recover from the surprise.

"I take it that's a thank-you," I mumbled, rubbing the spot on my cheek where the reaper's lips had touched me. They were warmer than I'd expected from a dead man.

Nash huffed, but he didn't really look mad. His brother's kiss spoke more of gratitude than anything else.

While he watched out for our exit, squinting beneath streetlights at regular intervals, I pulled my phone from my pocket. But before I could scroll through the call history for Addy's number, a small message at the bottom of the display popped up to tell me I'd missed five calls.

Crap. My dad had discovered my empty bed.

Please *tell me he didn't call the police!*

Three messages were from him, as expected. The first two had come in less than an hour after I'd left the house, while we were in the Netherworld bargaining with the fiend the first time. They were virtually identical—my father's angry voice demanding to know where I was, and what the *hell* I was doing. My dad didn't cuss much. Only when he was really, really mad. Or scared.

The third call was from Emma, warning me that my father had called her house at one o'clock in the morning. Which woke her mother up and led to all kinds of questions Emma'd had to dance around.

Oops. I made a mental note to bake a pan of brownies for Emma, too, to try to make up for the trouble I was getting her into.

Fortunately, her mother hadn't noticed the missing car, and it hadn't occurred to my father—yet, anyway— to ask if I'd borrowed it.

The fourth call was from Harmony, who was worried, and even sounded a little angry. She said my dad was "beside himself" and about two seconds from driving the streets in search of me. Then she wanted to know if I'd seen Nash, who wasn't answering his phone, either. Which meant he would have messages, too.

That was her way of warning us that she knew we were in this together—whatever *this* was—and that we'd better have a good explanation when we finally turned ourselves in.

I liked Harmony, and I was afraid that once she found out what we were doing, she'd shorten the long leash Nash had enjoyed since way before I'd met him. And that would be my fault, too.

The fifth call was from my dad again, saying he was going to drive around town looking for me, and if he hadn't heard from me by three, he'd go to the police.

Wonderful.

A quick glance at the clock on my phone display said it was two fifty-four in the morning. "I gotta call my dad," I said, glancing at Nash in dread. He nodded grimly, having obviously heard at least part of the messages.

As my dad's phone rang in my ear, I tugged my pants leg down and set my foot on the floor, gasping when even that slight movement made the accumulated fluid slosh.

"Kaylee?" my dad barked into my ear. "Is that you?"

"Yeah, it's me. I'm fine," I added before he could ask. And that was true, relatively speaking. I hadn't been mugged, or kidnapped, or turned out on the streets. "Look, I don't have much time to talk, but the bottom line is that I'm sorry I snuck out, but I *had* to. I have to finish something important, then I'll be home. A couple of hours, at most."

"Is Nash with you?"

I sighed, and let my head fall back against the headrest, watching as the highway lights passed over us in a steady, hypnotic rhythm. "This isn't his fault," I insisted. "I asked him to help. I'll explain everything when I get home."

"Kaylee—"

"I gotta go, Dad. I just wanted to tell you I'm okay.

And please don't go to the police. They won't understand." With that, I slid my phone closed and pressed
the button to ignore the incoming call when it began
to ring an instant later. Instead of answering, I called
Addison. She answered on the first ring and assured me
that Regan was up, if not exactly perky.

I told her to funnel another Jolt down her sister's throat and get her dressed. We'd be there in ten
minutes.

Again, Addy met us at the door, but this time Regan
sat on the couch in designer jeans and a couple of snug,
layered, long-sleeved tees. She stared across the room
with those weird, solid-white eyes until our arrival
caught her attention and she smiled blankly at me, her
lips barely curling up enough to qualify as an actual
expression.

"She's gonna have to put her contacts in," I said,
forcing myself to look somewhere other than Regan's
eyes. Anywhere else. "She can't go out like that."

Addison crossed the room toward her sister, a brown
leather jacket folded over one arm. "I don't think I can
get them in her eyes, and she's not up to it yet. Can't she
just wear sunglasses?"

"It's the middle of the night." I picked up one of
Regan's listless arms and slid it through the jacket sleeve
her sister held.

"We're not trying to make a fashion statement, Kaylee." Addy stuffed her sister's remaining hand through its sleeve. "We're just trying to avoid notice."

"Will we have to worry about paparazzi at three in the morning?" I asked as Addison knelt to slide a pair of glittery canvas shoes on her sister's bare feet. Not exactly winter attire, but it would work in a pinch. As would the sunglasses.

"Not in your car," the pop princess said, and I didn't bother to tell her it wasn't my car. She would have been much more embarrassed to appear in mine than in Emma's. "Not unless someone tipped them off. And if that's the case, we have bigger things to worry about." She rose and pulled her sister up by both hands.

Regan just stood there.

"How much did you give her?" Nash stepped closer to the youngest Page with his arms out, as if to catch her. Because she looked pretty wobbly.

"You mean Jolt or pills?"

"Pills."

"Two. But I think part of this is shock."

Nash exhaled deeply, frowning. "Grab another Jolt for the road." He wrapped one arm around Regan's shoulders and led her toward the door. Addy ducked into the kitchen while I snatched a pair of oversize, super-dark sunglasses from the bar between the living room and kitchen, sliding them in place over Regan's ears right before Nash pushed her gently over the threshold and onto the porch.

Addy sat by her sister in the back, and I slid into the passenger seat, buckling my seat belt as Nash started the engine. I resisted the urge to take another look at my ankle because I didn't want Addy or Regan to see it.

I didn't really want to see it, either.

"Regan, can you hear me?" Nash asked, as we took the on-ramp back onto the highway.

"Yeah…" Regan said, frowning slightly.

"Here, drink this." Addison popped the top on the drink can and held it to her sister's lips.

"No…" Regan pushed sluggishly at the can, and Addy pulled it back to keep from spilling.

"We need you coherent, Regan," I said, wishing I had Nash's Influence rather than my own much harsher abilities. "Don't you want to get your soul back?"

Regan shrugged, and I couldn't even tell if she was looking at me from behind those huge sunglasses.

"Keep making her drink." I settled into my seat, concentrating on the pain in my leg to keep from falling asleep.

My eyes were just starting to close when my phone buzzed in my pocket. My dad had called me twice more on the way to Addy's house, but I checked the display just in case. It was Tod, calling on Nash's phone.

"Hello?" I jabbed Nash's arm as I answered, then mouthed his brother's name.

"Kaylee? I found him. If you guys get here before he leaves, this might just work." Tod sucked in a tense, worried breath. "But, Kay, this place isn't like the stadium. It's…busy. You'll have to cross over in the parking lot, then bring everyone in through the side door, because the building's still closed in the human world. And be careful. Don't touch anything—"

"Like I haven't learned my lesson on that one…" I interrupted.

"And don't let Addy and Regan touch anything, either. Or talk to anyone."

"We'll be careful." I was as eager as the next person to walk out of this alive. "Make sure he doesn't leave. We're about fifteen minutes away." Fortunately, we were too early for morning rush-hour traffic, and most of our fellow highway drivers were truckers on overnight routes.

"I don't think he will. Everyone's here to absorb the bleed-through of human life force, and they're not going to leave before the workday starts. That's when the energy here will go through the roof." Another pause. "But hurry, just in case."

"We're going as fast as we can." Without getting splattered all over the highway.

By the time Nash pulled into a spot on the bottom floor of the Prime Life parking garage, Regan was starting to come around, either because the pills were wearing off, or because the Jolt was kicking in. Or maybe the importance of our mission was finally starting to sink in.

Her hand trembled as Nash helped her out of the car, and she rose unsteadily, almost knocking her sunglasses from her face when she tried to wipe her eyes. I stood, intending to help him with her, but the moment my right foot hit the ground, the echoes of my previous pain were swallowed in a wave of fresh agony so fierce I almost fell on my face right there in the parking lot.

Addison caught me. "What's wrong, Kaylee? Are you okay?" she asked, as I regained my balance and stepped carefully away from her.

"Yeah." I eased weight onto my injured leg, wincing as flames of pain flashed as far north as my hip. "I hurt my ankle earlier, and it's getting worse." I glanced up, smiling at Nash to assure him that I was okay.

"Let's get this done so we can take care of your leg," he said, one arm still around Regan, and I could only nod in agreement.

Moving slowly because of my limp and Regan's

chemically induced stupor, Nash led us to the locked glass doors, where we both turned to face Addison and Regan. "I'm going to cross us all over," I explained, "kind of like Bana did for you both, by holding your hand. When we get there, it won't be like last time. Tod says Prime Life is...populated this time of day in the Netherworld, so there are a couple of ground rules you need to follow, at all costs."

Both sisters nodded, Addison's fake-blue eyes wide with both fear and determination. I couldn't see Regan's eyes through her glasses—not that it would have mattered if I could—but I knew from the thin line her lips were pressed into that she was listening and taking me seriously.

Thank goodness.

I accidently put too much weight onto my bad leg and hissed in pain, so Nash continued while I breathed through it. "Don't touch anything," he began. "Don't make eye contact with anyone. Don't even look at anyone but us."

"And make sure you don't step on anything," I added, smiling wryly when my pain seemed to scare Regan. "Ready?" I asked. Both sisters nodded, taking the hands I held out. Nash held on to my arm, but I was afraid that if he wasn't actually touching my flesh, he couldn't come along for the ride, so I shoved up both my shirt and jacket sleeve, and he held on to my bare wrist.

Crossing over was a little harder this time, which left me oddly relieved, in light of Harmony's warning that it would eventually become too easy. This time, the pain in my leg was so distracting, it was hard to convince myself I actually wanted to return to the source of my injury. But after a few frustrating minutes, my need for closure transcended pain, and my intent to cross over became real.

I opened my eyes when Regan gasped, not surprised to find her staring in openmouthed wonder through the glass doors at my back. The Netherworld version of Prime Life was already open for business, and based on the number of beings I could now hear milling around inside, I had to wonder if they ever closed.

"What is this place?" Regan whispered, stepping closer to the door. She pulled her sunglasses off as if they impeded her vision, and I was almost as glad to see her finally returning to true consciousness as I was unnerved all over again by the sight of those eerie white eyes. They fit in much better here than they did in our world.

Nash must have been thinking the same thing. He glanced from Regan, holding her sunglasses, to Addy, wearing her contacts, to me and my normal, boring blue eyes. "Um, Addy, I think you'll be safer here without your contacts," he said. "And Regan, give Kaylee your glasses."

"Why?" she asked as Addison dug a plain white contact case from the pocket of her jeans, shooting Nash a questioning look almost identical to her sister's.

"Because most of the things in there—" I pointed over my shoulder; I hadn't yet worked up the nerve to actually *look* at the lion's den we'd be walking through "—have no reason to bother you if they know you have no soul. But my eyes will give me away in an instant."

Neither of them argued, and I almost felt guilty for not mentioning that some of them might try to eat us, whether or not we had souls. But not guilty enough for full disclosure, which might send them screaming into the Nether-night.

Regan handed me her glasses, which I slipped on immediately, then she held her sister's case while Addy took out her contacts. Nash seemed willing to go in with his eyes unguarded, and I had to trust that he'd crossed over more than I had, therefore knew what he was doing. And finally, when we were all ready to go inside, I made myself turn and look.

The shock of what I saw was almost as powerful as the pain shooting up my bad leg with every movement.

Though I'd never been in our world's version of

Prime Life, I was willing to bet my next paycheck that the world-anchor had pulled it through in its entirety. Furniture, marble floors, stone fountain, and all. But the creatures occupying that space had little in common with their real-world counterparts.

We should not be here, I thought as Nash pushed open the door. He held it for us as I led Addy and Regan inside. Though, once again, Regan needed a little push to get her going. Not that I could blame her.

When the door closed behind us, I concentrated on putting one foot in front of the other on the slick, marbled floor. *Step-ow! Step-ow!* Over and over again, breathing through the pain and doggedly avoiding eye contact with any of the creatures in the room. At least, any of them who actually had eyes.

Regan's breathing sped up until she was practically panting, and out of the corner of my eye, I saw her hand shaking. I wrapped my hand around hers and squeezed to tell her she was fine. Everything was okay. Then I made myself look up, though not at anything in particular, when I realized that walking with my eyes down practically advertized my status as prey.

And I would not be prey.

Near the fountain in the center of the room, two headless human-ish forms stood with their backs to us. One was male and one female, and she was bent to let her hand dangle in the flow of water that looked thick and smelled foul. When and if they turned, we'd find their facial features imbedded in their chests, as if they'd swallowed their own heads, and the lost parts were trying to break free from the inside. I knew that because I'd glimpsed this species briefly the day Emma died.

But what I hadn't known—since peeking renders everything in shades of gray—was that their skin tone would be a smooth, delicate pink, as if they'd never lost the soft flush of the birthing process. If creatures like that were even birthed in the first place.

"Just keep walking," Nash whispered, and I glanced quickly at his profile to find his jaw tense, his hands in his pockets. "Tod's waiting for us by the elevators. We're almost there."

I followed his line of sight. Tod was indeed waiting for us by a bank of very normal-looking elevators, his arms crossed over his chest. His expression was strong, closed-off, and arrogant, as if to say he might not belong there, but neither was he afraid.

But we were not almost there. We'd gone less than a quarter of the way—just far enough to attract attention.

As we crossed the room, oddly lilted, strangely pitched snippets of conversation began to fade into silence as one creature after another noticed our presence.

Then, as we passed an arrangement of formal, bur-
gundy-colored couches, that conversation started back
up, as if I'd just yawned to pop my ears and could suddenly hear again. This time I caught actual words here
and there.

"Overworlders..."

"...taste their fear..."

"...used-up husks..."

"...plump, soft flesh..."

"...beacons of energy..."

"...swimming in pain..."

"...strong, young hearts..."

Chills traveled up my arms and down my spine. I
became aware of a steady movement toward us, as the
creatures slowly converged, slinking, slithering, lurch-
ing, and gliding in our direction from every corner
of the room. I caught glimpses of extra arms, coiling
tails, and flashing eyes in all manner of *wrong* colors.
Whispered hisses followed us. Outstretched appendages
welcomed us.

Something brushed a strand of hair from my shoulder, then trailed lightly down my back. I swallowed a
shudder of revulsion and forced myself to face forward.
To keep walking.

"This one smells like warm rot...." a female voice
whispered into my ear, though as near as I could tell,

the speaker was all the way across the lobby, beside the reception desk. Skeletal hands peeked from beneath long, wide sleeves, but she stood on nothing that I could see. No feet. No paws. No flippers. She simply hung on the air, sunken eyes glowing a dark, eerie blue.

As we moved forward, the crowd parted reluctantly, some beings moving so slowly we had to wait for them to vacate our path. Oddly textured hems brushed my jeans. Scalding fingers tugged on mine. And something cold and airy, like a breeze somehow made solid, wound around my ankles, forming an almost physical resistance to my forward motion and introducing a new, prickly cold pain to the agony still throbbing in my leg.

When we finally reached Tod and the bank of elevators—I'd come to view them as salvation itself—my sigh of relief was audible. Without a word, he pressed a button on the wall, and a set of doors slid open. We stepped inside, and Addy jabbed the "close door" button repeatedly with one trembling finger.

When the door closed, she turned on us, tears welling in her oddly blank eyes. "What the *hell* was that?"

"Hell's about right," I mumbled, and she whirled on me, fierce anger overwhelming her fear for the first time.

I was glad to see it. Leaking fear in the Netherworld was like leaking blood in a shark tank.

"You could have warned us!"

"What did you think you were getting into when you sold your soul?" Nash demanded, and I glanced at him in surprise. Contempt shone in his eyes. "These creatures live off the human life force that bleeds through from our world to theirs. Some of them eat souls. Some of them eat flesh. Some of them just like new toys. Either way, walking through that lobby was like dangling a bloody steak in front of a tiger, and Kaylee and I did that for you two, even though she's in horrible pain and huge trouble with her father. And neither of us have a thing to gain from this. So if you have any further complaints, you can lodge them right up your own ass, *pop star,* because nobody here gives a damn who you are or how much you're worth. Without us, you're meat, pure and simple. Got it?"

Addison blinked her big, empty eyes. Then she nodded, still trembling, and I couldn't resist a smile.

But then the elevator binged and the doors slid open, and my heart jumped so far up my throat I could have spit it on the floor.

Tod stepped out first and we followed quickly, pleased to find the hallway deserted. And carpeted, which meant our shoes were silent. The reaper led us to a door near the end of the hall, where he stopped and turned to whisper. "He's in there. I peeked right before you got here." He hesitated, and forced a tense smile at Addy and Regan. "You guys ready?"

Addy nodded hesitantly and squeezed Regan's hand until she nodded, too.

"Good. Let's do this." Tod put one hand on the knob. My heart raced so fast I felt dizzy. He twisted the knob, and my pulse pumped scalding ribbons of adrenaline through my veins. He pushed the door open, and I had to swallow back vomit.

Behind a desk in the middle of a normal-looking office sat a normal-looking man in a suit, tie, and pair of sunglasses. He showed no surprise at our arrival. *This* was the hellion of greed?

"Avari?" Tod said, and the man nodded slowly, silently. "We're here to bargain for the souls of Addison and Regan Page."

And as the impossibility of what we were about to attempt truly sank in, I focused on one thought to keep myself calm: *Weirdest. Wednesday. Ever.*

19

Avari rose, placing both palms flat on the glossy work surface of a desk that stood empty in the Netherworld, but was probably cluttered with some worker-drone's papers, pens, and coffee mug in our world. "Come inside," he said, his words as smooth and dark as good fudge, but nowhere near as sweet.

His voice sent shivers through me, leaving tiny icicle shards to chill the blood in my veins.

Tod stepped inside and we followed him reluctantly. I brought up the rear, fighting to control the wince of pain my features wanted to form, and to deny the groan lodged in my throat. I would not expose myself as the weakest member of the herd.

With the casual wave of one hand, Avari closed the door behind us, from across the room. "Addison. Regan." The hellion nodded formally, rounding his desk to stand in front of it. "I assume you've come to invoke your respective out-clauses?"

"No." Addy spoke firmly and clearly, in spite of the trembling hands she clasped at her back. "We won't damn someone else to eternity with you. We're here to make a different sort of trade."

Avari sat with one hip on the corner of his desk, tugging the sleeves of an immaculate, coal-gray suit jacket into place. If not for the sunglasses—and the ability to close doors without touching them—he could have been any ordinary cog in the life-insurance machine. "What makes you think I'm open to such an exchange?" Power radiated from him in waves of bitter cold, drawing goose bumps from my skin, even beneath my jacket.

"You're a hellion of avarice," I began, but when the demon's head turned my way, the words froze in my throat, and I had to cough to force them up. "Why wouldn't you want more for less?"

Avari's brows rose above his sunglasses, and my heart thumped painfully from the knowledge that both his attention and his gaze were focused on me.

Being scrutinized by a hellion was definitely not part of the plan.

Nash stepped protectively closer to me, his hand brushing mine, but Avari took no notice.

"You reek, *bean sidhe*." The hellion's words wove through me on a gust of frigid air, coiling around my chest until I could hardly feel my heartbeat through the simultaneous numbing cold and stabbing, icy pressure. "The rot spreads inside you quickly. I smell it. I feel it, though you disguise your pain with uncommon strength and fortitude. Both qualities I find quite appetizing in a soul."

He rose from his desk and took a single stride toward me. I answered it with a backward step, swallowing a cry as my bad foot hit the floor. Needlelike pain shot down my foot and up my leg, this time enveloping my entire pelvis, as well.

I was getting worse. Fast.

The hellion's long, straight nose twitched as he inhaled, and a terrifying flash of hunger flickered across his otherwise empty expression. "I can eat your pain. I can spare your life."

Panic shot through me and I squelched it all, except the tremor in my hands. "When my death comes, you can't stop it, and I won't even try. If I'm supposed to die from crimson creeper venom, so be it." Not that I was exactly eager to go, but I would *not* die without my soul. Not even for the promise of a quick, painless death.

"And if you were not meant to die of such poison?" Avari's brows lifted once more as he stepped forward, and again I limped backward, my vision going gray with the sudden, harsh movement. "I see your lifeline spread before me like a length of road, and the miles should tick away your fleeting, insignificant life for some time to come. Yet the stench of death clings to you. It flows through your veins like a river through its channel, and the toxin will reach your heart within minutes."

He paused, and I thought I glimpsed a dark flash of pleasure, even through the opaque tint of his lenses. "If you stay in the Nether much longer, you will die here."

Fresh fear skittered up my spine to lodge in my throat, and my gaze flitted from Nash's horrified expression to the smug hellion. Then I asked the question he clearly wanted to hear, in spite of some strong instinct urging me to retreat into silence. I had to know. "But you said my lifeline goes on." I stopped to breathe through another agonizing wave of pain. "How can I die here?"

"The date stamped on your feeble body means nothing in the Netherworld. If you suffer a mortal injury or contract a deadly infection here, you will die among us. As one of us. But you have a few minutes yet. Enough time to barter for your friends. Or to escape to your own world."

Was he telling the truth?

Horror drew my hands into fists so tight my fingernails cut into my flesh. If I fled the Netherworld to save myself, there would be no one left to suspend Addy's and Regan's souls once the hellion released them, so Nash could guide them back into the proper bodies. But if I stayed to help them, I would die.

Unless I sold my soul to Avari.

"Which will it be, little *bean sidhe?*" The hellion's faux-sympathetic smile sent a spike of terror through my heart. "Your life, or your friends'? Or your soul?"

"Tod?" I turned on him, silently demanding the truth, keeping the hellion safely in my peripheral vision.

The reaper's tortured, conflicted expression greeted me. "Kaylee, he's just trying to buy your soul."

I knew that, of course. But I also knew Tod would say anything to save Addison's soul. He would also *not* say anything with that same goal in mind. "Tell me the truth, Tod. Can I die here?"

The reaper sighed but nodded. "Your expiration date means nothing here. You know, 'Offer not valid in the

Netherworld, the Bermuda Triangle, and various un-discovered warp zones across the globe....'"

I closed my eyes briefly and exhaled. "Awesome, Tod. Thanks for that." Anger flamed through me, thawing some of the chill Avari's voice had left in my veins. But it could do nothing to ease the agony clawing its way up my right leg and into my torso. "Thanks for warning me *before* we crossed over."

And suddenly I realized. I remembered. "You knew!" He'd almost said something in the car. He'd started to tell me my ankle couldn't wait. But then he didn't.

On the edge of my vision, Nash's hands curled into fists at his sides, and his eyes churned furiously in fear and rage.

"I'm sorry, Kay," Tod began as Addy and Regan stared at me in horror. "I'm so sorry...."

I turned my back on him, ignoring his silent plea for forgiveness. "If I die, it will be with my soul in my possession," I said to the hellion, summoning every ounce of that fortitude he'd mentioned. "It will never be yours." I paused, as cold, treacherous anger flowed swiftly over the demon's face. "Got that, Tod?"

"I got it," he whispered from behind me. He would take my soul if I died, to keep it from the demon. It was the least he owed me. That, and a few tears spilled over my grave...

"So be it, *bean sidhe*." Avari's voice was as still and deadly as an Arctic winter. He turned that toxic hunger on Addison. "What do you offer?"

Addy nodded at Tod, who'd recovered most of his composure. "Your colleague Bana is no longer with us," the reaper said. "Not in body, anyway."

The hellion's expression did not change, but I suffered in silence for several tense moments before he spoke again. "You have Bana's soul?"

"Yes." Tod let a slow smile stretch across his face. "She was more than one hundred years old. Her soul has more accumulated energy than both Addison's and Regan's combined, and I can personally attest to the quality of that energy." He patted his stomach, like he'd just eaten a particularly satisfying burger.

Again, Avari betrayed no thought or emotion, and frustration spiked with my pulse. I couldn't tell if he was even interested in our bait, much less how close we were to a deal.

The entire right side of my body throbbed during Avari's silence, pain cresting and falling with each beat of my heart. Small, sharp tongues of anguish licked at the base of my spine, replacing the numbing cold with a searing heat. I could almost feel the creeper venom flowing through me, taking over my body one cell at a time, one limb after another.

"No." Finally the hellion spoke, and I concentrated on his words to distract me from the pain that hunched my back and singed my nerve endings. "Human souls are pure, and particularly innocent are the souls of children." His gaze seemed to focus on Regan then, though I couldn't be sure with his eyes hidden. "If you want your souls back, you will offer a fair exchange. That is the agreement you signed."

Regan moaned, and Addy squeezed her sister's hand. "Please," the pop star begged, stepping in front of Regan to block her from the demon's sight, and vice versa. But the moment the word left her mouth, both Nash and Tod went stiff, and it didn't take me long to catch on. Addison had just shown the hellion another weak link in our chain, and exactly how to exploit it.

The demon smiled, and the temperature in the room plummeted. My goose bumps grew fatter, and my nose started to run, like I'd caught a cold. I began to shiver, and each small movement sent fresh waves of pain throughout my body, one after the other, cresting in my injured ankle.

"You want to save your sister?" Avari's voice pierced me like a massive icicle through the chest, and I couldn't hold back a gasp. I wasn't the only one; Regan looked like her blood had just frozen in her veins.

Addison hesitated, and Nash tried unsuccessfully to

catch her eye without speaking. "Yes," Addy said finally, her pretty face twisted with fear and desperation.

The hellion's smile widened almost imperceptibly, and some small motion caught my eye from his desk. I glanced down to see a thin, blue-tinted film of frost forming on the glass desktop, crawling across the surface in tiny, flat ice-vines. The frost branched steadily in all directions, a network of captured snowflakes. It was beautiful.

It was also one of the scariest things I'd ever seen.

"I will trade one unspoiled human soul for this reaper's accumulated energy." Avari's soft words rolled over me like thunder as ice continued to spread toward the edge of the desk. "Show me Bana's soul."

"You first," I gasped, clutching my abdomen as the toxin spreading within me set my stomach on fire. Soon the poison's flames would meet the ice Avari's words had driven through my chest, and I knew better than to hope the two would simply cancel each other out. "Give us the soul first," I repeated, ignoring the shocked faces staring at me. "Or there's no deal."

A growl rumbled from the demon's throat to shake the entire room, and a sudden gush of frigid power sent more frost surging over the edge of the desk and onto the floor. Avari ripped the sunglasses from his face and they froze in his hand, tiny icicles hanging from the earpieces and the left lens. His fist closed, and the frozen plastic shattered, clinking to the floor like glass.

His eyes, now exposed, were spheres of solid black, just like Addison had said. But what her words had failed to convey was the utter *darkness* encompassed in those obsidian orbs. Looking into Avari's eyes was like looking into the depths of oblivion. Into the distillation of nothingness.

He was the very absence of all things light and good, and staring into his eyes called forth my own worst fear: that if I were to look into my own heart and soul, I would find nothing more. That I would be just as empty. That my own void would mirror his.

But I wouldn't let it. If I had to die, at least I could die helping a friend.

"You dare make demands of me?" the hellion roared, shattering a heavy stalactite of ice that had grown from the ceiling. It crashed to the floor, and both Page sisters jumped.

I only smiled. I was a little light-headed, and more than a little out of my mind with pain and with the very thought of my rapidly approaching demise. "I *totally* dare. You don't scare me." I barely noticed the sick look on Nash's face, growing worse with every word

I spoke. He aimed eyebrow acrobatics my way, trying to shut me up, but I ignored him. What did I have to lose? "I'm going to die, anyway," I continued. "And if you don't release one soul now, Tod will take off with Bana's, as well as mine, and you'll have gained nothing from this little gathering."

How well did *that* concept sit with the demon of greed?

Avari growled again, and more spears of ice dropped from the ceiling to shatter at our feet. But then his growl died, and the floor went still beneath me, a temporary mercy for my tortured right leg. And when the sound faded, the hellion's lips turned up in the single most terrifying smile I'd ever seen.

"Fine. Have your soul, for what good it will do you…." He exhaled deeply, without sucking in a preparatory breath, and what I at first mistook for warm air puffing into the cold room soon revealed itself as a soul. A human soul.

We'd done it!

I glanced at Nash and Tod in relief and in pure joy, ignoring the pain that now wound its way over my ribs toward my right shoulder.

"Kaylee!" Nash whispered fiercely, desperately, and I followed his gaze to the soul now floating steadily toward the icicle-studded ceiling.

Oops. I'd forgotten the most important part. Since Regan wasn't actually dying, I'd had no urge to wail for her, and her soul was getting away. So I used what I'd learned from Harmony to call my wail up on demand, suspending the soul with the thin sliver of sound that leaked from my tightly sealed lips.

The soul bobbed just below the ceiling, surrounding one of the stalactites of ice. Sweat broke out on Nash's forehead, in spite of the freezing temperature, as he concentrated on guiding the soul into Regan's body while everyone else watched. Tod stared at his brother in relief, while Addy and Regan looked on in amazement—evidently in the Netherworld humans can see souls.

But Avari looked…amused?

Was I missing something?

I focused on my wail, on holding most of it back, to distract myself from the pain that now pierced my right shoulder and was inching its way down my arm. Nash brought the soul steadily closer to Regan, and in a sudden moment of comprehension, Addison pushed her sister toward the bobbing soul, to make Nash's work easier.

My heart beat harder in anticipation. The rush of adrenaline through my veins tried to overwhelm the pain in my bones. Any second, Regan and her soul would be reunited. We could claim success on the part of at least one Page sister.

We couldn't help Addy—she'd made her own choice—but we'd done what we could.

Nash's sudden wide-eyed, horrified expression was the first sign that something had gone wrong. "It doesn't fit!" he breathed, and I wasn't sure whether I'd actually heard him or read his lips. "It's not hers!"

Suddenly the hellion's unprecedented agreeableness and his amused expression made sense, and we all seemed to draw the same conclusion at once: Avari had tricked us.

He'd released Addison's soul instead of Regan's.

20

"No!" Addison shouted, her voice strong and shrill, powered by a singer's trained lungs. Which I could have used in that moment, as my muffled keening thinned. But her protest meant nothing to Avari.

"This is my offer," he said, softer than before, yet still his words sent cold, ethereal fingers over my flesh, making my goose-pimpled skin crawl. "The choice is yours."

"Nooo." Addison moaned that time. "No. Take me. You said you'd take my soul."

Avari shook his head slowly, a cruel teacher scolding a naive student. "You misinterpreted my words. That happens more than you might think."

As my wail wavered, my mind raced while I tried to remember everything the hellion had said. Had he actually said he'd trade Regan's soul for Bana's? Or just *a* soul? I couldn't remember....

"Choose." Avari clucked his tongue at Addison. "Your friends cannot hold your soul forever. Not with this one near death." The demon's gaze met mine, and suddenly his cruel truth sank in. I was dying. The poison had spread to my right hand, and now flowed over my left side on its way to my heart. I couldn't hold Addy's soul for long.

My gaze pleaded with her as I struggled to keep the sound steady in my throat.

Addison's eyes watered and she glanced from me to Regan, who stood frozen in terror, clenching her sister's hand so hard it had turned purple. Then her gaze swung my way, and she focused on something over my shoulder. And I thought I saw some glimmer of hope in her grotesquely blank eyes.

Was that possible? Had she thought of something?

Addy turned to Tod and mouthed something I couldn't interpret.

I was next, and what she said silently to me was "One more minute. Please." I closed my eyes briefly, then opened them and nodded. I would hold on, for just a little longer.

Addison smiled her thanks, then she nodded decisively, again looking over my shoulder.

An instant later, Addy collapsed. Her legs simply folded under her and her head smacked the frosted marble floor. Not that it mattered. She was dead before she hit the ground.

"No!" Regan shouted, tears pouring down her cheeks. She lurched toward her sister, but Tod held her back, wrapping his arms around her shoulders to keep her still.

Surprise dried up the trickle of sound flowing from my throat, and Addy's soul bobbed, until I keened again a second later. Then things got even weirder.

A figure stepped forward from behind me and to my right, her mouth open, already sucking in a long, thick stream of Demon's Breath from Addy's still form.

Libby. My heart ached as I realized Addison had seen her over my shoulder. She'd nodded to Libby, not to me.

Then Tod spoke, Regan now sobbing on his shoulder, and I began to put the pieces together. "The deal has changed, Avari. If you want Bana's soul, you take Addison's with it and return her sister's. Or else, we'll leave with both of the souls in our possession, and you'll keep only the one you have now."

Damn. Shock wound through me, blending with the

pain now arcing across every nerve ending in my body. Somehow, Addison had known who Libby was and why she'd come. Had Tod told her, or did understanding simply come in the last moments of her life?

Either way, with a single nod of her head, Addison had asked Libby to end her life, to force the hellion into trading her soul for Regan's. Because Addison's was ready to reap now, and Regan's wouldn't truly be his until she died, likely decades later.

Avari's face paled with rage, and the void in his eyes seemed to churn, though I could detect no motion when I looked directly into those dark spheres.

"Five seconds, or you're out of luck," Tod said as Nash continued to sweat, and my voice warbled. "We're in a bit of a rush." He gestured to me, and I realized he planned to get me home before I died. He was trying to save me, since he couldn't save Addison.

All I could do was sing. And watch Libby claim the Demon's Breath. And wait.

"Five… Four…" Tod taunted as Regan heaved with silent sobs and Avari bellowed in rage. The floor grew slick with ice beneath my feet, and my breath puffed visibly into the frigid air.

Then, just when I thought it was over—thought Addison's death had been for nothing—the hellion spat one short, powerful exhalation into the room, and Regan's soul bobbed near the ceiling.

At Nash's signal, I let go of Addison's soul and sang for her sister's. Libby swallowed the last of the Demon's Breath and popped out of existence without so much as a glance at the rest of us. Avari slurped up Addy's soul in a fraction of the time it took Nash to guide Regan's home. And only then did Tod release Bana's soul into the room.

While Avari devoured it, Nash rushed toward me across the slick floor, tugging a shocked Regan by one hand. I had a moment to notice that her eyes were again beautiful, and blue, and normal. Then they converged on me, sliding so quickly they almost bowled me over.

"Now!" Nash whispered desperately, tugging me into an agonizing squat so that I touched both him, Regan, and Addison's limp arm. "Take us back now!"

That time, intent to cross was no problem, and I was already keening. Avari's roar of fury faded swiftly from my ears. An instant later I collapsed to the floor of a generic office full of cubicles and cheap industrial carpet. Addy lay at my side, and Nash and Regan stared down at me, a mixture of grief and relief coursing over their features.

A moment later, Tod popped into existence next to his brother.

"Are you okay?" Nash knelt at my side, but by then I could only shake my head. I'd lost my voice completely, and was in so much pain it hurt to draw a breath. "Call Mom," Nash ordered, sliding one hand behind my back, the other beneath my knees. He carried me out of the office and into the hall while Regan followed, crying and scrolling through the entries in Nash's phone for a name she wouldn't even recognize, because Tod carried her sister's body.

Each second we waited for the elevator was pure agony. I hurt all over, and worse wherever he touched me. But I was grateful for that touch.

"You'll be fine," Nash whispered. "Your expiration date is in full effect here, so you won't die. But you're going to hurt like hell until we get this fixed."

I'd guessed as much.

I'd just decided that Prime Life shut down their elevators after hours when the mirrored doors slid open with a soft ding. Downstairs, we crossed the eerily empty lobby and Nash set me on a burgundy couch while he kicked open the locked glass doors leading to the parking garage. It took him three tries, but I was still impressed.

Harmony answered her phone as Nash buckled me

into the front seat, and Regan gave the phone to Tod as he closed the trunk, where he'd gently laid Addison. He explained the basics, demanding his mother meet us at my house with the necessary supplies. She said she'd be there in ten minutes.

It took us twenty, and once he'd dropped me and Nash off, Tod took the Page sisters home, where Regan would "find" her sister's body on the floor of her own room. Then he returned Emma's car.

My front door flew open before Nash and I even got to the porch, and my father took me from him without a word. His anger had momentarily been eclipsed by fear I hadn't seen since that long-ago day I barely re-membered.

The day my mother had died to save me.

"Not again," he muttered, laying me on the couch. I moaned, and tears overflowed his eyes.

"She'll be fine." Harmony pushed him aside gently. I hadn't even known she was there, but suddenly she was at my side, her fingers cold on my arm, a filled syringe ready in her other hand. "Tod said it's crimson creeper."

"Where the hell did she find crim—" His eyes widened in horror, and some of that anger returned. "Kaylee, what did you do?"

"She can explain it later, Aiden," Harmony said

firmly. The needle slid into my arm, and though it was blissfully cold, the medicine that invaded my body scalded like one of the original pinpricks from the creeper. "For now, let her sleep. She'll need another dose of this in four hours." She held a second syringe up for my father to see, and he nodded. "If the red webbing isn't gone four hours after that, call me."

But she'd be back to check on me before then. Nash would see to that.

"Come on, Nash," Harmony said, and the hard edge in her voice said he wouldn't get off easy, either.

"No…" I moaned, surprised when my voice actually produced the cracked, tortured sound. I grabbed his wrist with the last of my strength.

Harmony frowned at me, then at my father. "Can he stay, Aiden? She wants him to stay."

My father hedged, and I begged him with my eyes. I needed them both. I'd never hurt so badly in my life, but Nash's voice could help. I knew it could. "Fine," he said finally. "But you have to go to sleep, young lady."

We'd argue about the "young lady" part later. But I agreed with the rest of his statement.

The last thing I saw before sleep—blissful, pain-free sleep—claimed me were their faces, side by side, watching me with identical expressions of concern.

21

"THANKS FOR COMING." Regan smoothed her black dress over her flat stomach. Her perfect blue eyes were red from crying, but her expression was pure strength and poise. Her mother stood beside the coffin, staring past all the headstones in a chemically induced oblivion. She was coping with Addy's death the only way she knew how—with pills, and alcohol, and seclusion. She hadn't left her house in nearly a week, and had only come out this time for the funeral. Because Regan made her.

"We wouldn't have missed it," Nash said, and I nodded. He spoke for us both.

Regan had made all the arrangements, choosing her sister's favorite flowers, music, and poetry, as well as the coffin and the plot. It was a lot of responsibility for a thirteen-year-old already devastated by her sister's death—her sacrifice—and it broke my heart that she'd had to rise to such a tragic occasion.

But she would be fine. The determined line of her jaw and straight length of her spine said that clearly. Whatever else happened, Regan Page would be just fine.

Addy had seen to that.

Regan glanced briefly at her mother, then at the crowd of paparazzi gathered behind a long barricade before returning her attention to me. "How are you feeling?"

"I'm fine now. Really," I added, when doubt flickered behind her mercifully real eyes.

The red webbing had faded from my skin by the time the sun went down the day Addy died, but it took three more days before the last of the pain abated. And the puncture marks around my ankle left scars—a double ring of bright red dots. I'd missed school for the rest of that week, but Harmony had only let Nash miss Thursday, and only because we'd been up all of Wednesday night.

And since I was well enough for the funeral, I would be returning to school on Monday.

Addy's service was private, but Regan got us in. Tod cried through the whole thing, but I think I was the only one who could see him. Addy's death nearly killed him. Again. Levi had given him a couple of weeks off, and was personally covering his hospital shifts. And we hadn't seen Tod once between that night and the funeral.

I think he was having a lot of trouble with the knowledge that Addison's soul was now the property of a hellion of greed, and that the rest of her existence would be spent in agonizing pain, of every possible variety.

I wasn't dealing with that very well, either. I'd really wanted to save her. And I would have plenty of time to think about my failure, because I was grounded for a solid month. My father was unmoved by our altruistic intentions. He considered nothing else on the face of the planet—or in either world—worth risking my life.

After he said that, I found it pretty hard to complain about being grounded, even though I would only see Nash at school and at *bean sidhe* lessons.

The only positive thing to come out of the whole mess—other than returning Regan's soul—was the fact that we were never fingered for the "break in" at Prime Life. Thank goodness. That one would have been impossible to explain to the cops. It was no picnic to explain to my dad, either.

"So, what are you going to do?" I leaned into Nash's chest for both comfort and warmth.

Regan shrugged and tucked a strand of blond hair

behind her ear. "Take care of my mom, I guess. And stay far away from John Dekker."

I nodded. Regan had done us all proud. In honor of Addison's sacrifice, she'd already broken her contract with Dekker Media and was pursuing other acting opportunities. Rumor had it the Teen Network—Dekker's biggest competition—wanted her to do a pilot for them, but she wouldn't even accept their calls until she'd laid Addison to rest.

The fact that the wolves were already nipping at her heels made me wonder if anyone in the entertainment industry remained in possession of a soul.

As for Dekker Media, as far as I knew, they couldn't continue to provide souls for Avari without someone to ferry teenage stars to the Netherworld for them. So, for the moment at least, the adolescent population of Hollywood was secure. Though I still got a sick feeling every time I thought of all the soulless victims still waiting to suffer throughout the afterlife at Avari's hands.

But there was nothing I could do about that.

My dad said I couldn't save them all, and on my good days, I have to admit that he was right. Eventually, people have to learn to make their own choices, and to deal with the consequences.

Including me.

"I think that's your dad over there," Regan said, and I twisted to follow her gaze. Sure enough, my father—more handsome than ever in his dark suit—stood in front of his freshly washed car, waiting patiently for me.

"Yeah, I better go." I stepped away from Nash as Regan opened her arms to hug me.

"Thank you, Kaylee," she whispered into my ear, as she squeezed me so tight I could barely breathe. "Thank you so much." She sniffed, and her next words sounded thick, as if she were holding back more tears. "I won't forget what you did for me. What you helped Addy do."

I hugged her back, because I didn't know what to say.

No problem? But it was a problem. I'd nearly died.

Anyone else would have done the same? But that wasn't true, either.

I'd helped Addy and Regan because I couldn't *not* help them. Because in most cases, I believe that people deserve a second chance. And because I couldn't have lived with myself if I'd stood by and let them both die soulless, when I could have helped.

Finally, Regan stepped back and looked into my eyes, her own still brimming with tears. "I want you to know that I understand what Addy gave up for me. And I'm going to do my best to deserve it."

"I know you will." With that, I squeezed her hand, then turned toward Tod, who stared at the coffin from beneath the skeletal branches of a broad oak. I needed to talk to him before I left, because I wasn't sure when I'd see him next.

Or if Nash could see him at that moment. But then his hand stiffened on my arm when he saw where I was leading him, and I knew he could see his brother. "Kaylee, do we have to do this now? He's really hurting."

"So is Regan," I pointed out, and my free hand slid into the pocket of my formal black coat, bought just for Addy's funeral. "I have to know if he did this."

"Does it really matter?" Nash asked, and I looked up at him to find his eyes swirling slowly, though I couldn't quite identify the emotion. "What's done is done, and justice isn't always pretty. And, anyway, do you really want to know?"

"Yes. I need to hear it." Because part of me couldn't believe he'd actually done it.

Nash frowned, but tagged along. When we stopped beneath Tod's tree, Nash's body shielding us from the stragglers still loitering around the coffin, I pulled from my pocket a news clipping folded in half. "Do you know anything about this?"

Tod took the clipping and unfolded it. He couldn't have read more than the headline before handing it back to me, his face carefully blank, though rage churned violently in the cerulean depths of his eyes. The fact that I could see it surely meant he harbored it deep inside his soul. And that thought scared me.

"Kaylee, don't ask questions you don't want answered," the reaper said, his voice harder and more humorless than I'd ever heard it.

"You killed him," I accused, glancing at the headline for at least the fiftieth time.

BILLIONAIRE CEO MISSING; SISTER FEARS THE WORST

"No. Death is too good for John Dekker," Tod said without a hint of remorse. His ruthless expression gave me chills.

"Where is he?" Nash asked, when he realized his brother wasn't going to elaborate.

"I dropped him off in Avari's office."

My heart jumped into my throat, and suddenly I could hear my own pulse. "You stranded him in the Netherworld?"

The reaper shrugged. "A live plaything is rare on that side. They won't kill him."

"They'll do worse," I spat.

Tod cocked one eyebrow at me. "Does he deserve any less?"

I had to think about that. John Dekker had been responsible for dozens of teenagers losing their souls, and he'd worked to keep Addy and Regan from reclaiming theirs. Did he deserve any less than eternal torture?

Probably not. But that wasn't my call to make. The very thought of wielding so much power terrified me.

Though, it didn't seem to have bothered Tod.

"I can't believe you did that…."

"And yet you haven't asked me to bring him back." He ran one hand through his hair. "I think you have no trouble believing it. I think you wish you'd done it yourself."

"No." I shook my head, bothered by the spark of anger raging unchecked inside him. Was this why my father didn't want me hanging out with a reaper? Because, as he'd always insisted, Tod *was* dangerous?

I shook that thought off. It was too much to think about with Addy not yet in the ground, and my failure on her behalf haunting me. I took Nash's hand again and shoved the clipping deep into my pocket. "I have to go," I said, already turning toward my dad's car.

"Kaylee, just say it," Tod called after me, and I was glad no one else could hear him. Not even Nash, this time. I could tell from the relief on his face—he was happy to be walking away from his brother. "Say the word, and I'll bring him back. I'll rescue him from never-ending torture. It's your call…."

Hot, bitter tears filled my eyes, as horror filled my

heart. It wasn't my call. He couldn't put a decision like that on me. It wasn't right.

Yet as I headed toward my father with my boyfriend at my side, my lips remained sealed, and I was more terrified than I could express by the thought of what my silence probably said about me, deep down inside.

My dad started his engine, and Nash kissed me gently before I sank into the front passenger seat. Then I tucked my skirt beneath me and he closed the car door. I put John Dekker and Tod out of my mind. Forced them to the back of my brain to make room for Nash.

I would only think about Nash. I trusted Nash. I loved him. I understood him, like I would never understand his brother.

Nash waved at me in the side-view mirror as our car pulled forward slowly, my father carefully avoiding stray members of the press. I leaned with my head against the cold window, watching as his image grew smaller and smaller in the mirror. Trying not to think about how long it would be before we could be alone together again.

Three weeks, five days, and four hours until my grounding ends.

Three weeks, five days, four hours, and fifty-four seconds. Fifty-three seconds... Fifty-two seconds...

But who's counting?

Acknowledgments

Thanks, as always, to my husband, and to my critique partner, Rinda Elliott, for being my first sounding boards. Thanks to Alex Elliott, the first reader from my target audience. Thanks to my editor, Mary-Theresa Hussey, and to the entire editorial and production teams, for believing in this book.
And a huge thank you to my agent, Miriam Kriss, for holding my hand and keeping me sane.

Netherworld Survival Guide

A collection of entries salvaged from
Alec's personal journal during his
twenty-six year captivity in the Nether...

COMMON HAZARDOUS PLANTS

Note: Flora in the Netherworld is eighty-eight per cent carnivorous, ten per cent omnivorous, and less than two per cent docile. So keep in mind that if you see a plant, it probably wants to eat you.

Razor Wheat
- **Location** – Rural areas with little foot traffic.
- **Description** – Fields full of dense vegetation similar to wheat in structure, ranging in colour from deep red stalks to olive-hued seed clusters. Over six feet tall at mature height.
- **Dangers** – Razor wheat stalks shatters upon contact, raining tiny, sharp shards of plant that can slice through clothing and shred bare flesh.
- **Best Precaution** – Complete avoidance.
- **Second Best Precaution** – Long sleeves, full-length rubber waders and fishing boots, metal trash-can lid wielded like a shield.

Crimson Creeper
- **Location** – Anywhere it can get a foothold. Creeper can take root in as little as a quarter-inch wide crack in concrete and will grow to split the pavement open. It grows quickly and spreads voraciously, climbing walls, towers, trees and anything else that can be made to hold still.
- **Description** – A deep green vine growing up to four inches in diameter, bearing alternating leaves bleeding to crimson or blood red on variegated edges. Vines also sport needle-thin thorns between the leaves.
- **Dangers** – Though anchored by strong, deep roots, which have hallucinogenic properties when consumed, creeper vines slither autonomously and will actually wind around prey, injecting pre-digestive venom through its thorns. The vine will then coil around its meal and wait while the creature is slowly dissolved into liquid fertiliser from the inside out.
- **Best Precaution** – Complete avoidance.

- **Second Best Precaution** – Crimson creeper blooms can be made into a tea which acts as one of two known antidotes to the creeper venom; however, the vine blooms only once every three years. Blooms can be dried and preserved for up to two decades.

COMMON DANGEROUS CREATURES

Note: Whether it intends to consume your mind, body or soul, fauna in the Netherworld is ninety-nine per cent carnivorous, in one form or another. So keep in mind that if you see a creature, it probably wants to eat you.

Hellions
- **Location** – Everywhere. Anywhere. Never close your eyes.
- **Description** – Hellions can look like anything they want. They can be any size, shape or colour. Their only physical limitation is that they cannot exactly duplicate any other creature, living or dead.
- **Dangers** – Hellions feed from chaos in general, and individual emotions in particular. But what they really want is your soul—a never-ending buffet. Since souls cannot be stolen from the living, a hellion will try to bargain for or con you out of it. If you refuse—and even sometimes if you don't—the hellion will either kill you for your soul or torture you, *then* kill you for your soul.
- **Best Precaution** – Complete avoidance.
- **Second Best Precaution** – Pray.

Harpies
- **Location** – Found in large numbers near thin spots in the barrier between worlds, but individual harpies can live anywhere they choose, in either the human world or the Netherworld.
- **Description** – In the human world, harpies can pass for human at a glance, as long as they brush hair over their pointed ears and hide their compact, bat-like wings beneath clothing. In the Netherworld, harpies

appear less human, with mouths full of sharp, thin teeth, claws instead of hands and bird-like, clawed talons instead of feet.

- **Dangers** – Harpies are snatchers. Collectors. They will dive out of the air with no warning to grab whatever catches their eye, which can be anything from broken pots and pans to shiny rings—often still attached to human fingers. Also, they're carnivores and they don't distinguish between human and animal flesh.
- **Best Precaution** – Complete avoidance.
- **Second Best Precaution** – Stay inside or keep one eye trained on the sky and get ready to run.

ESCAPE AND EVASION

Note: The best way to escape a Netherworld threat is to leave the Netherworld, though that won't keep certain species, such as harpies, from crossing into the human world after you. If you are incapable of leaving under your own power, eventually something *will* eat you. But to help put that moment off as long as possible, here is a list of the most effective evasion tactics:

- Find shelter in rural areas. Netherworld creatures are attracted to heavily populated areas, where the overflow of human energy they feed from is most concentrated.
- Fibres from the *dissimulatus* plant can be woven together and worn to disguise your energy signature and keep predators from identifying you as human and thus edible.

Kaylee only thinks she's done fighting evil.
What will she do when a Netherworld
element infiltrates her school?

Turn the page for a sneak peek at

My Soul to Keep

the chilling third instalment in the
Soul Screamers series.

"SO, HOW DOES IT FEEL to be free again?" Nash leaned against my car, flashing that smile I couldn't resist. The one that made his dimples stand out and his eyes shine, and made me melt like chocolate in the sun, in spite of the mid-December chill.

I sucked in a deep, cold breath. "Like I'm seeing the sun for the first time in a month." I pushed my car door closed and twisted the key in the lock. I didn't like parking on the street; it didn't seem like a very safe place to leave my most valuable possession. Not that my car was expensive, or anything. It was more than a decade old, and hardly anything to *oooh* over. But it was mine, and it was paid for, and unlike some of my more financially fortunate classmates, I'd never be able to afford another one, should some idiot veer too close to the curb. But Scott Carter's driveway was full long before we'd arrived, and the street was lined with cars, most much nicer than mine. Of course, they all probably had more than liability coverage…

Fortunately, the party was in a very good section of our little Dallas suburb, where the lawn manicures cost more than my father made in six months.

"Relax, Kaylee." Nash pulled me close as we walked. "You look like you'd rather gouge your own eyes out than hang for a couple of hours with some friends."

"They're your friends, not mine," I insisted as we passed the third convertible on our way to the well-lit house at the end of the cul-de-sac, already thumping with some bass-heavy song I couldn't yet identify.

"They'd be yours if you'd get to know them."

I couldn't help rolling my eyes. "Yeah, I'm sure the glitter-and-gloss throng is waiting for *me* to give *them* a chance."

Nash shrugged. "They know all they need to know about you —you're smart, pretty, and crazy in love with me," he teased, squeezing me tighter.

I laughed. "Who started *that* vicious rumor?" I'd never said it, because as addictive as Nash was—as special as he made me feel—I wasn't going to toss off words like *love* and *forever* until I was sure. Until I was sure *he* was sure. Forever can be a very long time for *bean sidhes*, and so far his track record looked more like the fifty-yard dash than the Boston marathon. I'd been burned before by guys without much staying power.

When I looked up, I found Nash watching me, his hazel eyes swirling with streaks of green and brown in the orange glow from the streetlights. I almost felt sorry for all the humans who wouldn't be able to see that—to read emotion in another's eyes.

That was a *bean sidhe* thing, and easily my favorite part of my recently discovered heritage.

"All I'm saying is it would be nice to get to hang out with my friends and my girlfriend at the same time."

I rolled my eyes again. "Oh, fine. I'll play nice with the pretty people." At least Emma would be there to keep me company —she'd started going out with one of Nash's teammates while I was grounded. And the truth was that most of Nash's friends weren't that bad. Their girlfriends were another story.

Speaking of bloodthirsty hyenas…

A car door slammed in the driveway ahead and my cousin, Sophie, stood next to Scott Carter's metallic-blue convertible, her huge green eyes shadowed dramatically by the streetlight overhead. "Nash!" She smiled at him, ignoring me in spite of the fact that we'd shared a home for the past thirteen of her fifteen years, until my dad had moved back from Ireland in late September.

Or maybe *because* of that.

"Can you give me a hand?" As we stepped onto the driveway, she rounded the end of her boyfriend's car in a slinky, sleeveless pink top and designer jeans, a case of beer clutched awkwardly to her chest. Two more cases sat at her feet, and I glanced around to see if any of the neighbors were watching my fifteen-year-old cousin show off an armload of alcoholic beverages. But the neighbors were probably all out, spending their Saturday evening at the theater, or the ballet, or in some restaurant I couldn't even afford to park near. And most of their kids were at Scott's house, waiting for us to come in with the beer.

Nash let go of me to take the case from Sophie, then grabbed another one from the ground. Sophie beamed at him, then shot a haughty sneer at my plain jacket before turning on one wedge-heeled foot to strut after him. I sighed and picked up the remaining box, then followed them both inside. The front door opened before Nash could pound on it, and a tall, thick senior in a green-and-white letter jacket slapped Nash's shoulder and took one of the cases from him. Nash twisted with his empty arm extended, clearly ready to wrap it around me, but found Sophie instead. He sidestepped her—ignoring her plump-lipped pout—and took the case from me, then stood back to let me go in first.

"Hudson!" Scott Carter greeted Nash, shouting to be heard over the music. He took one of the cases and led us toward a large kitchen crowded with bodies, scantily clad and shiny with sweat. In spite of the winter chill outside, it was hot and humid indoors, the hormone level rising with each new song that played.

I took off my jacket, revealing my snug red blouse, and almost immediately wished I could cover myself back up. I didn't have much to show off, but it was all now on display, thanks to the top Emma had picked out for me that afternoon, which suddenly seemed much more daring than it had in the privacy of my own room.

Nash set the remaining case of beer on the counter as Scott slid the first one into the refrigerator. "Kaylee Cavanaugh," Scott said when he stood, having apparently noticed me for the first time. He eyed me up and down while I resisted the urge to cross my arms over my chest. "Lookin' good." He glanced from me to Sophie, then back, while my cousin tried to fry me alive with the heat of her glare. "I'm starting to see the family resemblance."

"All I see is you," Nash said, pulling me close when he realized Sophie and I weren't happy with the comparison.

I smiled and kissed him impulsively, convinced by the slow churn of colors in his irises that he meant what he said. Scott shoved the last case of beer into the fridge, then slapped a cold can into Nash's hand as I finally pulled away from him, my face flaming. "See? Family resemblance." Then he headed off into the crowd with Sophie, popping the top on a can of his own. Three steps later they were grinding to the music, one of Scott's hands around his drink, the other splayed across my cousin's lower back.

"Wow, that was…unexpected," Nash said, drawing my gaze from the familiar faces talking, dancing, drinking, and… otherwise engaged. And it took me a moment to realize he meant the kiss.

"Good unexpected, or bad unexpected?"

"Very, very good." He set his can on the counter at my back, then pulled me closer for a repeat performance, one hand sliding up my side. That time I didn't pull away until someone poked my shoulder. I twisted in Nash's arms to find Emma Marshall, my best friend, watching us with an amused half smile.

"Hey." Her grin grew as she glanced from me to Nash, then back. "You're blocking the fridge."

"There's a cooler in the other room." Nash nodded toward the main part of the house. Emma shrugged. "Yeah, but no one's making out in front of it." She pulled open the fridge, grabbed a beer, then popped the can open as she pushed the door shut with a toss of one shapely hip. It wasn't fair. Emma and her sisters inherited crazy curves—a genetic jackpot—and all I got from my relatives was a really gnarled family tree.

There were times when I would gladly have traded all my *bean sidhe* "gifts"—did a glass-shattering screech and the ability to travel between the human world and the Netherworld even count as gifts?—for a little more of what she had. But this was not one of those times. Not while Nash's hands were on my waist, his taste still on my lips, and the greens and browns in his eyes swirling languorously with blatant desire.

For *me*.

Em drank from her can, and I grabbed the car keys dangling from her hand, then showed them to her before stuffing them into my hip pocket, along with my own. She could stay the night with me, and I'd bring her back for her car in the morning.

Emma smiled and nodded, already moving to the music when someone called her name from the living-room doorway.

"Hey, Em!" a voice called over the music, and I turned to see Doug Fuller leaning with one bulging arm on the door frame. "Come dance with me."

Emma smiled, drained her can, then danced into the living room with Doug's hands on her already swaying hips. Nash and I joined them, and he returned greeting after greeting from the glitter crowd writhing around us. But then he was mine. We moved with the music as if the room was empty but for the stereo and the heat we shared.

I had stolen Nash from a room full of his adoring devotees with nothing but the secret connection we shared. A connection no other girl could possibly compete with. We'd combined our *bean sidhe* abilities to bring my best friend back from the dead and to reclaim a damned soul from the hellion who'd bought it. We'd literally saved lives, fought evil, and almost died together. No mere pretty face could compete with that, no matter how much gloss and mascara she applied.

An hour later, Em tapped my shoulder and pointed toward the kitchen. I shook my head—after a month without him, I could have danced with Nash all night—but after Emma left, Nash kept glancing at the kitchen door like it was going to suddenly slam closed and lock us out.

"Need a break?" I asked, and he smiled in relief.

"Just for a minute." He tugged me through the crowd while my heart still raced to the beat, both of us damp with sweat. In the kitchen, Emma drank from a fresh can of beer while Doug argued with Brant Williams about a bad call during some basketball game I hadn't seen.

"Here." Nash handed me a cold soda. "I'll be right back."

Then he pushed his way through the crowd without a backward glance. I looked at Emma with both brows raised, but she only shrugged. I popped open my Coke and noticed that Doug and Brant's argument had become a whispered conversation I couldn't follow, and Emma hadn't even noticed. For several minutes, she prattled about her sister refusing to lend her a blouse that made Cara look lumpy, anyway. Before I could decide how to respond, someone called my name, and I looked up to find Brant watching me. "Yeah?"

Obviously I'd missed a question.

"I said, 'Where's your boyfriend?'"

"Um…bathroom," I said, unwilling to admit that I wasn't sure. Brant shook his head slowly. "Hudson's falling down on the job. You wanna dance till he gets back? I won't bite." He held out one large brown hand for mine, and I took it.

Brant Williams was tall, and dark, and always smiling. He was the football team's kicker, a senior, and the friendliest jock I'd ever met, not counting Nash. He was also the only other person in the house I would dance with, other than Emma.

I danced with Brant for two songs, glancing around for Nash the whole time. I was just starting to wonder if he'd gotten sick when I spotted him across the room, standing with Sophie in an arched doorway leading to a dark hall. He brushed a strand of hair from her forehead, then leaned closer to be heard over the music.

My chest ached like I couldn't breathe.

When he saw me looking, he stepped away from Sophie and scowled at my partner, then waved me over. I thanked Brant for the dance, then made my way across the room, dread building inside me like heartburn. Nash had ditched me at a party, then showed up with Sophie. Deep down, I'd known this day would come. I'd figured he'd eventually look elsewhere for what he hadn't had in the two and a half months we'd been going out. But with Sophie? A flash of anger burned in my cheeks. He may as well have just spit in my face!

Please, please be imagining things, Kaylee…

I stopped five feet away, my heart bruising my chest with each labored beat. Yes, Sophie had a boyfriend, but that didn't mean she wouldn't try to take mine.

Nash took one look at my face, at my eyes, which were surely swirling with pain and anger I couldn't hide, then followed my gaze to Sophie. His eyes widened with comprehension.

Then he smiled and grabbed my hand.

"Sophie was just looking for Scott. Right?" But then he tugged me down the dark hall before she could answer, leaving my cousin all alone in the crowd. "We can talk in here," Nash whispered, pressing me into a closed door. The full body contact was promising, but I couldn't banish doubt. "Were you talking to her the whole time?" I asked around the hitch in my breath as his cheek brushed mine.

"I just went outside to cool off, and when I came back in, she cornered me. That's it." He fumbled for the handle near my hip, and the door swung open, revealing Scott's dad's posh office.

"Swear?"

"Do I really need to?" Nash stepped back so I could see his eyes in the dim light of the desk lamp, and I saw the truth swirling in them. He didn't want Sophie, no matter what she might do that I hadn't. I felt myself flush. "Sorry. I just thought—"

Nash closed the door and cut my apology off with a kiss.

Meghan Chase has a secret destiny...

Meghan has never quite fitted in at school...or at home. But she could never have guessed that she is the daughter of a mythical faery king and a pawn in a deadly war.

Now Meghan will learn just how far she'll go to save someone she cares about...and to find love with a prince who might rather see her dead than let her touch his icy heart.

First in the stunning *Iron Fey* series

Available 21st January 2011

www.miraink.co.uk